Flyover Fictic

DATE DUE

The Floor

UNIVERSITY OF NEBRASKA PRESS : LINCOLN & LONDON

Pamela Carter Joern

of the Sky

Manufactured in the United States of America
Typeset in Minion & designed by R. Eckersley
⊗

Library of Congress Cataloging-in-Publication Data
Joern, Pamela Carter, 1948–
The floor of the sky / Pamela Carter Joern.
p. cm – (Flyover fiction)
ISBN-13: 978-0-8032-7631-4 (pbk.: alk. paper)
ISBN-10: 0-8032-7631-1 (pbk.: alk. paper)
1. Grandmothers – Fiction. 2. Granddaughters –
Fiction. 3. Nebraska – Fiction. 4. Domestic
fiction. I. Title. II. Series.
PS3610.025F58 2006   813'.6–dc22   2006001983

For Brad

Elsewhere the sky is the roof of the world; but here the earth was the floor of the sky.

— Willa Cather, *Death Comes for the Archbishop*, 1927

ACKNOWLEDGMENTS

My sincere thanks to the people of western Nebraska, especially Mark and Teresa Bowman, whose love for the land inspired this story; Sheila O'Connor for mentoring me through the whole process; Mary Rockcastle for saying, "You're going to be a real writer out there"; Kathy Jursek, Kathryn Quaintance, Bonnie Reiland, Jackie Thureson, and Eve Winters, who graciously agreed to read a work in progress for their book club; Kathy Houser Weihe, Mary Bednarowski, and Sally Hill, who read versions of the manuscript; the Minnesota State Arts Board, whose Artist Assistance Fellowship helped make this book possible; Ladette Randolph and her colleagues at University of Nebraska Press for bringing it out; my students and the staff at the Loft Literary Center, who inspire me to believe that words matter; Scott Edelstein for good advice; my friends and family, who've listened patiently to my dreaming; Shannon and Matt, Raegan and Jacob for sending me flowers and giving me hope in the future; Brad for everything, always.

In addition, I wish to thank these authors: Teresa Jordan, *Riding the White Horse Home* (Vintage Departures, 1994) for teaching me about riding to the bones; Margaret A. MacKichan and Bob Ross, *In the Kingdom of Grass* (University of Nebraska Press, 1992) for helping me picture life in the Sandhills from a winter study in Minneapolis; Jo Chytka, whose article "Branding Like Days Gone By . . . Keeping the Tradition Alive" (*Business Farmer*, July 6, 2001) gave me a window onto a custom I never had the privilege to witness.

Thanks to Kenny and Lyndy Ireland, hosts of the Triangle Ranch B and B, who live in a Sears model Alhambra that became the inspiration for Toby's house. In my book I used the decorative façade to underscore Luther Bolden's questionable character, but Lyndy's great-grandparents' house is a thing of beauty rising up where the Bad River meets the prairie.

The Floor of the Sky

Toby

Everyone calls her Toby. Her real name is Gwendolyn, but few know that. For sixty-nine years she's been Toby, ever since her brother John called her Gwendolyn, and she spat peas from her seat in the high chair and said, "That sumbitch called me Gwenlum. My name not Gwenlum. My's Toby." The dog's name. The name stuck, long after the dog died, and now only she and John remember how she got the name, and John, once a falling-down drunk, either can't tell or no one would believe him.

She looks out the upstairs bedroom window of her foursquare house nestled deep in the Sandhills of Nebraska. The sun knifes off the roof of the empty machine shed and stabs at her eyes. She cups her hand over her brow. She'll have to haul water out to the old windmill, rescue the blue morning glories that have started their summer climb. Buttoning her shirt, she automatically recites a childhood rhyme: *doctor, lawyer, merchant, chief.* She changes the wording for the last four buttons: *banker, rascal, shyster, thief.* Smoothing her wiry gray hair with a glance in the mirror, she voices her concerns to a god she's not sure she believes in, "Give Lila a safe flight. And grant Malcolm Lord a miserable day. It might do the little wretch some good."

Running her palm down the worn stair banister, Toby thinks she'll see Malcolm Lord in hell before she'll give up this place. Her parents built this house in 1920, eleven years before she was born. They ordered it as a kit from Sears, hauled it thirty-five miles overland by wagon from the nearest train depot. She loves everything in this house: the creak in the oak floor at the foot of the landing, the rough maroon bricks of the fireplace, the smell of dust when the furnace kicks in. The red and blue Oriental rug chosen by her mother, frayed in spots, the fringe tangled in

1

lumps to trip over. The leaded glass doors on the half-wall book-cases, where she and her sister used to hoard bags of candy purchased on rare trips to town. The kitchen window facing west. A loud ticking clock. The same corner table her parents used, one leg propped by a wad of cardboard. The wide bay window, where she stands now, looking out on a sweeping canopy of sky.

The outside façade, however, tells a different story. The designers called it the Alhambra, after a Spanish palace that doubled as a fortress. Cream stucco, black trim, a scalloped header stretching up from the roof, elaborately carved front columns. Anywhere else, the house might have seemed elegant, or at least exotic. Plopped in the Nebraska Sandhills, it looked ridiculous, a fact missed by Toby's father, who had chosen it because it was the most ostentatious of all the models available. As he intended, the Alhambra stood as a monument to Luther Bolden's success on the Bluestem Ranch. When Toby was a girl, this house lit up the prairie for miles, people arriving by wagon and buggy and early autos to sing cowboy songs around a campfire, drink beer and whiskey on the front porch, dance in the cleared-out sunroom. Luther paraded her shy mother, spun Rosemary around in a red taffeta dress he'd ordered from another catalog, his grip tight on her upper arm. King of the Sandhills.

Toby knows that the neighbors smirked behind her father's back. They held grudges, every one of them, justified by her father's legendary ruthlessness. Still, they came to his home and drank his liquor, because they were lonesome and starved for a drop of pleasure, and he knew how to throw a fine party. And most of them, one way or another, owed Luther Bolden.

Even if Toby could scrape together the money, she wouldn't alter the façade. She keeps the false scallops, the hint of fallen aristocracy, because the exterior of her house reminds her of what she does not want to become – another Luther.

Gertie's already sitting at the kitchen table. She's dressed for town in one of those outfits old women wear, two-piece polyester, Wal-Mart or K-Mart specials. Peach pants, a white blousy top with peach, mint, and blue flowers made of twisted ribbons. Washable, lightweight, and cheap. Toby refuses such clothes, making her mind up, as she has throughout life, not to be like Gertie. Ten years older than Toby, Gertie's her advance warning, her red light flashing. Instead, Toby wears a plaid cotton shirt, tails out over the bunchy elastic waistline of her jeans. She does allow herself elastic. She's not a fool.

Toby moves to get juice out of the refrigerator, bends and retrieves a pan from the Hoosier cupboard, reaches down the box of oatmeal. Gertie sits, the Queen of Sheba. More like Luther every day. Toby knows she's behaving like her mother, passively resentful. Sooner or later she'll have to do something about it, but today's not the day. Today they have problems sufficient unto themselves.

She thinks this last, a vestige of some forgotten Bible verse, and then realizes that Gertie is paging through her Bible. The King James version, red-letter edition. Worn and dried-out leather framed by jagged zipper teeth. The zipper hasn't worked for years, clogged by the tangled tassel of a red crocheted cross that serves as a bookmark. Gertie roams the pages with her magnifying glass, head cocked to one side, her center vision robbed by encroaching macular degeneration. Toby leans over to see what book Gertie's opened up this morning, preparing herself for the onslaught that's sure to come. She hopes it's not any of the letters of the Apostle Paul, that bossy old patrician. Not the book of Revelation, with its promises of damnation and woe. She sees that it's the book of Ruth and breathes a little easier. Well. Two women finding a way to manage, manipulating men to get what they need, not a bad precedent for what's in store for all of them. She doubts Gertie will see it that way, but she likes feeling she has some leverage if Gertie gets going on the shalts and shalt nots of their lives in this hardscrabble place.

"You want me to come with you?" Gertie asks.

"No, I think I better go alone. She'll be overwhelmed as it is." Toby pours Gertie's coffee, sets the steaming mug in front of her.

Gertie doesn't look up. "You coddle her too much. Just like you did Nola Jean."

"Let's don't get started down that road."

"I'm just saying."

Toby says nothing. She rests her hips against the counter, cradles her coffee cup.

"I s'pose you'll be wanting to give her that front bedroom. I can move down the hall."

Toby studies Gertie, the roundness of her, the squint of her eyes through thick glasses. Gertie's out here for the summer because she hates her little house in town and because Howard's in the nursing home with Alzheimer's. Her eyes, too, getting worse. Gertie's daughter lives in Denver and doesn't want her. Her son's dead, his wife and Gertie not on speaking terms. That leaves only her grandson, Clay, who Gertie blames for everything that's gone wrong. And Toby. Toby's the last car on Gertie's train.

"All right," Toby says. She knows Gertie has no intention of moving out of that front bedroom. Toby had offered her the downstairs study, a small room with a bath that was added on after the accident that confined Toby's father to a wheelchair. All they had to do was swap the desk for a bed. But Gertie wanted

4

the room that was hers when they were kids in this house. "Maybe that would be best," Toby adds. She lifts her cup, the coffee bitter on her tongue.

She watches Gertie turn pink, like a live lobster she once dropped in a pan of boiling water when she and Walter took a cruise. She thinks about that lobster and wonders why it amuses her to see Gertie's discomfort. What kind of monster is she? She ate that lobster without blinking an eye.

"I might just as well go on back to town. I know when I'm not wanted." Gertie's high, nasal voice is not her best feature. Walter used to say it was in a dog's range and beyond human comprehension.

Toby raises an eyebrow and looks at Gertie. She's had some tough luck, old Gert. Or divine retribution. Either way, Toby's in no mood to play her games this morning.

"Suit yourself, Gertie. I got to be going, or I'll miss that plane. I don't want Lila thinking I forgot her."

The long drive out to the main road passes the family cemetery. Barbed wire fence, white gravestones peeking out from grama grass. Here and there a yucca with stalks of papery white flowers. Old boots atop six fence posts, the toes pointing home. For all the lost souls, Walter used to say. Toby's grandparents and parents are buried here, alongside Toby's brother who died in infancy. Toby's husband, Walter, too, his heart having exploded one spring during a difficult calving. He died surprised, his arm caught up to the elbow inside a cow. When George, the hired hand, came to tell Toby, Walter was already laid out on the prairie grass. The old cow was done for, bleeding and torn, too weak to rise, her newborn calf standing over her. Toby crouched and laid her hand on Walter's cheek. Without a word she walked to

George's pickup, took his shotgun down off the gun rack, fished two shells out of the glove compartment, loaded the gun, walked over, and shot the cow in the head. George said nothing. He helped her load Walter in the bed of the pickup. Then he scooped up the motherless calf and climbed into the truck beside Walter's body with the animal shivering in his arms. Toby drove back to the ranch house, weeping finally, and unable to say whether she was crying for Walter or for the motherless calf.

As Toby passes the small green house in the hollow, she takes note of the white picket fence, the crown of bluegrass shaping the front lawn, the cottonwood shimmering in the sun. Her brother John sits in a chair on the porch, wrapped in a blanket, a cup in his hand. George is not in sight, probably cursing the weeds among his tomatoes in the fenced area behind the house. He could be in the barn swabbing the horses down, keeping the black flies from ringing their eyes. She hasn't told either John or George about Lila. They'll have to know, but there's time for that.

Toby waits in the lounge of the Scottsbluff airport. Nobody much flies to this part of Nebraska, so the airport's small. A coffee shop off to one side, maybe twenty padded chairs, blue tweed upholstery on beige plastic frames. Two women's voices rise and fall like a distant flock of geese. She looks out at the runway, notices how the glass makes the air wobble. She's driven an hour and a half to get here, off the ranch, down a gravel road to the highway, west through four little towns. Her fingers are busy, rolling and unrolling the hem of her shirt.

She watches three people climb out of the airplane: a middle-aged man carrying a briefcase, an older woman who needs assistance from the pilot, and Lila. Toby studies the girl. She's wearing wide-legged jeans with frayed hems, a plaid flannel shirt with the sleeves cut out at the armpit. Her short dark hair spikes up in tufts like singed dandelion seed. When she gets close enough, Toby can see the multiple rings in her ears, one more in her right eyebrow, a glittering stud in her nose.

The three people enter the hallway where the luggage comes through. Toby watches through glass. Since the bombing of the World Trade Center towers, airport security won't allow anyone but passengers in this area. Lila struggles to lift a heavy suitcase off a platform. The middle-aged man reaches over her shoulder, hefts the bag for her. He smiles at her. She glares back. She manages a smaller bag on her own and walks through the sliding doors, towing both suitcases behind her.

Toby notices the belly now. Lila's showing, all right, the bottom two buttons of the shirt left undone. She hides it better than some, being a tall girl, like all the women in Toby's family. That's a coincidence, of course. Toby forgets, now and then, that her daughter is adopted. Some things get passed down – hand gestures, a certain inflection of the voice – but she can't take credit for her granddaughter's height.

Lila stops in front of her. She looks down at her feet. Toby won't speak to her until she looks up. She'll have to learn to carry herself proud through this. People will take their cues from her.

When Lila raises her head, her eyes are clear and blue like the Sandhills lakes in summer. She has always been a beautiful girl to Toby: skin golden and burnished, those blue eyes, that dark hair. The eyes are her dad's, but that hair and skin reveal traces of an unknown ancestor.

"Mom sent me here because she can't stand to look at me," Lila says. She offers this matter-of-factly, and while Toby guesses it's the truth, she's appalled that the girl knows it. Still, she can't lie to reassure her.

"Well. Maybe so." She reaches out and hauls her granddaughter into her arms.

They don't say much during the first forty miles or so. Toby watches Lila out of the corner of her eye, the girl's face turned toward the window. She can't guess what Lila might be thinking, but she figures she's scared.

"Air conditioner's broke," Toby says.

Lila does not turn her head, but offers her hand in a noncommittal wave.

"You feeling all right?"

No response.

"How long's it been since you've been out here?" Toby asks. She means only to pass the time, but Lila bristles. She turns with a sneer on her face.

"I'm barely old enough to drive, you know. I can't exactly bring myself."

Toby gnaws at her lip when Lila turns away. Still, she tries again.

"Four years ago, wasn't it? For your granddad's funeral. Your mother hasn't been out here since then, either. If I didn't make it to Minneapolis once in a while, you'd never know you had any Nebraska relation at all."

"Two Christmases ago," Lila says.

"What's that?" Toby's watching closely, not wanting to miss the junction off Highway 26.

Lila turns her face to her. There's accusation in it, even before she opens her mouth. "That's the last time I saw you. Two Christmases ago."

Toby doesn't answer. She has no defense this girl could understand. Four years or two years, that's a lifetime to someone her age.

8

"Your mother off this week? To Paris, I mean?"

"Yeah. I guess. She put me on the plane first." Lila's fingers fiddle with the dials and buttons on the radio. She hasn't turned it on, but her fingers are busy there, like a pianist whose hands are habitually trained. Her left knee bobs up and down to some interior beat or maybe out of anxiety or teenage adrenaline.

"How's your dad?"

"How would I know?"

Toby's surprised at the bitterness in Lila's voice. She knows Nola Jean blames Guy for their breakup, too many nights on the road playing jazz in what Nola Jean calls his Deadbeats Band. Fed up, she'd forced him to choose between her and his music, and Guy went with his true love. Somehow, Toby hadn't thought Lila would take her mother's side.

"Don't you see him?"

"He takes me out to eat once in a while."

Toby nods but can think of nothing to say. She's struck dumb with the realization of how alone this girl is.

"He'd like me better if I was musical," Lila says.

Toby gears up to deny Lila's statement, then stops. She knows it's true. She never could relate to Nola Jean, her love for fashion and what she calls the aesthetic life. Nola Jean flies to Paris regularly in her job as an airline hostess and sends Toby expensive blouses and bracelets, trinkets she has no use for. Nola Jean says she'd come home more often if she could fly here, but she can't stand all those hours in a car. She could fly to Scottsbluff, cut the drive down to a couple of hours, but she doesn't trust small airplanes, even though she's willing now to stick Lila on one. Toby loves her daughter, but she's too old not to admit that she might like Nola Jean better if she had taken to ranching the least little bit.

9

They ride a few more miles before Toby speaks again. "Gertie's staying at the house. You remember Gertie, my sister?"

"Clay's grandma?" Lila turns, her face brightening.

"Yeah."

Lila smiles then. A lovely face, when she smiles. "How is Clay?"

Toby thinks hard for a minute. It's too early to tell Lila the whole story on Clay. "Oh, he's all right. He's farming out on Gertie's old place."

"George still around?" Lila asks.

Toby smiles, peering ahead down the winding road, watching it disappear into the hills. She remembers how George used to take Clay and Lila fishing, the three of them wandering off with poles slung over their shoulders like slender muskets. "That old man is rooted to the land. He's got my brother John with him now. George looks after him."

They've passed Elmyra and the ghostly remains of Perkins, headed off Highway 26 onto the gravel road that leads up into the hills. Toby drives fast but keeps a watchful eye for roaming cattle. Once in a while she spots a red-tailed hawk circling, its shadow flirting with the thin ribbon of road. On both sides the land stretches away, speckled with primroses and swathed with patches of purple larkspur. Here and there a blue lake dots the surface, formed by rainwater spilling down the side of a hill. Sometimes the water disappears and resurfaces lower as a wetland marsh. Or it might keep on going, down, down through secret passageways to the Ogallala Aquifer, a huge underground reservoir stretching all the way to Texas. When Toby was a girl she imagined herself living on a giant ship, cast atop a rolling ocean. She would lie on her stomach, put her ear to the dry ground, and listen for the sloshing of phantom waves.

They drive in silence onto the cow path that meanders past

George's house, past the family cemetery. They pull up in front of the Alhambra. The rose bushes by the front porch need trimming. The lilacs stray, shabby and overgrown. The lawn has gone to ruin. In the early morning wild turkeys can be heard nesting in the cottonwoods, but now the only sound is the buzzing of insects. That, and the sun, hot and loud, blaring on the roof and walls.

Lila stands looking up at the house, the hills at her back. "When I was a kid," she says, "I thought this was a palace."

Toby moves up alongside her granddaughter, tries to see the Alhambra through her eyes. "What do you think now?" she asks.

Lila shrugs. "I'm not a kid anymore."

With that, she picks up her largest suitcase and moves up onto the porch. Toby, stooping to the smaller bag, watches her struggle with the screen door. She props it open with her hip, lets it slam behind her, the sound reverberating across the empty yard.

Lila

Not much has changed in her grandmother's house. The speckled ceramic hen still roosts in the bay window. White lace doilies drape the arms of chairs. Everything is old. She detects a faint odor, antiseptic or talcum powder. She studies the pattern on the rug, finds the threadbare spot Toby tried to disguise by painting the design onto the backing. Only the TV looks new, though it sits in the same place as the old one. Things are tackier than she remembered. She picks up a blue floral teacup off the oak end table, turns it in her hand, half expects to find a crack or telltale glue.

"Don't break that. That was our mother's."

Lila places the cup back in its saucer, rattles it on purpose. She turns to the old woman standing in the doorway to the kitchen, back hunched, head straining forward, the witch from Hansel and Gretel leaning into her oven. Lila's mouth twitches. "Hi, Gertie," she says.

Gertie steps closer, tilts her head back to give Lila the once-over. Lila stands still, though she'd like to run. The smell of Gertie's foul breath kicks up a wave of nausea.

"Why'd you want to mess up your face with all that metal?" Gertie asks.

Why'd you get born with a messed-up face? Lila wants to say. Instead she shrugs. Who cares, anyway? It's not a capital offense. Maybe she'll dye her hair green while she's here.

"Leave her alone, Gertie. She's barely in the door," Toby says.

Toby helps her carry her luggage up to her old room. Nothing has changed here, either. White chenille bedspread, white lace curtains, pale blue walls. A stuffed dog lies on her pillow. She's way past toy animals.

"Is Gertie going to be here the whole summer?" Lila asks. She sits on the edge of the bed, runs her hands over the ridges in the chenille. When she falls asleep on this bed, she wakes with stripes gouged into her cheeks.

"Afraid so," Toby says. She's fussing with the tiebacks on the curtains.

"What's wrong with her house?" Lila stretches her arm and picks up the stuffed toy. Her fingers search out the bell sewn into one ear.

Toby tosses aside a blue and white afghan from the back of the wooden rocker, sits down on a cushion quilted in strips of blue calico. Everything in this room is blue or white, the pitcher on the bureau, the flowers embroidered on the old-fashioned

12

dresser scarf. All this matching color gives Lila the creeps. Maybe she'll hang orange ribbons from the light fixture, drape red and purple from the headboard.

"You know Grady died," Toby says.

"Yeah, Mom told me." Something about a heart attack while sitting in the stands at the rodeo. It's weird that Clay's dad died the same year her dad split.

"Gertie and Howard had just signed the farm over to Grady. Tax reasons, mostly."

Toby pauses. Still rolling Fluffy's ear bell between her thumb and fingers, Lila pictures Clay banging the screen door on his parents' house, tiptoeing with muddy feet across Gertie's oak floors in the big house a hundred yards away. In those days Lila spent a month here every summer. Though older than her by two and a half years, Clay was an only child, too, and they became inseparable. Fifteen miles between the ranch and the farm, but somebody went back and forth every few days. They'd sleep over at one house or the other, sneak out of separate bedrooms late at night and curl up on opposite ends of the sofa. The year that Lila found out her mother had been adopted, she and Clay sliced their palms with a pocketknife, held them together over an open Bible so they'd be true blood cousins. Afterward, they tore the splotched page out of the Bible and buried it under an elm tree. Then they spit in the dust three times and wrote their initials in the mud.

"You want me to help you unpack?" Toby says.

"I don't have much." She tosses the raggedy dog back to her pillow, reaches to straighten him when he lands upside down.

"Okay." Toby stoops to pick the afghan up off the floor, folds it over her forearm.

"Didn't Wanda get remarried?"

13

"She did. Frank Trevino, a fine man. But Gertie, she thought Frank married Wanda to get the farm. Some bad words got said. So Howard and Gertie moved to town. Clay's out there now, trying to make a go of it. He dropped out after one semester at Greeley. I was sorry to see that."

"Why isn't Gertie with Howard?"

"That's just it. Howard's in the nursing home."

Toby stands a moment with the afghan, tosses it onto the seat of the rocker. She manages a tight smile, her thin lips almost disappearing. "Well, you probably want to get settled in. Supper after a while."

After Toby is gone Lila moves over to the window. She looks out onto the yard, hard dirt rambling off into prairie grass. She leans forward until she can see the steps of the porch. She remembers music, "The Beer Barrel Polka," blasting from the old phonograph her granddad kept in the study. It was her twelfth birthday. Clay hadn't been around much, too busy helping his dad farm. Disappointed and bored, she'd called her parents to pick her up early. But here Clay holds his arms out to her, coaxing her to dance. She clings to the porch railing. He's handsome already at fourteen, and his man's body scares her a little. C'mon, he says. It's fun. And then she does it. She steps down, and Clay swings her around, step-together-step-hop, step-together-step-hop. When they get better at it, he shows her how to turn on the hop, and he spins her until they are both dizzy and fall to the ground laughing. Her granddad turns up the volume, and then he polkas her grandmother around the yard. Her dad pulls her mother down from the porch and into his arms. Lila and Clay watch for a bit before they scramble up and join them, the three couples twirling, narrowly missing each other, like perfectly timed buckets on the Tilt-a-Whirl.

Looking down from the window, Lila thinks if she had known that was to be the last summer, she would never have let Clay go, never have let her mom and dad out of her sight, never have forgotten to give her granddad a kiss good night. She would never have stopped dancing.

Toby

Gertie and Toby are knitting, waiting up for the 10:00 news. Lila's already gone to bed, in the blue room at the top of the stairs, across the hall from the green room where Toby has taken up residence since Walter died.

"She eats like a bird," Gertie says. She's on the couch, near the lamp. She doesn't need to see to knit, her practiced hands jabbing the needles swiftly, but she likes the warmth of the light.

"Maybe she's a vegetarian," Toby says. Gertie's city granddaughters have all gone through a vegetarian phase.

"Then she should speak up."

"Give her time."

"Did she say anything? On the ride here. Did she tell you anything?"

"Like what?"

"Like who the father is. What she plans to do."

Toby tightens her lips. "She only just got here."

"Wayward girls," Gertie mumbles.

"What did you say?"

Gertie shifts her weight in the chair, offers nothing.

"You don't start in on her. I won't have it. Times are different now."

"The Bible says fornication is a sin. That hasn't changed."

Toby's hands tighten on the arms of the chair. She's surprised, now, with Lila in the house, how the old anger rises within her. Her hatred stands up before her, a monster dripping with swamp ooze, and before she can stop herself, she imagines leaving Gertie sitting in the chair, finding her there in the morning, her heart stopped.

"Clay'll be coming to the branding," Toby says. She knows this is cruel. She can't help it. She's turning Gertie by the horns.

"Then I'll just stay up here at the house."

"You'd miss out on the fun, steaks over the open fire, just for spite?"

Gertie doesn't answer. Toby steals a look at her. The knitting needles click, click. The cable channel of the television flickers. They have that big satellite dish, but Toby still likes the traditional networks. Gertie watches CNN for hours, and it leaves her wrung out on an overdose of bad news.

"It's not the boy's fault," Toby says.

"He's the one gaining by it, ain't he?"

"You think living out there all by himself on your old place is what he had in mind? He's only nineteen. I don't guess it's too much fun for him, rattling around in that big house."

"He's got that Pickford boy out there."

"That's temporary. Besides, Tim's living in that old trailer."

"You don't say."

"That's what I heard."

They sit quietly for a few moments, Gertie picking up stitches with her clicking needles.

"Nothing good ever came from a Pickford." With that Gertie stands up. She drops her knitting on the floor, her glasses fall off her face.

Toby moves over to her sister, puts her hand on her arm. She bends down and retrieves the glasses, sets them on Gertie's face, tucks the earpieces under her gray hair. "Clay's all you got left of him."

Gertie brushes Toby's hand off her sleeve. "I'm going to bed," she says. Then Gertie walks across the room, her head slightly turned, using her peripheral vision. She looks like a bird, Toby thinks. Not an owl, not the birds with frontal lobes, but the ones whose eyes are on the sides of their heads. If they lose one eye, they're blind to predators on the other side.

"Gertie," she calls, as Gertie reaches the bottom of the stairs. Gertie stops but does not turn her head.

"You leave Lila alone. Or I swear, I'll put you in that nursing home with Howard."

Gertie stands still for a moment. "I believe you would," she says. She pauses. Turning her head then, not seeing, but offering her vacant eyes, she adds, "There are not many people could do that." She smacks her lips a couple of times, leaves the rest unfinished. Toby does not speak, stares at Gertie until she's hefted herself up the stairs. She hears Gertie's bedroom door close behind her.

Toby busies herself in the kitchen, rinses a cup in the sink, wipes off the counter. Out the west window, she spots a crescent moon. Luther used to say a swing dangled from it, and she spent hours looking for it.

Toby folds her pants and shirt over the back of a rocking chair. She takes off her bra, rubs the chafed skin under her breasts, slips on a nightgown. She kneels beside her bed before she climbs in, a childhood habit she's returned to since Walter died. She braces her arms on the quilt top. She hears crickets outside, an owl *who-whooing*. The air smells moist, the spring rains giving them a little boost into summer. Sometimes she recites the Twenty-third Psalm. Mostly she kneels in silence, letting her mind slip over the graces and troubles of the day. Long ago she lost faith in the old man god of her Lutheran upbringing; she might as well pray to the man in the moon. She doesn't have new language, slips into the familiar patterns because she knows them and they comfort her, but if pressed about what she actually believes, she'd have to confess that she trusts in the rhythm of seasons, the regularity of the sunrise, and the sure realization that love is better than bitterness. That's about it, and most times it's good enough to call on. She's got that girl here now, who's in trouble. She's got Gertie. Malcolm Lord closing in. She hears the owl again outside the window, knows it's hunting. Out loud she says, "I'm too old for this."

George

George Bates is standing on the small rise in back of his house when the lights go out in Toby's bedroom. He's climbed up here for a few reasons. To think about things under the stars, that's one. To watch Toby's lights go out, that's another. It's a habit of his, no harm in it. His way of saying good night. He knows that if the lights go out, then everything's all right up at the Alhambra.

He's been watching out for things on this ranch most of his adult life, ever since he showed up one winter morning in the waning years of the Great Depression. He had his wife, Ella, with him and David, his nine-year-old half brother. He'd met Ella when he and David made their way west from Illinois after their mother died of consumption in a sanatorium. Neither boy had ever known a father. It took George a long time to figure out that his mother was not pure like the Virgin Mary, and that the men she had lain with were probably employers in the houses she cleaned. It wasn't hard to promise his dying mother to look out for David. George would have taken an arrow in his heart before he'd let anyone harm the boy. He took that job working for Ella's brothers on a small spread in South Dakota because a one-room shack went with it, and David could walk to school, and because Ella had smiled kindly at him while he stood with his hat in his hand. He couldn't take his eyes off her bright yellow hair, the proud way she carried herself, and when Ella's mother died from stomach cancer, he married her. He knew what it meant to be an orphan in this world.

Ella's brothers ended up squabbling over the land left to them to share. Once it got parceled out, there wasn't enough work to keep a hired hand. Somebody directed them to the Bluestem Ranch, so they traveled south. To their good fortune, Rosemary opened the door and not Luther. She looked past them at the dilapidated car in the drive and the white expanse of snow and could not turn them away. They moved into the original house built by Toby's grandfather, and George has never left. Except for his mother, all the family he's ever known is buried on this land.

He searches the skies for Orion, the Hunter, his favorite among the constellations. He can't decide whether the star man has his arm raised to fight or to pay homage, perhaps to impart a blessing. It is this ambiguity that has kept him coming back, year after year, night after night, to study the planted feet, the three lights of the belt, the shield held against the onslaught of the world, and then the upraised arm.

He likes to think about these things. He ponders, in his own life, the times when he has raised his fists to fight. He doesn't like violent ways, although he admits sometimes they are unavoidable, men being what they are and slow to learn, but lately, since he is turning down the last road of his life, he likes to think Orion, the Hunter, raises his arm in gratitude for all that he has been given.

Tonight, gazing up and following the curved swipe of the Milky Way, he is troubled. Toby is not telling him something. It could be Malcolm Lord, the taxes. Some new pressure the weasel man has found to pry Toby off her land.

The wind shifts slightly, the breeze tickling his cheeks. He feels uneasy, the play of the wind warning him of change. If he stands still long enough, could he feel the earth move beneath his feet? With the shifting of the night air, his gut tenses. Whatever it is, he hopes they are ready for it.

He cocks his ear to the late-night sounds. The horses in the corral are restless, too. He hears a low whinny, the snorting and tramping of feet. He waits for the mournful coyote, the solemn night owl, the chorus of crickets – all of them speak and the sounds comfort him. These are the things he knows: these voices, the star man behind his shield with the raising of his ambiguous salute, and the heart of the woman who sleeps at the Alhambra.

Toby

Next morning when Lila comes downstairs, the clock reads 10:15. Toby's sitting with Gertie at the kitchen table. She's working in a book of crossword puzzles while Gertie polishes her fingernails. Out of the corner of her eye, Toby watches Gertie dab a blob in the middle of each finger, smear it to the edges, wipe off the excess with a cotton ball. She makes a mess of it, but the polish is light.

"There you are," Toby says. The girl stands in the doorway, hands stuffed in her back jeans pockets, chin tilted up.

"How about an egg today?" Toby offers.

"I hate eggs," Lila says.

"You need to keep your strength up. You're eating for two now," Gertie says.

Lila slams the milk carton she's retrieved from the refrigerator on the counter. She stands with her back to the two old women. She looks out the window and up at the sky.

Toby watches Lila and shakes her head. She thought kids these days knew about condoms. She might have gotten AIDS, for Christ's sake. She waits until Lila turns around, relieved to see that she's drinking the glass of milk she poured herself.

"Today we're going into town," Toby says.

"Okay." Lila's voice sounds detached, most of her still floating out the window.

"I thought we'd see if we can find you some clothes."

Lila smoothes her shirt over her expanding belly. She folds her arms across her front.

"Maybe some bigger shirts. Something with sleeves – you'll need more protection on your arms at the branding."

"She ought to have some decent maternity clothes," Gertie says.

Both Lila and Toby turn and glare at her.

"New jeans, too," Toby offers. She raises her shirt, pulls out the elastic waistband of her pants. "Something like this. You can just leave them behind at the end of the summer."

Lila nods but doesn't sit at the table. She stands at the counter with her arms folded over her abdomen, her hair sticking straight up.

"You had hair just like that when you was a baby," Gertie says.

"Not so dark, but it stuck straight up like that. Like you'd stuck your finger in a light socket. Like a shock of wheat, gone wild. Your momma couldn't wait 'til you'd outgrow it. And now look at you."

The three of them drive into Elmyra in the late morning. They drive down out of the green rolling hills, through the tableland where Gertie's old farm lies. This is transition land, held by farmers who raise a few cattle, maybe hogs, a field or two of corn or alfalfa. Gertie never did make the switch from being a rancher's daughter to a farmer's wife. She married Howard Hoffman, kept his home, bore two children, but she never made peace with having to turn over every clod of dirt on the place.

They reach the north edge of Perkins, a dried-up town. They roll on past the prairie cemetery where graves are marked out by rocks and patches of gravel, past the deserted drug store, an empty gas station. One block off the highway is the Lutheran church that Gertie and Toby still attend. They drive west along the North Platte River, past irrigation farms of beans, potatoes, and sugar beets. More corn here, too. The valley, carved between the dry tableland of the south and the Sandhills on the north, was once the route west for both the Oregon and Mormon trails. The people who dropped from the wagon trains and stayed – Czechs, Germans, Britons, Poles, Swedes – were later joined by an influx of Greeks and Italians, Latinos who came first as migrant workers, a few Indians from the reservations in South Dakota. One local man married a Filipino woman after World War II, and there have been a scattering of Japanese families. The only African Americans ever seen in these parts are delinquent or homeless boys from Omaha and Chicago who are sent by a judge to the Boys' Ranch. Over the years some of these kids have been Walter's best summer hands, once he trained them to know the front end of a cow from the back. Toby still chuckles over the gangly kid who spent weeks riding with Walter, then one day while standing under one of the windmills that pull up water from the Ogallala Aquifer, asked, Do these big fans really keep the cows cool?

They cross the river at North Bridge, a ghost town that was once a thriving river port and train stop. Across the bridge, they enter Elmyra, the Meredith County Seat, 1,658 people with eleven churches: Methodist, two Baptist (one split off from the other, proving they are a cantankerous lot), Presbyterian, Missouri Synod Lutheran, Episcopalian, Seventh-Day Adventist, Catholic, Mormon, Church of Christ, Assembly of God. The Greeks have to drive fifteen miles farther west to the Orthodox church in Huntsville. Four bars, two banks, a historic courthouse, a Class C high school, a Hardee's, a vacant lot that once held the Trail Theater (a grand old movie house with velvet seats and western-theme tapestries on the side walls, left to the town when Mr. Schmidt died but fatally burdened with unpaid taxes), a laundromat, a small bakery, Bea's Floral Shop, a fabric store, a swimming pool, a Jack 'n' Jill and Sonny's (the latter with a pharmacy), two general stores where you can find furniture, appliances, weed killer, a garment or two, new window shades, a flapper for your leaky toilet tank, trash bags, lawnmowers, jigsaw puzzles, rain gear, fishing tackle, Go Big Red sweatshirts, and an assortment of nuts, bolts, screws, fasteners, and geegaws. For a little town, it's not doing too bad, though there's no longer a jewelry store. Piggoty's and the Rainbow Cafe have gone under. Murphy's, the Five 'n' Dime, Bert's Drugs, two women's dress shops, all gone. People now drive to Scottsbluff to shop at Wal-Mart or K-Mart, or for a really big spree, they head to Cheyenne or Denver. Many of the old storefronts are vacant. Others are filled with a parade of antique and gift shops that come and go, the town being too far off the beaten track to attract tourists.

The primary hope of Elmyra is the new community center, where Toby drops Gertie off. Built with money given by Mike Trevino, the Greek land baron of Meredith County, the community center offers services to the several hundred elderly widows who populate Elmyra and to a handful of teens, kids, and young mothers. The Prairie Points Center also boasts conference capabilities, caters weddings and reunions, and has sparked a new vision for Elmyra. The idea was first voted down on the local ballot, people grousing and complaining about the cost – why do we need that when we've got the Legion Hall? – but Mike gave such a large gift that the town council couldn't ignore it. With the mayor's support, the building had gone up. Nothing spectacular, metal siding, a big rectangle like an overgrown machine shed, but inside two full-sized basketball courts, a walking track, exercise equipment, a fully equipped kitchen, and several meeting rooms with padded chairs and air-conditioning.

Grudgingly, people began to use the services. They had to admit that Prairie Points was a good idea, but if Mike thought he could buy their respect, he was wrong about that. Mike sat back while other farmers overextended in the seventies and eighties, then bought up one bankrupt farm after another. Rumors were that he was funded by the Greek Mafia, filtering drug money through Denver. Toby thinks Mike's just smarter than most of these valley farmers, whose dreams got too big too fast, but they'll not be easily won over by the man who profited from their losses. Gertie, who can hold a grudge longer than anybody, resents Mike more than most, since it's Mike's nephew who married Grady's widow. She believes the Trevino family has designs on her old farm, the one she loathed all the years she lived there, and she's not about to forgive him for it.

"I hate to go in there," Gertie says, while she's getting out of the car.

"Go on, Gertie. You'll have a good time."

"I hate to give him the satisfaction."

Gertie grumbles, but she gets out of the car, her love for pinochle and companionship overriding her hatred for Mike Trevino and his kin. Toby thinks about telling Gertie that she doubts whether Mike's keeping track of her comings and goings, but she holds her tongue. Pride might be about all Gertie's got left.

Toby drives down Main Street, turns at the corner of the old Blues Hotel, which for years housed drifters and other men of low account, heads onto First Street, past the park, turns right, and pulls up across the street from the hospital, in front of the doctor's office. She knows she should have warned Lila. She turns to her now and says, "This is Dr. Sadler's office. I called ahead for an appointment."

"What's the matter with you?" Lila asks.

Toby searches her face for hints of sarcasm, but sees none. "Not me. You. The appointment is for you."

For a moment Toby thinks Lila will bolt and run. She actually reaches for the handle of the door. She turns her head, looks at an odd angle up through the window at the sky. She says nothing. Toby waits. After a while she decides to fill up the silence with words, although she has no idea what to say.

"I know this is difficult. I'll go with you. If it matters, Dr. Sadler is a woman. She's the first woman doctor we've had in these parts."

Lila doesn't move.

"She took over the practice after her dad died. Old Dr. Sadler.

He was my doctor. He died just before Walter did." There, she's trying to say. I can say the hard words. Walter died. It's not so terrible. You can do it, too. You can say the words – baby, pregnancy – they're just words. She tries to convey this to Lila through her thoughts.

"Okay," Lila says finally.

"Okay?" Toby echoes. "Okay. Well, then." She unlocks the car doors, opens hers, and steps out. Lila gets out, stands on the curb. Toby comes around, steps in front of Lila. She waits for her to look up, and then she nods and walks ahead of her into the doctor's office.

When they call her name, Lila rises but does not move forward. Billie Mae, the office nurse, calls her name a second time. Toby, alarmed, stands up beside Lila. "Do you want me to come?" Toby whispers, and Lila nods. While Billie Mae takes Lila's history, Toby sits in a chair and looks around the room. Sterile. White. The hospital bed laid over with paper. Silver stirrups. She never went through this, of course. One adopted child. And then that other time, no one took her to a doctor, that's for sure.

She flinches when Billie Mae tells Lila to put her feet in the stirrups. She's had pelvic exams, of course, she knows all about what's coming now. She'd like to reach out and take Lila's hand, but that might only frighten her. Besides, Lila's not a baby. Billie Mae drapes blue paper over Lila, then she's gone. Lila shuts her eyes, and Toby watches her breathing, up and down. She seems okay.

Dr. Sadler comes in the door with a smile. "Hi, Toby," she says. She's a slender woman, warm brown eyes. She wears a white lab coat over blue jeans, a Wonder Woman button pinned to the lapel, a gift, Toby guesses, from a grateful patient.

"Penny." Toby nods hello.

When the doctor has finished, she washes her hands again at the sink. "Everything looks good," the doctor says. Toby nods her head.

"I'd say about six months, although we can't be sure. We'll know more after the ultrasound."

"No ultrasound," Lila says. Toby's surprised to discover that the girl has been listening.

"Under the circumstances, I think it would be a good idea," Dr. Sadler says.

"No," Lila says again. She sits up, the blue paper fluttering to the floor. She struggles to stand and grabs for her jeans.

Dr. Sadler turns to Toby. "We'd have a lot better idea when the baby is due. It's standard procedure these days. We'd know if there are problems."

"What if there are?" Lila asks. She's got her bra on now, her arms slipping into the cut-out armholes of her shirt. "It's too late to do anything about it." She stoops to tie her shoelaces.

"You could be jeopardizing your baby's health. It doesn't hurt. There's nothing to it. Talk to her, Toby."

Toby lays a quieting hand on the doctor's shoulder. "Thanks, Penny," she says. "We'll call that good for today."

Toby follows Lila out of the examining room, into the outer office. Three people sit in mauve chairs against a white wall: old man Kuxhausen, with chronic arthritis, Speed Olson, the local Allstate agent, who has prostate problems, Elsie Yardley, who has her blood pressure checked monthly. Lila stops in the middle of the waiting room and glares at every one of them. She puts her hands on her hips, sticks her belly out. "What are you staring at?" she spits at poor old Mr. Kuxhausen.

Mr. Kuxhausen, confused, turns to Toby. "What's the matter

with her?" he asks, and before Toby can think what to say, she sees Lila outside and heading up the street.

Toby throws a smile at Mr. Kuxhausen and scoots out the door. She gets to the end of the walk in time to see Lila heading across the street toward the park. Toby hangs her head and considers. Lila can't get very far. The town's not that big. She figures the best thing to do is sit in the car and wait. She thinks this even while her feet are carrying her to the park, especially when she sits down in the swing next to the one Lila is sitting in. Lila has twisted the chains round and round, her head thrown back studying the sky. Her feet, in red high-top tennis shoes, dig at the dirt. She's rocking herself back and forth. Toby sits quietly. A couple little girls ride the merry-go-round, shrieking as an older boy pushes them. They look familiar, but Toby can't place them.

After a while, Lila pulls herself upright. She looks down at her shoes. Her arms are tight at the elbows, the crook of each arm holding the swing's chains. She lifts her hands, palms up, and shrugs. Toby chuckles and nods. She turns her head and looks away from Lila, and then she says, "It's not going to go away."

Lila is silent.

"Look. I'll tell you how it's going to be if you stay here. You got to take care of yourself. You got to eat decent and get some sleep. You got to come in to the doc every other week, like she says. You don't have to have that ultrasound. I guess women have been birthing babies long before ultrasound was invented. Soon, not right away, maybe not until next month, you have to make some decisions."

"I'm giving it away."

Toby turns then and looks into Lila's stony face. She can't fathom what the girl is thinking, but she can see she's determined.

"Well, that's fine. But then we got to set things in motion."

"I won't be talked out of it."

"I won't try."

"I'm too young. And anyway . . ."

Lila lets her voice trail off. Toby waits a moment.

"C'mon," Toby says, and then hefts herself to her feet. "Let's go see if Gambles has any clothes fit to wear."

They almost have fun looking through the jeans in the Gambles store. There's not much choice, and Lila obediently tries on the pants that Toby points out to her. She comes out of the dressing room and models, puts her hand in the elastic waist and pulls it out. She turns around and looks at her butt in the mirror, the extra fabric hanging. She sighs, and Toby, watching her, thinks it's a good sign when a young girl cares how she looks.

"Never mind that now," Toby says.

Lila turns toward her, eyebrows up.

"You'll get your figure back soon enough. That's one good thing about being so young."

Toby watches to see how Lila will take this, if she'll get defensive, but the girl surprises her. She actually grins, the smile lighting up her face enough to make Toby sit back hard in her chair.

When Lila comes out of the dressing room, she hands the jeans to Toby. "I think two pairs of grandma pants will be enough, don't you?"

"What about some shorts? Gets hot on the ranch."

They riffle through the racks of shorts, seersucker with fitted waists, plaid and sea green and peach, nothing Lila would wear if she could fit into them, and it's clear that she can't.

"Lord-a-mighty," Toby says. "Maybe we need to make a trip to Scottsbluff."

29

"These are good enough," Lila says. "If I need shorts, I can cut off some of the old jeans I brought along."

They find a couple shirts, a blue chambray with long sleeves, size large, a couple oversized T-shirts. Nothing maternity. They round the corner with their pile of purchases, head for the checkout counter, and run smack into Malcolm Lord. Little man. White shirt, blue checkerboard tie. His face red and puckered from drinking too much or too much sun on that fair skin. He's holding a plumbing pipe in his hand. Stuffing dollar bills back into his billfold. He's paid, then. He won't be here long.

"Well, well. Toby, nice to see you."

"Malcolm," Toby says, nods.

Malcolm turns toward Lila. Toby sees his eyes fall on Lila's full belly. "Everybody around here calls me Booger," he says. Terrible nickname, Booger, but it's been with Malcolm since childhood. He doesn't seem to take offense. In fact, he prides himself on being a big-shot banker with the name of Booger Lord. Toby, who sees through his good ol' boy act, will not grant him the satisfaction. Nor will she lower her dignity to call the banker about to foreclose on her ranch by a name derived from such a filthy habit as nose picking. She might as well call him Fat Ass, which he also has.

Toby watches Lila appraise Booger. She does not offer any information. She merely looks at him, her eyes wary and darting.

"Who's this?" Booger asks Toby. He nods toward Lila and raises his eyebrows. God, how she hates the little buzzard.

"Lila is my granddaughter."

"Nola Jean's girl?" Booger's voice rises with amazement. Toby thinks at any moment he will throw out his chest and start to crow. Instead he merely laughs, a low sniveling snicker, and moves away.

"Who was that?" Lila asks, looking after him.

"That was our local banker."

"He's short," Lila says, staring after Booger.

Toby smiles, wondering how much meaning this girl intends.

"He's never gotten over the fact that your momma turned him down for the senior prom."

Later, they pick Gertie up at Prairie Points and head over to the rest home.

"You don't have to come in if you don't want to," Toby says.

Gertie gets out of the car and slams her door. Toby's still leaning over the front seat, waiting to hear Lila's answer.

Lila bites her fingernails. "Okay. I'll wait here."

"Okay," Toby says. She slips the keys out of the ignition. She hopes it looks natural. She hopes it looks like an automatic reflex and not like she's afraid her only grandchild might steal her car and run away.

Gertie

Howard is not in his room. Again. He's taken to wandering, and Gertie's been warned that he may have to be locked in his room. This is not a specialty nursing home. They don't have enough staff to look after the far-gone Alzheimer's patients.

Gertie sets her lips in a hard line. She knows where Howard is. He's with that woman. The same woman she found him with the last time she visited. That Stewart woman, frizzy gray hair, beady blue eyes, dim now with cataracts. Before, Howard never would have looked at her. She's trashy. She lived in a trailer down by the river. She dyed her hair and wore too much makeup. She pierced her ears and wore long silvery dangles so the holes in the lobes were stretched into teardrops. She has the look of wanton living and excess. Her children turned out badly, one daughter divorced three times, a son who ended up in the pen somewhere back east. She's in here now on public welfare, Gertie's sure of it. Not costing her a dime, while Howard's stay here is robbing her retirement out from under her.

She marches down the hall toward the Stewart woman's room. Toby follows behind her. Gertie wishes Toby wouldn't come with her on these visits. She hates to have anyone see Howard like this. He used to be so handsome, fastidious even. She's sorry that she complained about the scattered whiskers on the sink when he trimmed his beard. Why didn't she make more rhubarb pie, his favorite? She doesn't like rhubarb herself, but what difference does that make? Toby made rhubarb pie, and Howard went on and on about it. Gertie said to him once, You go on about Toby like she's the only woman who ever rolled a piecrust. And he looked at her, that sad-eyed look he could get. He reached out and patted her hand and said, Now, don't go on; you know it don't mean nothing. She should have made those pies herself. She's slow to see things. But she doesn't have to think too hard to figure out why Toby comes along on these visits. Revenge, pure and simple. Toby gloats about what's happened to them, how far they've fallen.

The Stewart woman isn't in her room either. The bed is mussed. At least they aren't lying together in it. Gertie closes her eyes, shakes her head as if to clear the ugly images. The nurses told her that Howard sometimes climbs in bed with that woman. It's common, they say, with these patients. But the woman gets frightened, and they have to take Howard back to his room. This is part of the warning. Keep your husband away from the Stewart hussy.

The place smells. Disinfectant. The stink of unwashed bodies. A half-eaten bread crust lies soggy in a coffee saucer on the bedside tray. There's a bunch of greeting cards, all with roses, taped to the off-white walls. Gertie listens to the soft steps of nurse's shoes, the shuffle of old feet. It's too much, this whole nightmare. Toby grabs her arm as she wobbles, leads her to a chair. They are still in that Stewart woman's room, and Gertie doesn't want to sit. She's afraid the woman has lice or some scent that won't wash off. But Toby presses her down. Leans on her shoulder.

"Breathe, Gertie," Toby says. Standing over her, as if she's her keeper. It's a zoo, this place.

"Where is he?" Gertie grinds out.

Toby pats her shoulder. Irritating, that pat, but Gertie doesn't push the hand away.

"Maybe he's in the halls. Shall I take a look?"

Gertie grabs onto Toby's hand. She grabs it and can't let go, frozen as a tongue on a winter flagpole. She tries to loosen her fingers, but they clamp. To her horror, she starts to cry.

Toby kneels down. She looks Gertie in the eye. "Now, now, Gertie. What's the matter? He can't be far away. We'll find him."

Gertie looks into Toby's face. She tries to read what's written there. Promise me. Promise me, she wants to say, that you won't put me in here, just for spite. Her hand shakes and she moves it to her brow, rubs her forehead. Her Howard, a man who taught Bible classes. Who believed in sex only in marriage and even then hardly ever laid a hand on her. What a cruel joke God has played.

Suddenly Gertie stands. She shrugs Toby's hand off. "He's probably down in the TV room," Gertie says. And so he is. They find him sitting on a couch with Meeks Middleton, a man he has

33

known all his life, a friend, you might say, and they are both staring at the TV screen. The picture has gone awry, rolling over and over, no one has had the time to stop and adjust the vertical hold, and Meeks and Howard sit there, watching images tumble like clothes in a dryer.

Lila

When Toby and Gertie have disappeared into the nursing home, Lila decides to take a stroll. She figures they'll be in there at least half an hour, maybe longer. She's got time to walk the three blocks to the swimming pool. It feels good to stretch her legs. She squints up at a sky fluffed with white pillows. She passes a row of tall hollyhocks, pink and bloodred. Her fingers itch to pluck them, turn the bell-shaped flowers upside down into hoop skirts for clothespin dolls, but she's too old for that now.

The pool sits at the end of a curved gravel lane. There used to be pine trees, the grounds cool and shaded, dotted with picnic tables. Now, except for a dying elm, the pool and grass are exposed to the prairie sun. A low stone fence circles the area. Lila walks atop it for old time's sake. She's turning toward the front walk when she hears a voice coming at her from a parked pickup. It's a beat-up Ford, red; the voice growls low and raspy.

"Hey, girl. Don't I know you?"

Her stomach ties in knots. This is a small town, the middle of the day, but she's conditioned. She keeps walking.

"Hey," calls the voice. She hears the pickup door open and slam. "Wait up." She glances in his direction, sees a tall man, torn jeans. She fixes her eyes on the two women sitting on a bench outside the pool fence, wonders how long it will take them to react when she yells.

When she feels the grip on her right elbow, she turns with her left fist swinging. The man reaches out his hand and stops her fist, grips her wrist hard enough to make her wince. "Hey, Lila, what's the matter with you?"

"Clay?" She looks up into the face of her cousin. He's standing over her, grinning, tall and lean, his hair wavy and sun-bleached. He's cute, better looking than she remembered. He's wearing a work shirt rolled up to his elbows. He looks big and out of reach. The hug she has imagined is impossible.

"I heard you were coming," he says. "Good thing I was warned. I wouldn't have known you."

"Me either. You, I mean," she says.

"You're all growed up. Look at you." He's dropped her hand, her elbow, stepped back a full step. He's staring at her belly.

She tosses her head, runs her hand through her short-cropped hair. "I got knocked up."

He looks away, then takes a sharp breath. "Well, hey," he says.

They stand there for a moment, dragging their toes in the dirt. She can't look at him, turns from side to side like she's surveying the place, getting a feel for the old familiar.

"It's been a while," he says.

"Yeah. You could say that." She still can't look at him. She hooks her hands in her back jeans pockets.

"I just did," he says. Then a low chuckle. She feels a smile tug at her lips. She looks at him finally, shakes her head and gives a small laugh.

"A lot's happened since you were here," he says.

She studies the widow's peak in his hair. "I know," she says.

He twists his mouth in a wry grimace. "My dad died."

"Yeah. I heard. I'm sorry."

He rubs his hand across his mouth.

"My mom and dad split up," she says.

"Really?"

"You didn't know?"

He shrugs. "Maybe I heard. Things have been pretty confusing."

She nods. She can't get words around the knot in her throat.

"That sucks," he says.

She puts her hand on her belly, takes a deep breath. He reaches toward her but doesn't touch her. One tear slides down her cheek, and she wipes it away by raising her shoulder.

"You here for the summer?" Gentle now. His voice easing her into this world.

She nods.

"Good," he says.

"You going to be around?" She tries not to sound like she's ten and waiting for him to finish his chores.

"When I can. I got lots of work to do."

"Yeah." She raises her chin, looks over his right shoulder at the empty road stretching behind him.

"I'm farming now," he says.

"On Gertie's old place."

"Dad's place. And mine. I lived there my whole life."

"I didn't mean. . ."

He waves his hand, cutting her off. She smiles at the familiar gesture, Clay's old shorthand for Never mind.

"Frank's helping me," he says. "He's Mom's new husband. Frank Trevino."

"I heard."

"Small town, huh?"

"Toby told me."

"Yeah, well, I needed a part for the irrigation pump, so I just stopped around here for a break."

"At the swimming pool?"

He laughs and raises his hands, like this is a stickup and she's the thief.

"C'mon," he says. "I want to show you something."

He half drags her up the hill toward the baby pool. She doesn't want to look at the little kids, but Clay barrels ahead. She lets him bully her because it feels good to have his arm around her shoulder. She can't figure out what's propelling him until she sees the body of the young woman laid out at the edge of the pool. She can't be much more than twenty, and she's slathered with lotion. She's lying on her stomach with the back of her swimsuit top undone, the zebra-striped bottoms cut high on the leg. She's skinny, like a fashion model.

"Hey, Alicia," Clay croons. He's still got one arm around Lila's shoulders. The other hand claws into the chain-link fence.

The girl on the towel raises her head. She has green eyes and auburn hair. Not quite pretty, her chin too soft, dark circles under her eyes, something fragile about her. Feeling both dowdy and clumsy, Lila notices a red-haired toddler paddling in the water astride an inflated duck.

"Hi, Clay," Alicia says. She reaches behind her and hooks her top, then swings her legs around and sits sideways. She moves like a girl used to being looked at. Lila tries to imagine herself doing that, tries to see herself wearing a zebra-striped bikini. She's studying the pose, looking for a name for it, while Alicia makes her way over to the fence. She puts her hand over Clay's, her long tapered fingers folding over his, her nails painted peach and gold metallic. Somewhere inside Lila, it registers that Clay lied to her about needing an irrigation part.

"That your kid?" she asks.

"Yeah. That's Amber," Alicia says. She grins at Clay again, and Lila can see that he's drowning.

"This is my cousin," Clay says. "From Minneapolis. Lila." He's not looking at her. She's invisible.

"Hi," Alicia says, turning her radiance on Lila. It's lost on her, though, which Alicia quickly figures out.

"I gotta go," Lila says, nudging Clay with her elbow.

"Okay," he says, still gazing at Alicia. "Guess I better, too." Not moving.

Lila tugs at his shirt. "C'mon. Toby'll be worried." She's not leaving without him. Let Alicia get that straight.

"You know Toby," Clay says to Alicia. "She's Lila's grand-mother."

"You call your grandmother Toby?" Alicia says, her voice high and perky. All she needs are pom-poms.

"Everybody calls her Toby," Lila says. "That's her name."

They all laugh then, a false, tinny sound. Clay mouths some excuse, moves away with Lila, watching Alicia back over his shoulder. Lila doesn't turn around, but she'd bet Alicia is posed against the fence, one knee bent, hips turned to accentuate the curve of her waist, a hand raised with delicately bent fingers. Clay nearly stumbles moving down the hill. When they get near his car, he stops and bangs on the fender.

"Damn. She's pretty."

Lila says nothing. She feels fat. Huge. Swollen.

"She's something, isn't she?" Clay says.

"Is she married?"

Clay looks down at his boots. He goes for the country boy act.

"Aw, she's a neighbor, that's all. She and Randy live up on the Canaday place, about a mile from me."

"Uh-huh."

He takes the challenge, drops the charade. He throws his next line at her straight as a spear. "We're friends."

"Randy, too?"

"It's not like that."

"It never is."

He softens his tone. Tries a reasonable approach. "She's lonely. Randy . . . he just wants to go hunting with the guys and hang out at Carl's shooting pool."

"He doesn't understand her." She's shocked at how snotty her voice sounds.

Clay flares back. "No, he don't, come to think of it."

"What about the kid?"

"Amber?" His voice trips on her name. It's clear the kid isn't on his radar.

"God!" Her arms rise and fall at her sides. It's Clay standing there, but she's watching her father throw his packed bags into the trunk of his Camaro, not even a glance in her direction.

"Look," Clay says. "I wasn't born yesterday. And from the looks of you, I'd say you wasn't neither."

She glares at him for a long moment. Her hand flutters over her belly. She opens her mouth and closes it. She leaves him standing there. Behind her, she hears him mumbling an apology, but it's too late. She knows he would have offered her a ride if he had any intention of leaving. She doesn't look back. What the hell. He wants to wreck his life, let him.

Toby

Toby sits in Malcolm Lord's office. She's left Gertie and Lila at Hardee's, not speaking to each other while they down french fries, hamburgers, and milk shakes. She faces the window, sees Main Street, the old brick building, catty-cornered, that was good enough for Malcolm's father, but not good enough for him. That's the bank that was shut down in the thirties. Carried a WANTED poster for Charles Starkweather in the fifties, when he and his fourteen-year-old girlfriend tore across Nebraska murdering eleven people. Now the bank's empty, the old vault barren. Everything in this new slick building, with its automated teller and drive-up window, seems tawdry in comparison. That's what happens when you grow old. Nothing seems as good as it used to be. Modern translates to cheap. Improved means clever marketing.

Malcolm sits behind his desk. His pudgy hand scrubs the top of his balding head, eyes poring over sheets of paper. He's manufactured a look of distress. It's supposed to convey his concern to Toby, his pained concern. The bastard.

"The numbers aren't there, Toby. Even if you could repay last year's loan, there's this year's taxes. Gladys Slokum sold that place of hers for well over a million dollars. That's good news, if you want to sell, but it pushes the taxes higher."

"It's a damn funny world when my land is worth over a million dollars, and I can't afford to live on it."

Malcolm shakes his head. "I know, I know. It's too bad Walter didn't invest in life insurance."

"I don't guess he planned on dying."

"Everybody dies, Toby. Ranchers just think it won't happen to them."

Toby bites down hard. She's not going to discuss her husband with this little man. She wouldn't own the ranch at all if it hadn't been for Walter. He'd married Toby and quietly bided his time. When Luther died he bought John's share of the ranch. Gertie's, too. Turned out Walter had money set aside from a great-aunt who'd made a fortune running a whorehouse in Deadwood. He put every cent back into the ranch, and then he died. One man can't be expected to think of everything. With no insurance and no family left to help out, she'd been forced to sell off the herd. She kept two horses for riding, Cream and Sugar, and leased her land to her neighbors, a fine arrangement until taxes soared out of sight.

"Malcolm, my father did business with your father. Walter and I, too. He trusted us. Some years we damn near lost everything, and Curtis would say, Don't you worry. I can help you out. We'll work out the terms later."

Malcolm sits back in his chair, taps the tips of his fingers together. "Toby, you know things don't work the way they used to."

"I do know that. For sure."

"If my dad was alive today, he'd tell you the same thing."

Toby looks around Malcolm's office, his college diploma hanging on wood-paneled walls, fake geraniums in a plastic flowerpot on the credenza, a picture of Malcolm's two small sons who live with their mother. "I'm sure your father would be the first to admit that things have not turned out like he imagined." She smiles. Malcolm's red face is her reward. "A good man, your father."

Malcolm waves his hand, shooing away spirits.

"What do you want that ranch for anyway? Nola Jean sure won't want to come back here."

"No, I don't expect she will."

"You hanging on for that granddaughter? Don't look to me like she's the ranching type either."

Toby raises her chin. Leave her family out of this.

"You could try diversifying, I guess. Turn that old barn of a house into a B and B. They're springing up all over the West. You'd be surprised how many people, back east and from the cities, want to spend a weekend on the prairie."

"You mean like Hazel Lloyd has done?"

"Hazel. And others. Some're making a pretty good go of it. You got, what? Four bedrooms. Then that little house George and John live in. You could fix that up, too."

"What about us? Gertie? George and John? Where are we supposed to live while city slickers occupy our rooms?"

Malcolm shrugs his shoulders, raises his palms. "I don't know, Toby. Looks to me like you're going to have to make some kind of sacrifices."

Toby sits up straighter. She knows he's trying to bait her. She could recite a litany of sacrifices that would bruise Malcolm's ears, but it wouldn't make a dent.

"Now, I got a buyer anytime you're ready. You know that."

"Western Cattle?" Toby cannot keep the sneer out of her voice.

"Say what you will, but these big conglomerates are the way of the future. They're the only ones can make a go of it these days."

"They don't care about the land."

"They're in it for the profits, that's true. You can't blame them for that."

Toby says nothing. Only glares.

"I wish I could say I can find you a deal that excludes your house, but that house of yours has attracted some attention. One of the accountants has his eye on it."

"Accountant?"

"Western Cattle has quite a corporate crew. They like to keep some of them close to the property, keep an eye on it. You can understand that."

"Not for sale."

"You'd have enough to buy a nice house in town. Don't you think you're getting . . . well, it will only get more difficult to live so far out."

"If I sell it would ruin Royce and Julia."

"It'd be hard on them. But you ain't running a welfare business out there, are you, Toby?"

"You been listening to too much gossip, Malcolm."

"It's my business to know what's going on in these parts. Royce and Julia been off to some of them newfangled outfits . . . "

"Holistic Land Practices."

"Whatever. They think they can run their herd without cutting hay. Leaving the cows out on the range through the winter. Calving late. It's laughable."

"That's how it was done in the thirties and forties. It's not such a newfangled idea."

"Well. People learned better, didn't they? First bad winter comes along, Royce'll lose half his cows. Maybe more."

"Suppose I were to tell you that Royce has showed more profit, per head, than anybody else? What would you say to that?"

Malcolm waves his hand. "Don't matter. People can't work it the way Royce does. Other people got families. They got lives. Royce and Julia run, what," – here he stops to shuffle papers – "five thousand acres of their own, six thousand of yours, three thousand from the government set-aside, that's fourteen thousand acres, twenty-two square miles, by themselves, no hired help, and it takes fourteen thousand acres to sustain two of them. How long you think that's gonna last?"

Toby studies the signs across the street. She knots her hands in her lap. She worries her lip. Part of her fears that Malcolm is right. She's never known any young couple to work so hard. Royce and Julia have no children, no hobbies. Both of them are up at dawn, moving herds or repairing fences. They haven't had a vacation in years. But she's also seen results. They are making it. Profit. And they're doing it without using chemicals. They rotate their herd in small bunches from pasture to pasture, sending them on before insects have time to hatch in the manure. She's seen varieties of grass coming back that she hasn't seen for years – not just grama grass, but big and little bluestem, buffalo grass. Most of their neighbors shake their heads. They scoff and laugh, reminding Toby of the fools who watched while Noah built an ark. Even when Royce shows his results on paper, the old diehards can't give up their land-wasting practices. But Royce and Julia need her land. They couldn't find enough grazing on Royce's five thousand acres. They'd be wiped out, and the conglomerate would take them over, its tentacles stretching that much farther, squeezing out all the old homesteaders.

Toby stands. She does not reach out to shake Malcolm's hand. "How much time have I got, Malcolm?" she asks.

Malcolm rises and hitches at his pants. He runs his hand over the top of his balding head. "I can give you the summer."

Toby's eyes flare at his choice of words. Give. Like it's a gift.

Malcolm smacks his lips. "That's the best I can do."

Lila

Lila has made her way to the family cemetery. It's dusk, and the sweet scent of grass hangs in the air. She's only been here, what, a day, and already she's seen a doctor, chanced on Clay and his road to ruin, gathered a whole new wardrobe of old-lady jeans and baggy shirts. She lifts up the looped barbed wire, pulls the gate back, leaves it lying on the ground. The grass grows higher here inside the fence, so she keeps her eyes on the ground to watch out for rattlers. She hates snakes. When they were younger Clay never seemed to mind if they came on a snake. If it was a bull snake he'd take her hand and lead her past the snake without harming it. If a rattler he'd find rocks and stone it to death. Once he used his boot heel to step flat on the snake's head.

She's lucky today and doesn't see anything slithering or hiding behind the flat white tombstones. She finds her grandfather's stone first. Four years ago she stood out here beside her mother. It was early March, the wind cold and icy. Her mother had on black cowboy boots she'd bought at the airport in Denver, a long fur coat. She looked elegant but foreign. Her dad had been here, too, and he held her hand. Toby stood across the hole in the ground from them. The wind whipped at her black pantsuit, the long black parka that she wore. She had a triangular paisley-printed headscarf tied under her chin. George stood, with one arm under John's elbow, behind Toby and off to one side. Lila squints her eyes, trying to recall the scene. Clay must have been here. His mom and dad, too. And Gertie. Probably Gertie's husband, Howard. But she doesn't remember any of that. She only sees her grandmother, braced against the wind, her face set and unflinching while the minister read from the Bible and prayed.

She looks at the words on her grandfather's stone: Walter Jenkins, February 6, 1926–March 4, 1998. She pictures him, tall, severe. Kindhearted, though. He always seemed busy, coming and going, stopping once in a while to ruffle her hair when he swept through the room. When he died Lila's mother said, No reason to go home anymore. He was the best thing about that place.

Lila starts, then recognizes that George has come up behind her. She didn't hear him. Lost in her own thoughts, partly, but also George moves silently. He wears jeans, a cowboy shirt, boots. His gray hair is pulled back and tied with rawhide at the base of his neck. George once told her and Clay that his hair used to be fiery red, his main inheritance from Red O'Brien, the hard-drinking Irishman who might have been his father. He'd never met the man, but he'd seen pictures hidden in his mother's bureau drawer. George's black hat is banded in rattlesnake hide, probably from a snake he skinned himself. His weathered face falls in folds around high cheekbones, a strong nose, laughing eyes.

"Toby told me you were here," George says. He smiles at her and holds out his hand. His eyes have not once strayed to her big belly but instead hold a lock on her face.

"Hi, George." Lila takes his hand. The skin feels loose on the bones. Rough. A working hand still.

"You out here to ask questions of the dead?"

"Visiting Granddad's grave, I guess. Do you miss him?"

"Walter was a good man."

"What're those?" Lila asks.

"Snapdragons."

George moves past Walter's stone, past Luther and Rosemary and the baby they lost. In the corner of the cemetery are two headstones. He takes his hat off, gently separates the flowers, lays half in front of one stone. He raises his fingers to his lips. Then he stands and crouches again by the second stone, laying down the other half of the bouquet. Again, the fingers to the lips. Lila watches him and wonders how anybody can keep love alive that long.

46

George stands silently, holds his hat in his hand. Lila moves up beside him, but says nothing. She knows this is George's wife. The other stone is George's brother, David. They've both been dead a long time.

"Was David sick a lot?"

George takes a deep breath, lets it out in a long sigh. He puts his hat on his head. The leather cord hangs long under his chin. "Nope," he says.

He turns to go. Lila scurries to follow him. Once George starts moving, he covers ground fast. She stops to shut the gate, and while she slips the loop of wire over the post, she glances at Luther's headstone. Her mother had been a little girl when he died. All she remembered was him sitting in his wheelchair, cussing out somebody, hollering so you could hear him all the way out to the barns and the chicken house. Rosemary's stone stands next to Luther's. The white granite has mottled over the years, settled lower into the ground. Lila stops with her hand on the gate. She lets George disappear from sight. Funny how she never noticed that before. Rosemary's day of death is the same day as David's, June 10, 1948.

That evening after supper, Lila finds her grandmother sitting in a wicker rocking chair on the porch. Toby holds a coffee cup, but it's not coffee she's drinking. Lila smells alcohol. Wine, maybe. Or something stronger. The TV blares from inside. Gertie's got it punched up high, watching to see which new corporate executive is revealed to be a crook or whether President Bush gets his way about waging war on Iraq.

Lila sits in a wicker chair at a right angle to Toby's. She doesn't want to crowd her grandmother. She tucks her feet up under her. Together they look out on the darkening scene, clumps of sage poking up like stalled jackrabbits, the seam of the horizon dissolving so that it's hard to tell earth from sky. Higher above the hills, the eastern sky glows aquamarine, intense, from the reflected light of the setting sun. Once her eyes adjust, Lila begins to see stars, one or two twinkling low on the horizon.

"I saw George," Lila ventures.

"Mmm," Toby murmurs.

Lila bites at her fingernails. She gnaws off a loose chunk, spits it out.

"He was up at the old cemetery."

Toby turns and looks at her, says nothing.

Lila hears a warble, a bird she should recognize. The sound is low and plaintive. But beautiful. She cocks her ear to it.

"Meadowlark," Toby says.

"Where is it?"

"Perched on a post. A wire. They're tough old birds. They sing like that in the twilight. Their most beautiful song in the dying day."

Lila closes her eyes, sails on the bird's song. She has never known anyone who could sit as silently as her grandmother. No questions. No jiggling of her foot. Just that stillness, like the rock of ages.

"What are you drinking?" Lila asks. She waits for the lie. She can't stand the way grown-ups lie to kids. Then they lie to themselves about why they did it. For your own good. Yeah, right.

"Whiskey," Toby says.

Lila nods, surprised that her grandmother told her. Still. Does she do this every night?

"I'd offer you some, but you shouldn't drink while you're pregnant," Toby says.

"That's okay."

A few beats of silence. Lila doesn't know what to say. A stuffed dog on her pillow, now this? Does Toby think she's old enough for whiskey?

"You don't have to worry," Toby says. "I only drink about a shot's worth. Penny says it's good for me."

"Okay," Lila says, though she's not convinced.

They sit for a while without talking. Toby sips from her mug. Lila shifts her weight, swings her feet back and forth. Finally she takes a breath and opens her mouth. Even to her, her voice sounds far away.

"How did your mother die?" Lila asks.

Toby raises her eyebrows. "Car accident."

"The same one that crippled Luther?"

"Yep."

"Was he driving?"

"He never let her drive."

"Was it bad weather?"

Toby pauses. "You might say."

Lila waits a moment. She can't think what question to ask. Instead, she blurts out what she knows.

"She died the same day as David."

Toby takes a swallow of her whiskey. Lila thinks she detects a small tremor in Toby's hands. "That was a sad, sad time."

"What happened to David?"

Toby waits. She rests the coffee cup on the handle of her rocking chair. "You'll have to ask George about that."

"Why? Was he in trouble?"

Her grandmother leans forward. She sets her mug down on the porch railing. She seems to be taking a long time, thinking through what to say, how much to tell.

"David was a good man."

"But you won't tell me."

"It was a long time ago."

Lila sits quiet for a while. David was a young man when he died. It could have been anything. He could have been thrown from his horse, shot in the back. Maybe he'd been drinking. Or trying to scam somebody who got mad. Maybe the fact that he died on the same day that Rosemary bled to death in a ditch and Luther ended up in a wheelchair, mad as hell for the rest of his life, is nothing but a coincidence. An unlucky convention of stars.

"Do you have anything of hers?"

"My mother's?"

"You weren't very old when she died."

"Nope. Sixteen. Your age."

"I'll be seventeen in August."

"I know. I'm your grandmother."

At that Lila laughs a little. She starts to relax. The crickets have cranked up their night song. The sky has grown blacker, the stars as thick as Minnesota mosquitoes.

Toby goes on then. "She loved this house. I guess that's what's hers, mostly. Every morning I put my hand on the stair railing, I think of her. She had the smallest hands, pure white. I remember thinking, even then, that her hand was like a child's hand. She wasn't cut out for this life. She'd come from Ohio, met my father at a family wedding. I have an old garnet necklace of hers. She wore it sometimes at parties. All decked out in a red taffeta dress and that necklace around her neck. She looked like a flower. That's their wedding picture hanging on the landing."

Toby stops abruptly. Lila can't tell if the memories have upset her or if she's embarrassed for talking too long.

"Could I see it sometime? The garnet necklace?"

"Sure. I guess you like jewelry. Like your mother."

"Not hardly." Her mother wouldn't be caught dead with a nose stud or an eyebrow ring.

Toby purses her lips. "I didn't want to be like my mother either. I wasn't going to end up a rancher's wife."

Lila chews this over, how Toby ended up being exactly what she never wanted to be. She's not going to let that happen to her.

"There's a baby's grave, too," Lila says.

"He would have been my little brother. Born when I was about five, I'd guess. He only lived two days. It wasn't uncommon then, no hospitals way out here. It's a wonder Momma didn't die, too. She never was the same after that. Gertie's ten years older than me, John in the middle. Momma had three miscarriages between us, then a couple after I was born. She took it real hard when that little boy died. And Luther. My father. He was sorely disappointed. That boy was going to make up for Gertie and me being daughters, even things up a bit."

"George's wife died a long time ago."

"Ella died in childbirth. Momma went to her. They were fast friends in those days."

"I didn't see another baby's grave."

"No. George buried that baby with her mother. Both in the same coffin. Wrapped in the same blanket."

"This is a tough place for women and babies."

Toby turns. Her voice drops into a different zone. Lila feels her grandmother's hand, laid on her arm. "Things are different now. Don't you worry."

Lila stands. When she's at the screen door, she turns. She rests her head on the opened door, doesn't look at her grandmother but speaks back over her shoulder.

"Toby?"

"What, honey?"

Lila pauses. She hears the rocker stop, knows Toby is waiting. She feels a sting behind her closed eyelids. There's something solid stuck in her throat, so she has to swallow to get air. "Just . . . good night," she says.

On the way upstairs, Lila stops on the landing to look at the wedding picture of Luther and Rosemary. It's a sepia print, ornate oval frame. Rosemary's hair parts in the middle and swoops up in back. She's wearing a white dress with a round collar, pearl buttons down the front. She smiles with her lips closed, big eyes. Her head tips slightly so that it rests against Luther's. He's flat-out grinning, straight at the camera, not a whiff of shyness. Lila knows there's nothing in her that came from these people. Her own mother has none of their blood. Still, she reaches out a finger and touches Rosemary's cheek.

Late at night, lying in bed, Lila puts her hands on her belly, the surface ruffled like corrugated cardboard. Tears leak from the corners of her eyes, run down the side of her face. She thinks of that corny country western title, "I Got Tears in My Ears from Lyin' on My Back and Cryin' over You." That's the sort of stuff she used to laugh about with her dad. Now it makes her cry harder.

She turns on her side, bends her top leg so the baby inside her womb can rest on the bed. She wants this baby to belong. Not like her. She doesn't fit anywhere. She's got money and a house to live in, but all the same she's homeless.

Why didn't you have an abortion? That's what her mother said when Lila's gym teacher called and told her mother she thought Lila was pregnant. She hadn't even noticed that Lila wore nothing but baggy shirts. Her mother called a family conference, a name for what passes as communication among them these days. As soon as they all sat down, her mother made that abortion crack. Her father said, It's too late for that now. They started yelling back and forth, and Lila left the room. She didn't bother to explain that she hadn't known she was pregnant until it was already too late. The boy had a new girlfriend, and when she told him, he said he wanted nothing to do with it. He called his own baby It. She knew she'd ask him for nothing.

Not knowing what else to do, she'd gotten up every morning, picked her jeans up off the floor, pulled them on over her thickening body, and trudged off to class. She never had morning sickness. Sometimes she felt a fluttering inside that she hoped was her period. When the blood didn't come, she taught herself to ignore the flutter, the way she'd taught herself to ignore her parents fighting. She stayed on the softball team where she played first base, continued to get decent grades, told her mother she had no interest in the prom. She'd already stopped seeing her girlfriends when she took up with the boy, so it wasn't hard to avoid them. After a while, the whole thing seemed like a bad dream that she did not want to talk about. A nightmare that would fade with time. She stopped looking in the mirror. She felt invisible and saw no reason why she couldn't hide forever.

Lying in the dark in her grandmother's house, she can't believe what a fool she was. Make-believe, kid stuff. She has someone else to think about now. She can't talk to her mother. She hardly knows her grandmother anymore. What shall I do, Rosemary? she breathes.

She hangs onto things. She still has rocks collected from the North Shore in a jar shoved on the top shelf of her closet. Her baby blanket, shredded from dragging it around behind her, hidden in the bottom dresser drawer. Pictures of Wolf, the dog that died when she was six. How can she give this baby away to strangers?

She could keep the baby. She'd finish high school, there's that program, MICE, Mothers in Continuing Education, she could visit the baby between classes. She could make a home, she knows how to cook, does her own laundry. But then what?

She could search for her baby's adoptive parents herself. She'd know what to look for. She could find somebody this summer, and maybe, even, the new parents would be okay with the child knowing Toby. Toby could walk the child through the family cemetery, tell the stories. Maybe. She'd know that her child looked out every day on this wide sky, these rolling hills. She could put a star on a map.

She's tired. So tired. She could sleep for months, years, wake up when she's old. Somebody else would have to decide. Somebody would harvest the baby from her, like grain from a field of wheat, like organs from comatose donors in a horror movie she saw. She wouldn't even have to know.

Rosemary, Rosemary, she whispers, and she falls asleep thinking of stars, wishing on the name Rosemary.

Toby

Toby sits for a long while on the porch. She hears the television go off. Gertie calls good night through the screen door and Toby calls back. Toby rocks and looks out on her land. There's little moonlight, and still Toby knows the contour of the hills. She can't see the break or the canyon behind the ridge, but her heart takes her there. She roams over every acre, the lake at the bottom of the old summer pasture, the shores teeming with killdeer and marsh wrens. She treks to every windmill, scrambles to the top of Breakneck Ridge. She opens a picnic basket under a lone cottonwood, sits down on a blanket, lets Walter kiss her for the first time. She visits the cemetery, runs her hands over the rough stones, presses her cheek against the grass atop her mother's grave. She stops to talk to Walter. Such dreams we had, she says. In front of David's grave she stoops and places her hand on the cold dark grass. She stands there for a long moment, her breath a shivering sigh.

All this she does from her front porch. She knows she's going to lose this land, one way or another. Nola Jean doesn't want the place. She only hoped to die first. She's in a race now. She needs to get this girl through the summer. Then, before the conglomerate takes her land, before some slack-jawed accountant moves into her mother's house, she's got to find a way to die. It can't look like suicide. But there are plenty of ways to have an accident in this desolate place. Plenty of ways. And she sets her mind to finding one.

Lila

On the afternoon before the branding starts, Lila and her grandmother drive over to the Hendersons' to help Julia load up the chuck wagon. Gertie has refused to come. She's home, miserable, avoiding Clay and watching the soaps on television. Tomorrow George will be here. Maybe John, if he's having a good day. Gertie will still be at home.

Except during the trip to Elmyra, Lila's met no one. Her days are filled with monotony, reading, trailing Toby around, pulling weeds out of George's vegetable patch. She's hooked on one of

Gertie's soaps. Can't miss the *Oprah* show. At least at this branding there will be real people, even if they are cowboys and hicks.

Lila's wearing one of her pairs of grandma jeans, her red hightops, her shirt with the sleeves cut out. She's showing more, but no one says anything. Toby seems excited on the way over, like they're going to a party instead of two days of backbreaking work.

"I don't get what all the fuss is about," Lila says. She's got her hand out the window, riding the waves of the wind. Dust kicks up around them. Lila's throat closes off, and she has to cough. Already it's hot, and the air-conditioner's still broke.

"A branding is a big ol' party. Everybody shows up. Especially for Royce's."

"Why's that?"

"Two reasons, I guess. First off, Royce helps everybody else. He spends a whole month going from ranch to ranch. Makes it tough on Julia to keep up at home, but that's the way it works out here. We got to help each other or nobody would make it."

"What's the other reason?" Lila shouts to get her voice heard above the noise of the tires on gravel, skimming ruts. Now and then the car hits a sandy spot and scuttles sideways.

"Royce and Julia brand the old-fashioned way. It's a real shindig. Ever since Royce rode along on a Centennial cattle drive from the old Spade Ranch to Alliance, he's been doing this. People come out of curiosity. Mostly locals. But some from two or three states away."

They drive over a cattle gate and begin the long descent into the Hendersons' yard. Toby makes the turn, wrestles the car through a shaggy sand dune before she goes on. "They load up three big wagons and pull them with teams of horses. Julia sets up a chuck wagon. Some time today somebody'll get a fire pit dug. Lots of the wives come around for dinner, so they bring salads and desserts, but everything else Julia manages out of the back of that wagon. Hamburgers. Prime rib she buys precooked, so all she's got to do is heat it up. New York steaks you can cut with a fork. Cajun beans and cowboy fries.

"Cowboy fries? Is that what I think it is?"

"Naw. You're thinking of calf fries. Rocky Mountain oysters. We'll have those, too. The guys'll clean them after the first day's work. Cowboy fries are a mixture of bacon, onions, spuds, and Sprite."

"Yuk!"

Toby barks out a laugh. Lila hasn't seen her in this good a mood since she's been here. "Oh, there's plenty of other stuff: scalloped potatoes, hominy, BBQ kraut, potato salad, green beans, pineapple and rhubarb cobbler, homemade rolls. Julia feeds everybody mighty well, that's part of it."

"Couldn't they just go to a restaurant?"

"Child, you are missing the spirit of this whole adventure. Royce builds a wood fire. Burns old fence posts. Most ranchers these days use propane."

"So?"

"Propane burns hot, but it's noisy. Smells, too."

"Sounds like a lot less work."

"Yeah, but less work also takes the fun out of it."

"So we should go back to cooking over a woodstove?" Lila watches her grandmother's mouth tighten. She's doesn't know why she's arguing about this. She could care less whether they burn propane, wood, or buffalo chips. It's dumb to mix up the past with romance, that's all. She gets that all the time from her dad, talking about the heyday of American jazz in a voice that sounds like it belongs in church. If the good old days were so

57

damn good, why does everybody want to leave them behind? You wouldn't catch her mother doing without a microwave or her cell phone. Nobody wants to go back to outdoor plumbing.

Toby goes on talking then. Her voice has lost some of its shine. "Most of the guys camp overnight. Takes two days, since they move the whole site three or four times. It's easier to load up the wagons and portable pens and move people than it is to collect the whole herd. Then, when all the work is done, they heel up one of the longhorn cows and Royce gets on and rides. He's getting too old, the fool, but he says it takes him back to his rodeo days. It's the talk for a whole year."

By now Toby has pulled the car up alongside a barn with a corral attached. Three wooden wagons crowd the yard. Six monster horses wait in the corral, two black, two gray with a scattering of white stars on their backs, and two the color of a Florida beach. The sandy ones have furry feet and long tails.

"They going to ride those?" Lila asks.

"Those are draft horses," Toby says. "They pull the wagons. Percherons and Clydesdales. The gray and black ones are borrowed. But the roans are Royce's. Chip and Dale."

Crossing the yard to the house, Lila spots Clay. He's hauling what looks like camping gear from the barn to one of the wagons. "Clay," she calls. He disappears into the wagon bed without hearing her. Either that or he's ignoring her.

Lila hurries to catch up with Toby, who's halfway up the walk. Inside the picket gate, Royce and Julia's small house bends in an L-shape. Wood siding, painted white. One story. Two rangy dogs come barking out from under the front porch. Toby holds her hand out, coos softly, and the dogs back off. "Wiley and Fritter," Toby says, pointing to one dog and then the other. They look identical to Lila, black mutts with white blotches. She's not going anywhere near either of them. Toby stops to rub the dogs' ears, and both of them jump up, offering to lick her face. Lila stares at a long flowerbox fitted out with weathered wagon wheels and white, sun-bleached cattle skulls.

"Julia says that's reminiscent of Georgia O'Keefe," Toby says. Then she leans in closer. "I think it looks like hell."

They pound on the front door and after giving a holler, Toby lets herself in. Lila follows behind, enters a kitchen opening off into a combination living room and dining area. Wood paneled, the living room holds a brown leather couch, two rough-hewn wooden chairs with leather seats, a loveseat upholstered in white- and brown-spotted cowhide. Above a television set, a massive animal head is mounted on the wall, the horns curved up toward the ceiling. An ox, maybe. A loop of barbed wire hangs on one horn, as if someone plays an indoor game of horseshoes. Real horseshoes, welded together end to end, form two lamp stands, the shades of painted parchment, or it could be hide, something translucent and thick, one depicting cattle brands, the other an elaborate scene of buffalo running on green grass against a backdrop of blue sky, both laced and trimmed with lengths of rawhide, the kind George uses to tie his hair back. A few scattered rugs dot the wooden floors. They look handwoven, Indian patterns. In the bay window, a collection of wild-ranging cactus. The whole scene reminds Lila of *Butch Cassidy and the Sundance Kid*. On the kitchen refrigerator, a bucking horse magnet holds a bumper sticker that reads: Eat Beef: The West Wasn't Won by Salad.

Everywhere around the continuous flow of rooms, boxes are stacked with cooking utensils, bags of onions and beans and potatoes, plastic bins of cabbages and carrots. A huge cast iron Dutch oven takes up one corner. Two giant skillets, big enough to hold Lila's feet end to end, lean against the leg of the oak dining table. A case of Sprite is piled on top of another box marked "Kitchen Crap" in black marker. Jars of hominy, plastic bottles of ketchup and steak sauce, gallon cans of pickles, enough food for a small army, and in the middle stands a woman with a list in her hand, checking things off like a grocer. She's wiry. Her blondish-red hair waves, as if it's been crimped, and she wears it loose and long. No makeup, her face tanned and lined by the sun. Blue eyes. She looks hardened and competent, standing there in her white western shirt tucked into tight-hipped jeans.

"Hey, Toby," she says, not looking up.

"I brought a recruit," Toby says. The woman glances up then. Her eyes widen slightly. Lila's getting used to this. It's the belly. Maybe the eyebrow ring and the hair. She looks out of place here. Normal is out of place here. What kind of people want to sit their butts on cowhide furniture?

Julia sticks her hand out. "Julia," she says.

Her hand grips Lila's, rough-skinned and strong. Lila tries not to wince or shy back. She's conscious of her own hand, white and soft. Useless. "Lila," she says.

Julia smiles, and Lila can understand why Royce stopped riding the rodeo circuit. She wonders why they don't have kids. Julia looks like she could be in her late thirties or early forties. Maybe they're too old to have their own. Still, not too old to consider. Maybe there's more to them than this Wild West show atmosphere.

Lila excuses herself to go to the bathroom, something she has to do more often these days. The bathroom looks ordinary enough, clean. Above the stool, a Far Side cartoon, the one about chickens carrying a baby out of the house, passing the people who've just robbed their nest of eggs. Stolen babies. Cripes. On the way down the hall, she peeks into their bedroom. Holy shit, she breathes, staring at the long horn that makes up the bed's headboard. She runs her hand over the sharp point, the smooth curves. Okay, it's weird, but not that different from Minnesotans who make furniture out of birch logs. Or decorate their cabins with pine trees, loons, and moose. Fish everywhere. She's reassured by the rest of the bedroom furniture, plain knotty pine.

She pokes her head in a small office with a massive oak desk and computer. An elaborate chart on the wall. She decides that it's a listing of the pastures on the land, Crow Meadow, Rodgers Valley, Billy Rice. George told her that most of the places are named after the original homesteaders. So Royce and Julia are computer literate. They aren't playing games here, that's for sure.

She gets back to the kitchen and grabs a heavy box with pots and pans. She strains to lift it when Julia comes up behind her. "Here. You shouldn't be doing that." Julia leans over and picks up the box easily. Strong, Lila thinks. And kind.

She wanders over and picks up a different box, marked "Towels." She follows Julia out to the wagon, stands on the ground and lifts it up to her over the tailgate. Toby's inside the wagon, shoving boxes around, packing things in tight.

"What're you smiling about?" Toby asks. She's crouching with her hands on her knees, looking at Lila from the depths of the wagon.

Lila shrugs. "Nothing."

The next morning, Lila and Toby drive out to the branding site early, about 6:30. Lila's still shaking herself out of a dream, hardly awake, but already the forty to fifty helpers are out gathering cattle. A handful of men stand in front of the fire pit drinking coffee and munching on pastries. George is there. John, too, plunked down in a lawn chair that George toted in the back of the pickup. Already hot and muggy, the air barely moves. The gnats pick at Lila's ears, her eyelids. She shakes her head to be rid of them, but it does little good.

"You need a hat," George says.

"Have to have a tall one to cover that hair," a stranger says. He's wide, his feet planted down square, his eyes covered by dark glasses. George gives her a shove with his elbow, to let her know the man is kidding. She reaches up and rubs her hand through her hair, feels the sticky gel between her fingers.

"Guess so," she manages, though she doesn't like being the butt of their jokes. She's still wearing all the rings in her ears, her eyebrow, the nose stud. She's not going to lose herself in this outback country.

"You and them little calves going to have something in common today," the man says, guffawing loudly. "Ain't that so, boys?"

He raises his coffee cup to the others, asking them to be his straight man.

"Why's that?" This man has curly hair sticking out from under a black hat.

"Them baby calves going to get their ears tagged today."

He laughs again and takes a swig from his coffee mug. Lila twists her mouth. She studies George to see if has a hint for her, but his face is unreadable. She draws herself up tall. She knows this routine. She's played it out on city streets, on school buses. Next it will be something about her belly. She tries to get ready for it.

"Well," George says, his voice mild, soothing even. "Guess she won't be the only one."

The swaggering man turns to George. "What do you mean there, George?"

62

George doesn't move. Lila throws a glance at John, camped in his lawn chair across the fire pit, but she doesn't expect a response.

"As I hear it, the boy calves are being castrated today. Losing their balls," George says.

The silence hangs in the air for a second too long, and then John starts to laugh. He's so tickled that his sides heave. His coffee sloshes dangerously out of his mug, splashing on the dirt beside his chair, the curly-haired man doing a quickstep to avoid getting coffee on his boots. At that the burly stranger laughs, and then they all join in.

Lila steals a look at George, whose face hardly moves, except for a slight twitch at the corner of his mouth.

The riders come in then, driving enough cattle to flood a movie set. They herd the swarm of calves and cows into the portable branding pen. Calves bawling, riders kicking up dust, cowboy hats bobbing – Lila doesn't know where to stand to be out of the way. She wants to see what's going on, but there's so much flurry, so much hollering, and then it's all business, too, and not knowing where to run, she feels George's hand on her shoulder.

"Come," he says. She follows him, and he heads away from the pen, the riders, Julia and Toby and the few women at the chuck wagon. He threads his way around behind a ridge of sandstone, and they climb it from the back. "Keep your eyes peeled for rattlers," he says. Lila's tennies slip on the grass. Once she has to put her hands down and tug at a clump of sage to pull herself over a rock. At last they crest the ridge, and they are high, high above the scene below, but not so far that they can't watch everything that's happening. George spreads an Indian blanket on the grass. He holds her hand to help her sit, like a courtly gentleman. She watches, thinking this is what a bird sees, an eagle hovering over the scene, and she loves how they all look small and not quite human and yet humming with motion. She watched an ant farm once like this, trying to figure out the purpose of the activities. George helps her decipher it. There, in the center of the pen, the branding wagon, dropped table on the end. Buckets on the ground. Five riders heel out calves and drag them to wrestlers on either side of the wagon. In addition to the wrestler, each side has a cutter, an implanter, and a vaccinator. The branding fire blazes hot, but quiet. Male calves are castrated, their testicles dropped into a bucket before their flesh is seared by a hot iron, a lazy B, the ranch's calf brand. The heifers are pregnancy tested, and if keepers, they get a second brand, a quarter moon. George explains the whole process to her, says the teams average 125 calves an hour, and she watches from high on her perch.

At first she cringes at the bawling calves, their heels dragging as they are pulled away from their mothers. Her nostrils curl at the stench of charred hair and flesh. She watches Clay dust himself off with his hat, wipe his face on his shirtsleeve. One calf breaks free from a roper, caroms into the pen's walls. The man curses, and other men laugh. The red glowing irons burn and sizzle, and her eyes smart.

After a while she gets used to the noise and the dirt, and then she notices the precision with which the men work. Red irons wave through the air, but no one gets burned. The squirming calf gets tagged, vaccinated, implanted, castrated, and branded by a group of men who bend forward and then out of the way, like pistons on a huge machine. She saw a dance piece like this once. She and her dad went to the Ordway in downtown St. Paul, sat on plush seats and watched a troop of young women and men drop off ledges and land on mats, throw themselves, one after another, against a backdrop, timed with absolute precision, the thumping and falling of their bodies forming an underlying rhythm like the heartbeat of life itself.

About noon Lila stands in line along with the rest of the kitchen help to fill her plate. She wants none of the dripping meat that covers the eight-foot fire pit. She heaps her plate with potato salad, baked beans, and hominy. The cowboy fries look good, little flags of bacon poking out. When she stretches for the spoon, someone jars her elbow.

"S'cuse me." She turns, annoyed, and looks into the face of a man who can't be much older than her. Eighteen, maybe. She noticed him earlier, riding beside Clay. He, alone of the cowboys, looked awkward astride his horse. He hung onto the saddle horn with one hand, tried to lift the reins with the other, but he seemed off balance. He wasn't much use with the actual work going on. He mostly sat his horse and rode aimlessly around the corral, trying to stay out of the way. His hat looked too big for him, sat down on his ears. Another greenhorn, she thought, watching him. Now she looks into his face, and he grins at her. He's got a scar that rakes across his forehead, a little scruffy beard.

"You better have a scoop of those," he says. He points at the big bucket of breaded calf fries. The thought turns her stomach. It seems cannibalistic to her, eating flesh you've cut off a living beast. Worse yet, sex glands. Way worse than eating meat from a butchered carcass, and she doesn't want any of that either.

"I don't think so." She starts to edge away.

"Clay says you're from Minneapolis."

She studies him. People crowd forward in the line, so she's got to move on. She knows that if she tells this young man anything at all, he'll walk her to some spot on the ground and sit down next to her.

"Where is Clay?" She cranes her neck to look around. Maybe she wouldn't mind talking to this guy if Clay was there, too.

"Over there." The man nods his head in the direction of the bed wagon. Clay is leaned up against it, talking to a woman with a plate in her hand. The woman's auburn hair plays against a pale blue shirt.

"What's she doing here?"

Before the man can respond, Lila turns on her heel and walks over to Clay and Alicia. When she gets closer, she sees that their heads are tipped toward each other. Alicia feeds Clay cobbler from her plate, her fingers lingering on his lips.

"Need a fork?" Lila asks, walking up and standing close to Alicia.

Clay shoots her a warning glance. Lila raises her eyebrows at him, does her Groucho Marx imitation. He laughs, as he always did. Alicia wipes her hand on her jeans, turns slightly so she's aimed at Lila and not toward Clay's heart.

"I guess you remember me, from the swimming pool," she says to Alicia.

Alicia looks Lila over. She lingers on her belly. She touches her own eyebrow and then her nose. "I don't see how I could forget you, Lila."

"Where's your husband? Haven't forgot him, have you?"

Alicia turns her attention to Clay. She shifts her shoulders, so Lila gets the back side of her. "Think I'll check on how the cobbler's doing," Alicia says. She steps between them, her arm brushing against Clay's chest.

Lila turns and braces her back against the wagon. She dives into her plateful of food. She hasn't had anything to eat since pastries this morning, and she's starving. Clay leans his arm on the wagon. Shakes his head at her.

"Stay out of it," he says. His voice sounds dark.

"Where is old Randy?"

"Home. Amber's with Alicia's aunt. This is Alicia's day out."

Lila stifles a laugh. "I'll say."

"You don't know her."

Lila watches Clay. He's got his head down, kicking the toe of his boots. Stooped shoulders, gray smudges under his eyes.

"You look tired," she says.

"Yeah, well. You try roping and hauling calves for hours."

She mops at her baked bean sauce with her bread. "That all it is?"

Clay turns and leans his back against the wagon. Hooks his thumbs in his belt. "Things catch up to you after a while."

"I know what you mean," she says.

Clay lets the silence stretch a little, and then asks, "Grandma wouldn't come today?"

"She didn't want to miss her shows, I guess." Lila tosses this out, curious to see if Clay'll run with it.

"She didn't want to see me."

"What's going on, Clay?"

Clay strings out a long pause. When he does start talking, his voice is slow. He doesn't turn to look at Lila. He's watching Alicia laugh into somebody else's face over by the chuck wagon. "I don't know, really. She's always been hard, stubborn. After Dad had that heart attack, everybody went crazy."

"Must have been hard on your mom."

"She took to drinking. You probably heard that." Clay unties his neckerchief, uses it to mop the dust off his face. "I was a senior in high school then. I'd come home, house'd be empty. I'd find her in some bar. Take her home. Put her to bed. Grandma couldn't much handle that. You know how she is about booze."

"So Gertie and Howard moved to town?"

"Legally the farm belonged to Mom. Grandma said Mom wanted her out of that house so's she could move in. I think Grandpa was starting to lose it by then, only we didn't know it. He didn't put up much fight. Didn't sort things out, the way he used to. I found him one day digging ditches around the front yard, talking about pipes and things that made no sense. So they moved off the farm. Mom and me, we moved over to the big house. She didn't want to stay in that other house. Not without dad."

"So I still don't get why Gertie's mad at you."

"She's got to have somebody to be mad at. And she doesn't trust me. She thinks I'm too young and I'll botch everything, and then the farm'll be gone. She hated that place all her life, but she can't stand the thought of losing it out of the family. She won't speak to Mom, 'specially since she married Frank. Calls her a tramp and a whore."

Lila stands with her empty plate. She looks out across the open space. One of Royce's dogs has finally given up on the pile of food scraped off plates for him. Several of the cowboys are lying down, their heads shaded under the wagons, boots sticking out, resting up before the whole operation gets reloaded and moved ten miles or so for the afternoon branding session.

"At least your mom is on your side," Lila says, after a long silence.

"Mom's okay."

Lila watches Toby, over by the chuck wagon with Julia and a few other women, scrubbing pots and pans in soapy water. They carried the water from the tank at the base of the windmill some fifty yards away.

"Sometimes . . ." She pauses, then figures she might as well finish the thought. "I wish my dad had died."

"No, you don't."

"I could pretend, you know, that he wanted to be with us."

He makes a sound, a low grunt. She can see him taking that in, weighing it.

"Well," he says. "My grandma thinks I'm dirt."

"Gertie thinks most everybody's dirt."

They laugh a little then. She wonders if he's thinking about the times they got in trouble, Gertie preaching to them about little sins turning into big ones, making them stand facing the closet wall. When she caught them smoking the cigar stubs Howard pitched off the front porch, she sat them at the kitchen table and made them smoke until they were both retching in the bathroom. She hovered over them, quoting from the Bible, *as ye sow, so shall ye reap*, a little Sodom and Gomorrah thrown in.

She stands with Clay a few more minutes. He watches Alicia the whole time. He's got it bad, Lila can see. He's not that careful, either. It sticks out all over him.

The young man with the too-big hat is leaning on the gate of the branding pen. It's empty now, except for a few horses. He's got his hat in his hand and keeps looking over at Clay and Lila. She knows he's trying to decide if he can bust in on their conversation.

"Who's that?" she asks Clay. She nods slightly toward the man.

"That's Tim Pickford. Buddy of mine. He's staying out at the farm. In an old trailer."

"He's kind of cute."

"Look, Lila. He's a bad risk."

"I thought you said he was a buddy of yours."

"Well, he is. Kind of. He had no place else to go."

"What's he do?"

"Do?"

"He doesn't look like much of a rancher. Or a farmer."

"No, I guess not. He's got a little side business. Trying to figure some things out. He helps out where he can."

Lila turns to Clay. She puts her free hand on his chest, looks up into his face. "You in over your head, Clay?"

He nods. "In every way." He grins at her, that lopsided smile that she knows can turn a girl's heart.

Toby

Late evening, and Toby stands with George looking over the campsite. After two shifts of branding, everybody's tuckered out. Some of the helpers have driven home to sleep in their own beds, but twenty-five or so have camped out on the prairie with tents and sleeping bags. Toby'd like to stay herself, but she doesn't think it'd be good for Lila. Besides, it's been a long while since her bones took to lying on the hard ground for a night. She breathes in the scent of campfire smoke, the lingering pungency of seared calf hair, sweat and horses, manure, grease from the hamburgers cooked over another fire pit. The sun lowers itself majestically in the west, squatting down on orange haunches. The hills are shadowed and deep, mysteries folded in nooks and crannies.

"Gertie wouldn't come?" George says.

Toby shakes her head.

"Foolish old woman." George bends and scoops a handful of dirt. He lets it trail through his fingers.

Toby watches Lila. She's helping Julia with the last of the cleanup from the evening meal, rolling a white dish towel over pots and pans.

"Lila's asking Julia a lot of questions."

"That right?" George waits, sitting on his heels. He can sit this way for hours.

"Did she ever want kids? Did she grow up with kids around? Does she like kids?"

George chuckles. "Well. She could do worse."

"You know that won't work. You should know better than most people."

She leaves George and walks to where her brother John sits in his lawn chair. Luther ruined John, one more thing Toby will never forgive him for. John came back from the war in the Pacific with nightmares, his nerves shot. Luther rode John hard, reducing his grown son to quaking and tears. After Luther died John sold his share of the ranch to Walter and escaped to Cheyenne, where he lost his money gambling and fell further into the drinking habit he'd cultivated to numb himself to Luther's rages. Toby got a phone call one night, and the next morning she and George drove to Cheyenne, collected John from the VA hospital and brought him home. She puts her hand on his shoulder, not wanting to wake him if he is truly sleeping. He stirs and turns to her, his eyes glazed with that one-dimensional look. Then he smiles sweetly.

"Sister," he says.

"Hey, Johnny. How'd it go today?"

His fingers grab at the air, flail, and she catches them. He clings to her, and she struggles to maintain her balance as he pulls her closer. She leans over him, presses her cheek to his. He quiets a little. She murmurs in his ear, "It's all right. You're safe here. George will take you home soon." He nods his head. She stands, keeping her hand on his shoulder. She looks off in the distance, thinking this may be her last branding. This may be the last year she sets foot on her own land. She lets her eyes follow the line of the horizon, past that high ridge. A hawk trails through the sky overhead. She keeps her hand on her brother's shoulder, drawing strength from his broken body, knowing that as much as he hated this place when Luther was alive, it is, and always will be, home.

On the morning of the second day of branding, while the men work the herd and Julia and Toby bang pots and pans and George leans on the portable pen watching and Tim Pickford sits uncomfortably astride a big bay gelding and Lila rests off her feet in a chair next to John, a black Jeep Cherokee pulls up. Toby straightens, her hand against her lower back, shields her eyes from the sun, takes in the Wyoming license plate. How the hell did they find their way out here?

She watches while a tall, lanky man unfolds himself from the car. He's wearing town clothes, gabardine pants, western shirt with pearl buttons, string tie. She can't see his boots, but she's betting they're inlaid with rattlesnake skin or bits of turquoise. From the rider's side, slinking around the front fender, is Malcolm Lord. Well. So this must be the accountant.

Toby rubs her mouth with the back of her hand. Julia has come up beside her.

"Great. More mouths to feed."

"They won't be staying," Toby says.

Toby walks out to meet the two men. She squares her shoulders, sets her jaw.

"Mornin', Toby," Malcolm says. "This here is Jack Wesson."

He hooks his thumb in the direction of the stranger. Malcolm's grammar always slides when he's trying to look like one of the boys. It irritates Toby, no end.

"Malcolm," Toby nods. "Mr. Wesson."

"Jack here," Malcolm stops to kick the ground. He can't look at Toby. At least the little worm knows what's he up to. "Jack here, he wanted to see what a real branding was like."

"You're from Western Cattle."

Jack tips his hat. "Yes, ma'am, I am. We'd like to take a look around, if you don't mind."

"I do mind."

"Now, Toby," Malcolm starts. There's a warning in his voice. He raises one hand, pushes at the air between them. He shakes his head sideways.

"This branding is by invitation only, Mr. Wesson. You and Malcolm, you're trespassing."

The color rises in Jack Wesson's cheeks. Toby can see he's not accustomed to someone standing in his way.

"Forgive me, Mrs. Jenkins, I don't think this branding is your business."

"You're on my land."

"Toby, Toby," Malcolm waves his chubby hands in the air. He looks from her to Jack and back again. He's practically dancing. "Technically, this is Royce's land, he has the say-so, because he holds the lease."

Toby does not move. She stands her ground. She lets a vast silence open up. Malcolm looks like he'd rather be in Tokyo, but Jack Wesson holds fast. Toby admires his patience. Not many men can stand planted and silent in the face of an angry old woman. She's wondering who will make the first move when she feels a hand on her shoulder. Turning, she sees Julia has moved up, joined ranks with her. George steps up on her other side, and next to him, good lord, it's Lila, her belly sticking out, both hands cradled on her back. Like characters in an offbeat western, two old people, a pregnant girl, and a pretty woman face the evil outsider and his hired stoolie. Toby almost smiles; where is John Wayne when you need him? All the odds are on the side of the stranger and the banker. Except for one thing. George is bearing his shotgun.

"I expect you better move on out, Booger," Julia says.

Jack Wesson grins. A man spoiling for a fight. And liking it better all the time. "And who might you be?"

Malcolm intervenes. He can't take his eyes off George. "This here's Julia. She's Royce's wife. She and Royce lease this land." Malcolm underscores this last for Jack's sake.

George shifts the gun in his hands. A small, almost imperceptible move, but Malcolm shies like he's come up on a coiled diamondback.

"Go on, now," Julia says, her voice soft as butter. She could be coaxing a cow to give birth. She could be gentling a wild horse. She makes it easy for them.

Before getting into the Jeep, Jack Wesson stops to deliver one last glare. When the two men have finally driven away, Toby turns to George.

"You load that gun, George?"

"Nope," he says. "Didn't need to."

George turns and walks back to the branding pen, where the action has never faltered. Toby watches George walk away, knowing how he loves this role of protector. She only hopes he'll die before he finds out nothing can save her.

George

George makes his way back to the wagon bed, slower now. Lays the shotgun down the way he found it. Loaded. He'd put it there this morning thinking he might have to take down a wounded horse or blow the head off a poisonous snake.

He's breathing hard. Adrenaline. He'd known he could lift the gun, fire, hit the banker between the eyes. Twist, fire, bring the other one down before he'd have time to run. He hasn't used his gun against a man for a long time. But there's nothing he wouldn't do for Toby. Nothing. He let them see that in his face.

That girl, now. She's got spunk, for a city kid. Her stand-on-end hair the butt of half the men's jokes, those rings in her ears. The guys like her, though. She keeps to herself. She's tough and she doesn't ask a thousand questions.

He's seen Tim Pickford watching her. It's not Tim's fault that he's from a lousy family, his dad up on charges of murder, acquitted, even though most thought he probably did shoot Speck Granger. Tough load for a kid, and not his fault. It's up to Tim whether he's going to overcome his past or knuckle under to it. So far, from what George hears, his prospects don't look good.

He lets his heart slow down, his hand resting on the stock of the gun. Without even turning around, he's got his eye on Tim Pickford.

Lila

Lila follows Julia, matches her footsteps to hers exactly, as she moves from the fire pit to the wagon and back again. Julia has a long stride. As tall as Lila is, she has to stretch her legs to fit into

Julia's boot tracks. They're repacking everything, getting ready to roll home after Royce's ride.

Toby, George, John, and all the others are already lined up over by the branding pen. It's emptied out now, all the ranch hands standing around the perimeter, waiting to see Royce climb on top that longhorn and pump the air.

"C'mon, Julia," Lila says. "We're going to miss Royce's ride."

Julia runs her fingers over her lips, looks from the stack of pots to the wagon. She seems to be counting in her head. Lila can't figure it out. This is the first time she's seen Julia distracted. What's the matter with her?

"You go on," Julia says. She waves at Lila. "I got work to do here."

"It can't wait five minutes?"

"No. It can't."

Lila sees Toby looking around for them. She catches Toby's eye, lifts her shoulders in a shrug.

Toby nods. She leans over to say something to George. Then she breaks away from the jostling crowd and crosses to the chuck wagon. She doesn't hurry. She picks up a coffee cup somebody's left lying around, throws the coffee in the fire. The liquid sputters and sizzles on the coals.

"He'll be fine," Toby says.

"I know it."

Julia is tying twine around a box too small to hold its contents. She's turned the flaps up to extend the size. She knots the twine twice before she gets the knot to hold.

Lila watches while Julia ties and reties. Toby doesn't say a word. When Julia gets done, she stands and faces Toby. The two women look at each other. Julia lets out a gush of air. She turns her head and rubs the back of her neck.

"All right," Julia says. "Let's go."

She turns then and heads straight for the branding pen. Toby falls in line behind her and Lila scrambles to keep up. The circle of men parts automatically, and Julia takes her place. Toby moves alongside her. Lila stands on the other side. She can feel the heat off Julia's skin.

Royce stands inside the pen, across from Julia, yukking it up with a few of the men. He's wearing chaps with silver medallions down the side, his hat jammed down on his head. In the pen the curly-haired cowboy rides a chestnut horse with a black and gold saddle. There are two other men on horseback. They have a longhorn cow stretched out, a rope around her horns, another around her heels. Somebody points Julia out to Royce, and he turns. He doffs his hat to Julia, and Julia dips her head. Lila thinks, for a moment, that she's watching the beginning of a medieval dance, like something she saw on the history channel last year for school. Julia clenches her hand at her sides, but she manages to smile and look on while Royce swings up on the frightened cow. He holds his heels out from her sides, his hand groping for a hold on the back of her neck. He nods, and the ropers turn her loose. For a long moment the cow stands stock-still. Nobody breathes. A spray of white butterflies flits along the ground, and then the cow starts to flail. She twists her torso, shoots her heels at the sun, tries to go in two directions at once. The crowd yells encouragement, and Royce flings one hand into the air, his spurred boots gouging the cow's sides. The crowd roars when his hat flies off, groans when the cow's hoof lands squarely on the crown. They all lean forward to brace themselves as the curly-haired man rides up close to lift Royce off the frantic cow. Royce gets both feet on the ground, runs along for a few steps from the momentum of getting off the ride, and the crowd starts to cheer.

Lila cannot, the whole time, take her eyes off Julia's face. Julia's hands are pressed together, her fingers at her lips. Her eyes shine, and each time the crowd rolls with an ooh or an aah, Julia gasps. She's riveted onto Royce. It's beautiful, the way Julia holds onto him.

When Royce finishes his ride, Julia's is the first face he seeks. She walks to him. The crowd hushes as she lifts her hand and lays it on his cheek. Lila almost expects Royce to kneel and Julia to knight him with her own strong arm. Instead Royce slips an arm around her shoulders. With that the spell is broken and people start to walk away, laughing and calling out to Royce, naming him the king of riders for yet another year.

Lila's throat hurts, and she finds that she cannot move away. She watches Royce and Julia walk toward the wagon, sees Julia place her hand on Royce's shoulder then rub the back of his neck. They are magnets, drawing toward each other. She's trying to imagine what it would feel like to lean like that, knowing someone else would catch your fall, when she's startled by a hand on her own shoulder.

"Hey, Lila."

She turns, and Tim Pickford withdraws his hand. She could swear he's shaking. He tries to look at her, but he's gazing somewhere over her left shoulder.

"Could I see you sometime?" he asks.

She doesn't answer, and he goes on talking. "Maybe we could go into town, have supper. Or just go for a walk. Whatever you want."

She's watching true love. She's watching Julia and Royce together by the chuck wagon, Royce handing up boxes to Julia, their arms grazing against each other. She's watching the real thing, and she's got this boy who can't even look at her.

"I gotta go." Without once glancing to see the effect of her words on Tim Pickford, she walks away.

Gertie

Gertie sits in front of the television. It's past noon, they ought to be coming home soon. Must be getting time for Royce to get on some darn fool cow. She pictures the men leaning on the branding pen, goading him, ride, ride, ride 'em, cowboy. Women there, too, standing two and three deep, leaning against the backs of whatever man they're attached to. Pushing their breasts into him. Maybe one or two of the men reaches around, cups the buttocks of the woman clinging to him. The woman lets her hands slide low, past his belt buckle.

Gertie shifts her feet to get her mind off that scene. She never would have stood that way with Howard, but she's seen Toby with Walter. No shame, like that. Bending over and kissing him on the ear at the square dances. Pretending he was her one and only. Oh, there are things she could tell about her precious, high-and-mighty sister.

She didn't want to go to the branding. Why breathe in all that dirt? Smell burned flesh? She'd have had to see that boy. Clay. She hasn't run into him for months. They tell her at the rest home that he stops in now and again to see Howard. She doesn't want the boy upsetting Howard, but the nurses say it's good for Howard to have company. They say Howard seems to quiet to quiet in his presence. Don't that beat all? After everything, Howard gets quiet when Clay's around. When she visits she's got to track him to the room of that Stewart woman.

She waited last night until Toby and that girl came home. She waited up, sat in her chair long past her regular bedtime. They came in. Headed straight for bed. Hardly a howdy. She wanted news, but Toby could rot before she'd ask her for it. Toby's like that. Keeping things to herself. Knowing full well Gertie'd want to know how Clay seems, if he's managing all right, if he's tired out. If he had any news of his mother.

At the thought of Clay's mother, Gertie starts to cough. Her chest again. She feels the tightening. She heaves herself out of the chair and makes her way to the kitchen. Runs herself a glass of water from the kitchen sink. That spoiled girl, Lila, won't drink the water from the well. Has to have her bottled water in the refrigerator.

She looks out the window over the sink. She can't make out the outlines of the machine shed, but she's not looking for that anyway. She's waiting for the messengers. She's watching for Eliphaz, Bildad, and Zophar. She knows she's being tested, like Job. She's lost everything, hasn't she, and now it's time for the messengers to show up and tell her what it means. Why, when she has been so faithful, is she being punished?

Lila

Lila wants something, and she's waiting for the right moment to ask for it. She doesn't want to answer any questions, but her grandmother is sharp. Toby knows, for instance, that Gertie keeps a secret stash of chocolate bars in the Hoosier cupboard. When Lila accidentally knocked one off the shelf when reaching for the honey, Toby picked it up off the tile floor without a word. Gertie sat at the kitchen table paging through her worn-out

Bible, jabbering about Job and pestilence. Toby winked at Lila and put the bar back behind the rice. Hershey's Krackle.

Lila chooses a moment when Gertie is watching TV. Toby's in the kitchen, snapping beans. Lila sits at the table, picks up a few beans, and while popping ends off asks, "Do you have any other pictures of your mother?" She's been stopping every night on the landing to visit Rosemary. She focuses on Rosemary's face, but Luther grins back at her. She'd like to have Rosemary to herself.

Toby stops. Lila can feel her eyes studying her, but she keeps her attention on those beans. She doesn't dare look at Toby's face. "Got one in a small frame up on my dresser," Toby says.

"Oh." Lila tries not to show the disappointment.

"Guess I could loan it to you for a while."

Lila shrugs. She'd like to run up right now and get it. Instead, she snaps heads off beans, pings them against the edge of the metal pot.

That night in her room, she hears a tap on her door. She opens the door in a white V-necked T-shirt and her panties. Her bare belly bulges out between the bottom of the shirt and the top of her red bikini underwear. She hides as much as she can behind the door.

"I thought you might like to see that garnet necklace," Toby says.

Lila blinks a couple of times. "Yeah. Okay. Just a minute." She grabs an old quilt off the foot of her bed, wraps it around her shoulders, holds it in front so that she's mostly covered. When she turns, Toby is frowning.

"What?" Lila asks.

"Maybe I can find you a robe," Toby says.

She turns, and Lila follows her across the hall to her bedroom.

It's a small room, a high double bed taking up most of the space. The windows are hung with lace curtains. To one side sits a small oak chest with a gray marble top. Centered on the bureau, an oval picture frame, silver with raised roses forming an arch at the top. Lila doesn't make a move toward it.

Toby goes to a closet and pulls out a burgundy fleece robe. "It might be too warm for summer, but better than that quilt," she says.

Lila takes the robe. She turns her back to her grandmother, tosses the quilt on the end of the bed, wraps the robe around. It barely covers her in front, but she ties it anyway. It smells like her grandmother, some cross between apple spice and lavender soap. She smoothes her hands down the sides, catches her right thumb in a torn pocket flap.

"Thanks."

Toby has already gone to the small bureau. She opens a drawer and removes a rectangular jewelry box. The curved lid is painted with flowers and a cherubic female figure, pink rounds of rose petals and the cherub's cheeks lacquered to a high polished finish. Toby sits on the bed, lifts a gold hinged clasp, opens the box, and withdraws the garnet necklace. She holds it across her palm. "Sit down," she says. Her voice sounds husky.

Lila sits beside Toby on the bed. "Turn around," Toby says.

Lila turns and Toby reaches around her with the necklace. She fastens it at Lila's throat, then turns her so she can look at her. Toby smiles. "Looks good," she says. She nods toward the mirror above the bureau, a heavy wooden frame mounted on the wall. When Lila looks, the gems sparkle, red and dark. They shimmer like pools of wine against her skin. The beads are not smooth or round, but cut like diamonds. Lila raises her hand and rests her fingers on the necklace. She counts the generations: Rosemary, Toby, her mother, and her.

"Did my mom ever wear these?" she asks. Her voice comes out in a whisper.

"No."

That seems odd, but Toby doesn't offer more. Lila waits, but something's gone wrong. Her grandmother's hands twist over themselves in her lap. Lila reaches up and undoes the clasp. She hands the beads back to her grandmother. Toby slips them inside the box.

Without smiling, Toby stands and picks up the oval picture frame. "Here's that photo of Momma. I can part with it for the summer."

She holds it out to Lila. As soon as Lila takes it, Toby turns around, picks up a brush, tends to her hair. Lila lingers a moment but can't think what to do. "I'll take good care of it," she says. She starts back to her room when Toby calls after her.

"Don't forget that old quilt."

Lila stoops to pick it up from the corner post where she has draped it. Toby drags the brush through her hair, punishes her scalp with it. "Drunkard's Path," she says.

"What?"

"That's what that pattern's called."

Lila looks down at the blue and white squares, each square with two curved pieces fitted together, the pieces lined up to form a crooked trail. She tries to meet her grandmother's eyes in the mirror.

"Luther used that quilt in his wheelchair," Toby says. She never refers to her father by any name other than Luther. "I'd have thrown it out years ago except Momma made it."

Lila stands a moment, but it's clear that Toby has said all she's going to say. She throws Lila a tight smile over her shoulder. The two of them murmur good nights, and Lila goes back across the hall.

Sitting on her bed, she studies Rosemary's picture. Rosemary looks straight at the camera. Her dark hair frames her face, loose and curly. She's wearing a dark dress, big shoulder pads, large buttons down the front. She's smiling, lips slightly parted. In her arms she holds a baby wrapped in a blanket. The baby, who must be Toby, gazes up at her mother's face. Her eyes are wide open, her tulip mouth shaped in an open O. One of the baby's hands has wrested free of the blanket and reaches toward Rosemary's chin.

When she can tear her eyes away from it, Lila places Rosemary's picture on the oak dresser. She tries several spots, near the back, the front, turned on an angle, and finally she stands it opposite the blue and white ceramic pitcher that's stuffed with dried prairie grasses. Lila wonders if Rosemary's hands stitched the embroidery on the dresser scarf. Maybe she can ask Toby on another day.

Once she has the picture placed where she wants it, she sits in the rocker. She holds the quilt on her lap, runs her hands over the fine, even stitches. She knows it had to have been done by hand, Rosemary sitting in flickering firelight, her full attention to the rhythm of stitching. Lila begins to rock and watches the needle slide up and down. She takes a deep breath and lets it out.

She's thinking about Julia. Would she be a good mom? She's old enough to know what she's doing. And she's pretty. That's nice for a kid. To have a mom she can be proud of. She's strong. And kind. She loves Royce, that's good. She seems happy with her life, so she won't be going anywhere.

She closes her eyes and tries to picture Julia holding a baby. There's not much softness about her. Maybe it's not such a good idea. Why would any little kid want to grow up out in this remote place, anyway? She'd be riding a horse instead of a tricycle. Eating beef at every meal. Stranded far from civilization.

Lila rocks back and forth in the chair. Eyes closed. The quilt clutched in her hands. The word *stranded* has lumped in her throat. She's thinking of the photograph of Rosemary with Toby in her arms. Help me, Rosemary, she prays. Help me, help me.

Toby

Toby pulls her hairbrush through her coarse gray hair. She brushes back from her temples, up in the back, turns her head so that the bristles can reach every inch of scalp. Her arm tires from the raised motion, and still she keeps it up, brushing until her skin tingles, her hair in stiff meringue peaks. Long after Lila leaves the room, Toby sits on the edge of her bed. She presses her fingers into her eye sockets, pushes until she sees flares. Still she can see Nola Jean. It wasn't this room or this bed, but there's Nola Jean, six, nine, twelve, her hand in the drawer, taking out Rosemary's necklace, laying it on the blue and white quilt. Nola Jean with her silky yellow hair, her soft dimpled hand running up and down the faceted beads.

She was not an easy little girl, something strung tight inside her. It had been clear from the day they picked her up at the orphanage and drove her home from Omaha that Nola Jean would not take to this life. Two years old, she fell on her knees when they stood her on the ground, wiped dirt off her mouth, and promptly threw up. By the time she was a teenager, she and Toby were in open warfare. The more Toby tried to talk with her, the angrier Nola Jean got. Hurling accusations at her. Shouting ugly words – I won't be like you! I won't get stuck my whole life in this godforsaken hellhole! – until one day Toby had to face the truth. Nola Jean hated her. She hated this ranch, the land, everything Toby cared about. She did not want the life Toby had, and she was terrified. Walter shook his head, made excuses for her. He was somehow beyond the range of Nola Jean's fire. He was a man. Her daddy. He'd give her anything she asked for. And what she asked for was a ticket out of here. It shouldn't have felt like betrayal since all along they had planned for that. Scrimped and saved so that Nola Jean could go to college, knowing she wouldn't come back. What college-educated girl would come back to these parts, unless she wanted to ranch?

Sitting now on the edge of her bed, Toby slips her hand inside the lacquered box and fingers the beads. She should have thrown them out long ago. She should have buried them in the grave-yard, atop her mother's coffin. They belonged there, with Rose-mary, who was kind and gentle and who never would have done what Toby did.

It happened the day of Nola Jean's senior prom. She was dating the Everson boy. Scott. Nice young man, shock of dark brown hair. Quarterback on the high school team. Watching Nola Jean move through her senior year – honor roll, attendant for Homecoming Queen – was like reading a magazine with her daughter on the cover. The face looked vaguely familiar, but also like someone she'd never met. When she and Walter drove into town, people smiled and said, You must be so proud of Nola Jean. Toby could not reconcile the popular young woman who appeared in teachers' classrooms, in the downtown shops, in the lobby of the Trail Theater where she had a Saturday night job popping corn, with the spiteful, warring girl who shouted at her across the breakfast table. She was jealous of the attention and courtesy that Nola Jean extended to strangers, to her friends and teachers, to everyone but her own mother.

The day of the prom, Nola Jean drove into Elmyra. She had an appointment to get her hair done at Curl Up and Dye, the local beauty shop. Toby spent the morning cleaning the upstairs. She stayed out of Nola Jean's room, but from the doorway she could see the strapless white gown hanging by ribbons on the closet door. Silver strappy high-heeled sandals underneath. The dress floated in the breeze from the open window, danced in the morning sunlight. Nail polish, lipstick, eye shadow, mascara, all the things Toby knew little about, crowded the dresser top.

Nola Jean came home, ran a full bath, took her time pampering herself. She kept her door closed, and finally, late afternoon, she stepped out where Toby could get a look at her. Blond hair springy and curled, the white strapless dress floating around her, midcalf length. Silver hose and the heeled sandals with tiny straps. She looked like Marilyn Monroe, Toby was sure it must be on purpose, her choice of white and that hairdo. Nola Jean laughed and twirled.

"Momma, can I wear Grandma's garnet necklace?"

Toby swallowed. Why not? It would look beautiful with that white dress. Against Nola Jean's pale skin, pockets of fire.

Toby went upstairs to fetch the necklace, took it carefully from the drawer, unwrapped the tissue. She heard the front door slam, thought Nola Jean must have gone out to the barn to show Walter how she looked. She had about as much patience as a rabbit, that girl.

She waited downstairs for Nola Jean to come back from the barn. The necklace began to burn in her hands. What could be taking her so long? Remembering now, Toby shakes her head, sees herself put the necklace down on the dining room table, open the door, walk out to the barn. Why had she done that? She didn't want to be left out, was that it? Nola Jean had seemed so happy for once, and she wanted them to stand together as a family. She opened the door to the barn, and then she saw them, the man and the girl, her face turned up, his cheek on hers. His hand on her waist, her arms around his neck. She strained in the dim light to make out who the man was, clearly not Walter, too slender, and Walter would never have leaned into Nola Jean like that. So suggestive, the way they swayed together.

Blind with fury, Toby had rushed forward, must have, though she has no memory of moving from that doorway. She cannot forget the girl's face, openly defiant, her chin tilted. And then the laugh. Tinkling in the dim light of the barn. She remembers the slap, the feel of Nola Jean's cheek against her palm.

"You get up to the house," she said. Nola Jean ran out. The man stood before her, clumsy, torn jeans stained with cow shit. He'd been drinking and could scarcely stand on his feet. He was one of the hands, one of a chain of homeless cowboys who worked the rodeo circuit, then signed on for brief ranch stints when they ran out of money. He was young, this one, mid-twenties. Too old to be messing with Nola Jean.

"Tell me the truth, Nick. Has this happened before?"

"No, no." His hands batted at the air.

"Have you ever touched her?"

"We was dancin'. She said we could dance. That's all."

"You're drunk." She spit the words at him. "Get off the ranch. Go now, and I won't alert every rancher in these hills."

She could not force herself to go up to the house. She rammed around the yard, stirred up the hens in the henhouse, kicked at the dog, tore early radishes from their nest in the ground. She heard Walter drive in from the pasture. She heard the squeak of the garden gate, saw him disappear into the house where he would wash up. She imagined him finding Nola Jean flung across her bed, the white dress crushed under her, blond hair mussed and flying around her face. There, there, Walter would say. Nola Jean screaming her hatred at her mother, that bitch, that woman not her mother, there, there, and Walter's big hands fastening the clasp of the necklace. Toby stood, her feet planted in the dirt of her garden, her hands uselessly clamped around straggly bits of radish, when young Scott drove into the yard. She'd forgotten that he had agreed to drive all the way out here to pick up Nola Jean. She had packed a small overnight bag, planning to stay with Jenny Foster, as she had many times before, after late-night football and basketball games or play practices.

They came out of the house then. Nola Jean, radiant and smiling up at Scott, leaning on his black tuxedoed arm. Walter followed along in his jeans and boots, his camera catching the glint of the sun.

"Toby. To-o-oby," he called out to her. And she went. She greeted Scott. She smiled on while Walter took their picture. She watched them drive away. She went up the walk with Walter. She waited for him to tell her what Nola Jean had said, how he'd found her sobbing.

They moved into the house, to the kitchen, and Toby waited for him to accuse her. To ask questions. To hear her side. He said nothing, and then she understood. Nola Jean had not told him.

Toby moved through the mechanics of supper, boiled meat, green beans, cabbage slaw. She imagines now, although she can't remember, that there would have been pie. Walter loved pie. Perhaps lemon meringue or coconut cream. She washed the dishes.

She felt wooden, carved and stiff, old beyond imagining. She turned to go upstairs, Walter drooping in front of the television, and only when she got to their room did she recall that Nola Jean had not worn the necklace. Nola Jean had stood with Scott in front of the sagging porch roof, her shoulders white, throat bare, no jewelry except for the small pearl earrings Walter had given her for Christmas.

Toby turned into the room she shared with Walter. She slipped out of her shoes, reached for the light switch, felt something sharp under her heel. She knew before she reached down that it was one of the garnet beads. Standing with the bead in her palm, Toby closed her eyes and imagined Nola Jean's rage. She had snapped the string, flung the beads into the room. Cascading down the edge of the bed, chipping the mirror above the bureau, caught in the folds of the lace curtains at the window. It took Toby nearly an hour to retrieve them all, or nearly all – she would find one two years later, reaching into the pocket of a seldom-worn jacket, her fingers closing on the bead like a buried land mine.

Now, all these years later, Toby sits and folds her hands. She had never spoken of the slap or the beads again, not to Nola Jean, not to Walter. When Walter thought it odd that Nick had ridden off without pay, she nodded and said, You never can tell about drifters. She was gratified at first that Nola Jean said nothing. She reciprocated in kind. In fact, she hoarded the secret, mistook it as a bond with her daughter, an initiation into the complex world of women. Too late, she realized that their silence only widened the gap between them. She had restrung the beads herself and offered them to Nola Jean on her wedding day. She held them out to her, smiling, hoping. Nola Jean had smiled back, a new softness now that she'd found love. She refused them, said she didn't want red with her white dress, said the necklace didn't go with the wedding colors, and Toby accepted her reasons, nodded her head, moved away. How long, she wonders now, before forgiveness comes?

Lila

Lila looks for excuses to visit Royce and Julia. She delivers things. Pies. Cookies. She bakes them in the afternoon, sometimes with Gertie, who's turned out to be almost human in the kitchen. After supper she asks Toby if she can borrow her car. She has a license. It's only a few miles. She knows the way. Still it took a few times to wear her grandmother down. Finally she said the magic words: Don't you trust me? And Toby relented.

She knocks on Julia's door. Wiley and Fritter come out sniffing and barking, but she's learned to ignore them. The first two times Julia came to the door. This time it's Royce.

"Lookee here." He holds the screen door open for her. "Julia," he calls back into the house. "Our bakery girl is here."

They usher her in. Ask her if she wants coffee. Tonight there are papers strewn all over the table. Julia stacks them up, shoves them to one side. The three of them sit. Royce peeks under the aluminum foil at the brownies, but nobody dishes up any. Lila squirms in her chair.

"Working on something?" she asks.

Royce looks at Julia. "Going over some numbers," he says. He drums his fingers on the table.

"Everything all right at the Alhambra?" Julia asks.

"Yeah. I guess," Lila says. She leans forward. She can see it's a bad time. "Maybe I should get back."

"Okay," Julia says.

They stand with her, walk her to the door. Her hand is on the latch when she asks, "Could I use your computer?"

She's caught them off guard. Royce literally backs up a step.

"I mean sometime. Check my e-mail. Toby doesn't have one."

Royce lets out a gush of air. "Well, sure. Anytime."

"Right now, if you want," Julia says. She's looking past Lila at Royce, who nods his head.

They take her in the study, sit her at the desk. Royce shows her how to boot up the computer, though she's an old hand at this. They leave her then, and she hears them back at the numbers in the kitchen. Relieved, she guesses, that she's occupied.

She signs on as a guest to AOL. No e-mail. She hadn't thought she'd get any. She talks to her mom once or twice a week. Who else would contact her?

She types in google.com, and when the screen opens she fills in adoption. Bingo! A whole page of Web sites. She selects the first one, AdoptionNews.com. There's a picture of a family, the mother blond and smiling, the father tall and handsome, his arm wrapped around the mother, the baby bundled in a pink blanket. The perfect picture. How adorable. She clicks on "Photos of parents." People wanting babies. She wipes her sweaty palms on her lap. Licks her lips. Not ready to face parents, she clicks on "Who are we?" and finds out that this is a private agency. They have birth mothers and adoptive parents all over the United States and Canada. They specialize in personalizing the adoption process. The birth mother not only gets to select the parents, but together they decide how much the birth mother will be involved in the child's life. And money! Adoptive parents pay expenses. She shudders. Covers her face with her hands.

After breathing for a few minutes, she clicks again on "Photos of parents." You can choose by religion, ethnicity, or region. You can decide you want biracial Caucasian and Asian parents, Catholics who live in the Southwest. Or Muslim parents in California. Mormons. Oregonians or Georgians. There are pages and pages of people wanting babies.

She scrolls down through some of the photos. Beside each one is a brief statement to birth mothers about why this couple wants a child. They all sound alike, desperate and sad. *We have so much love to give; We've lost three children of our own through miscarriage; Thank you for this incredible gift.* Fat couples. Thin couples. Some look sickly. One man must be thirty years older than his wife. Some are dressed alike, navy turtlenecks for the serious and capable, chambray shirts for the fun-loving. All of them look like they have money.

She exits this Web site and clicks on another. State agencies. Pictures of older children, victims of abuse, sad-eyed lonely kids. Statements by people who've tried to adopt babies through state agencies: *Don't give up; It may take years; Some states are better than others.* She clicks on Nebraska and finds that there are no parents waiting for an infant in Nebraska. No one, it seems, is that desperate.

She feels sick. She thinks she might pass out. Sour waves ride up and down her throat. She manages to exit the Web site, get out of AOL, then she rushes for the door. Royce and Julia start to get up from the table, but she waves them down. "Gotta go. Thanks." She stumbles out into the thickening dark, herds Toby's car back along the dirt road. She's almost home, in the lane to the Alhambra, before she has to stop. She wrenches the car door open, heaves and shudders, and when it's over, she feels quieter, but spent. She sits in the open doorway of the car, her feet on the ground, straddling vomit. She leans her head against the door frame and tries to slow her breathing.

Toby will be worried if she doesn't hurry it up. But she can't make herself move. If she sits still, maybe she won't have to think. Won't have to see the sad faces of people who want somebody else's baby. Won't have to try to picture her child in the arms of strange Caucasians, any religion, Midwest.

George

The girl walks down to their small house sometimes in the evening. She says she can't stand Gertie and the television. She leaves Toby sitting on the porch, drinking whiskey.

She sits on their couch, a futon with arms shaped from gnarled wood. George made the frame himself, some time past. The cushion is dark green, worn in spots. John sits in the rocker that once belonged to Toby's grandfather, the one who fought in the Civil War and then came west to homestead this place. Lying injured in a field hospital, he swore that if he lived, he'd get as far away from the war as he could, and he did, bringing with him that chair, a Birdseye maple chest of drawers, and his second wife. Eleanor bore him four girls who all died the same winter of diphtheria. Robert Bolden built four small pine coffins, laid the girls out, tucked in with dolls and teddy bears, dressed in pinafores and calico dresses made by Eleanor's own hands. The coffins had to be stored in the horse barn until the ground thawed in the spring, and most days Robert found Eleanor draped over one or the other of her darlings' caskets, eyes dry and vacant, mouth slack with grief. In March Robert chose a spot in his own pasture, fenced it off, dug four graves, and lowered his daughters into the ground while his still ailing and depressed wife clung to his arm and wept. Robert carved the girls' names, ages, and the day they died into one stone: Sophie, 1 – Dec. 10; Lillian, 3 – Dec. 14; Mary, 4 – Dec. 12; Alice, 6 – Dec. 15. At the bottom the fateful year, 1885. Five years later, after two miscarriages, Eleanor gave birth to one more child. A boy this time. Luther. Eleanor looked at her new baby, turned an exhausted face toward Dr. Blackford, said, There now, Robert has his son, and died.

When they were younger men, Luther had told George this story, and they had argued good-naturedly over who had it worse, Luther growing up without a mother or George never knowing his father. It seemed to George then that Luther had the advantages, a landed father with money, an inheritance. George's mother had eked out a living caring for other people's children, cleaning strangers' houses, until she died in a sanatorium of tuberculosis. At twelve, George went to work setting type in a print shop, smelly, messy work, his hands stained black from ink, nostrils singed by chemicals. He knows now, measuring his beginnings against Luther's, that Luther lacked, and what he lacked could never be replaced. George doubts if anyone ever loved Luther. Not his father, hardened by the war and too many losses. Surely not Rosemary, who seemed afraid of him. He ruined his own chances with Toby and John. Perhaps Gertie. Gertie might have loved him, if Luther had given her half a chance. But of all his children, Gertie was the one Luther had the least use for.

The girl comes and they sit round the braided oval rug in front of the stone fireplace built by her great-great grandfather. Sometimes John has that granny-squared afghan thrown over him, the girl an old quilt spread over her legs, and George, who is old,

95

thinks he's got himself a couple of invalids. Her sickness will pass, of course. She's not ill or weak, it's only an illusion, that fragility men think women have when they're pregnant. He remembers Ella laboring, her face carved against the sinews and the bones, her fingers clawing into his arm. He knew then he'd never seen strength like that in any man. There's the worry, though. That child split his Ella in two. Strong enough to carry the child, but the blood, too much blood, and the cord wrapped wrong. He remembers how he and Walter sometimes had to saw a calf apart inside a mother cow. A wire passed through the calf's muscles and bones. Sacrifice the calf to save the cow – she could bear again, and the calf wouldn't live anyway. Watching Ella, the blood, her lips strained back, he wondered why it was possible to be kinder to a cow than to his own wife. He could not lift his hand against his own child. He let them both die, and that is his shame.

He tucks the quilt around the girl's legs. He doesn't touch her skin. He's an old man, but still, he wants to show his respect. He brews green tea in his kitchen and he brings the pot and sets it on the coffee table. He pours a cup for her. She takes it, sniffs, shrivels up her nose.

"Pond scum," she says. But she lifts it to her lips, and he is gratified.

He pours another, a mug with a large handle, and places it in John's hands. John nods, a man of few words. George has always liked that about him.

He pours a cup for himself. He sits on the far end of the couch away from the girl. And then the tales begin.

He tells her what it used to be like when they had calving season. The constant vigil over the cows, how most would just lie down in the grass and give birth without attention, then stand and lick the calf until it wobbled up on its own legs. Sometimes they grafted an orphan calf onto another mother. If she had lost her own calf, they would cover the orphan with the hide of the dead one so the mother would not refuse it. He tells her stories about mothers and babies, how when they rubbed dehorning salve on the nubbins, if one calf got upset and started bawling, the mothers would crowd round until they discovered, by scent, whose it was. He wants her to see the way of things, birthing and living, and that orphan calves are taken care of, and that mothers recover from losing their young.

In the old days, when more men worked on the ranch, it seemed that somebody was always injured. Pete broke his leg when a horse fell on him. Charlie smashed his thumb replacing a fence post. Andy broke his ankle the morning of branding and did not remove his boot until nightfall. All day he sat his horse and roped. People get hurt, and they survive. He wants her to know this.

He tells her that when you break a young colt, one day you ride it to a pile of bones. You find a gulch or a little draw where bones have collected, remains of coyotes or gophers or stray calves. At first the horse shies from the white bones, so stark against the grass. Eventually the horse learns not to fear. You ride the colt to the bones so that it will have more freedom and will not be afraid to move about the earth.

During these recitations, more often than not, John sits quietly, rocking and sipping his tea. He might nod his head, murmur um-hum.

One night she asks for a different story.

"Was it a coincidence that David and Rosemary died on the same day?"

George takes a sip of his tea. His hand is steady when he places it back on the table. "Did you ask Toby?"

97

"Yes. She said I should ask you how David died. She said Rosemary died in the car accident that crippled Luther."

George passes his hand over his eyes, rubs his brow. These are painful stories, but they belong to the girl. She has the right to know. He looks at John to ask him silently if he can bear the hearing. John returns his look with steady eyes.

"David was eighteen. A strong, good-looking young man. He and John were friends before John left for the war."

The girl shifts her gaze to John. She has large eyes, stillness like a doe.

"We used to hunt together," John says. He wipes at his wet face with the palm of his hand.

"David wanted to quit school," George continues. "I begged him to wait until he was eighteen. Finish high school. I knew how important his education would be."

George stops to sip from his cup. He watches the girl over the rim, takes her measure. She knows how to listen. She's hearing more than the words, and that is good.

"All the girls liked David, but he had eyes for only one."

"They grew up together," John says. "Couldn't hardly pry them apart when they was kids." This is a long speech for John. George watches the knowledge form in Lila's eyes.

"Toby." She states it. Not a question.

George nods. "She was seventeen that summer. The summer after they both graduated. And they were in love." George looks now at John. He wants a cue for how much he should tell this woman-child.

John scuffles his feet. He covers his jaw with a shaky hand, but when he does not look away, George goes on with the story.

"David was taking her to South Dakota, to Ella's people. He

98

had it in his head that they could be married there, without Luther's consent. And Luther would never give his consent."

"Because she was so young?" The girl is sitting up now. She's got her antennae working. She's a fox watching a lair, the hunt closing in.

George looks down at the leaves floating in the bottom of his teacup. He's too old for lies. "Because David wasn't good enough. To Luther. He was the kin of a hired man."

"They were just kids." John throws this out. George is surprised. Is he defending Luther? George looks over at John, sees John's hand waving back and forth, agitated. Still, George will not cut Luther slack. Not over this.

"I thought Luther'd come around in time. Anybody could see how it was with those two. I tried to urge caution. But David was young, and already the Korean conflict was heating up. He was afraid of another war. Afraid he'd have to leave her. He could not be persuaded to wait."

"Toby said there was bad weather?"

"Black-clouded sky. Winds. And David and Toby in that old Chevy. They set out in the afternoon. No one would have thought a thing. But Luther found out. And he went after them. He made Rosemary go, too. She didn't want to, but he blamed her, and he grabbed her and shoved her into the car. He and I pushed at each other, two bull buffalo, but in the end he went after them.

"I followed in my old truck. He drove like a madman, the car swerving and taking up the whole road. Gravel spit up from his tires, broke little stars in my windshield. And then up ahead I could see David's car. They weren't even hurrying. And Luther pulled his blue Buick up alongside David, reached into the backseat, took up his shotgun, and aimed it at David's head.

Rosemary, I think, lurched to stop him, and the gun went off. David lost control, his car careening into Luther, and Luther's car rolled, tumbled over and over again, and landed upside down in the ditch.

"I ran to David and Toby first. And there sat your grandmother, her foot on the brake, and David's head in her lap. Her face still and white, her dress blood-soaked. It was green, that dress, red blood on a field of green, and I remember thinking Christmas, and David's face blown apart by the blast. I stood there, I don't know how long, crazy and wild. But there was nobody else, and I had to leave him. I ran to Luther's car, upside down in the ditch. Both he and Rosemary had been thrown from the car.

"I found Luther first, against the ditch bank, his legs broken and him unconscious. I thought perhaps he was dead. I hoped he was dead, so I wouldn't have to kill him. I looked for Rosemary, but she was nowhere. I turned in every direction. And then I found a white hand. A white wrist.

"I couldn't raise the car by myself. I left Toby with all that blood and death, and I drove twenty-four miles to the nearest house. It was hours before we could get any help. Rosemary was dead. David was dead. Luther was taken to a hospital and came home in a wheelchair."

George stops talking. He has not looked up from his tea leaves since he started this tale. Now he risks a look at the girl's face. She is horrified, barely breathing.

"It was a long time ago," he says.

"Luther shot David?"

"Luther shot. And David died."

"Was there a trial?"

"No."

100

"Why not?"

"He claimed he never meant for the gun to go off. He said if Rosemary hadn't grabbed at him, he never would have fired it. He just wanted to scare them."

"You believed him?"

George only looks at the girl. John makes a small sound, a whimper, a dog who's been mistreated too many times.

"But why did you stay? How could you stand it?"

"I stayed for Toby."

It's only later, after more tea and more silence, when the girl is standing on his front porch ready to retrace her steps back to Toby's house, that she asks the question George has been trying to avoid. He can see she's been chewing on it for a while.

"Did you know they were going?"

"I did," he says. "They came to me that morning."

He watches her weigh the situation. He wonders if she has any idea how many times he has gone over this in his head.

"But you didn't tell Luther," she says.

He shakes his head. He had not. Maybe, if he had told Luther, David and Rosemary would not have died. He could have told Luther and held him at gunpoint. He could have shot Luther when he set off in his car. At the very least he could have slammed his fist into Luther's face, bloodied him until he couldn't see to drive. He says none of this to the girl.

"How did Luther find out?"

George looks up at the night-dark sky. The Big Dipper leans toward the Little Dipper, the Milky Way stretches wide. Fireflies dance around the yard.

"Luther and Rosemary were down in the west pasture. She took some coffee out to him, same as she did every day. Next thing I know, they came tearing into the yard. They must've climbed to the top of the hill, seen David's car in the distance. Put two and two together." He turns to the girl, lets her see the grief in his face. "That's the only thing I've been able to figure out."

When she leaves, he watches until she is out of sight. Then he turns once more to search the sky. He knows there are no answers but can't help looking.

Lila

"Now ease up off the clutch while you give it some gas. A little gas." The pickup lurches forward, grinds, shudders, and dies. Lila leans her forehead against the steering wheel. It seems like they've been out in this pasture for hours.

"I can't do it," she says. "I can't push in with one foot and let up with the other. It's not natural."

"Sure it is." Clay chuckles. "It's like walking. You push off with one foot while you stretch the other in front of you. Same thing. You do it all the time."

Lila stares at Clay, trying to decide what planet he comes from. Why isn't he cussing and slamming his fist against the door? How can he sit there, in the falling daylight, and go through this over and over? She wants to scream, and he's as patient as a Buddha.

She stretches her arms at the wheel. Her belly, hard as a basketball, is perched on her lap. She'd like to remove it, just for an hour, so she could glance down and see her feet on the pedals. Last night she gave herself a good look-over in the mirror. The heart-shaped birthmark on her lower right side is bent all out of whack. She put her hands around the front of her belly. She tried to imagine something living in there, in the dark, sloshing in water. It scared her. If she were carrying a baby in a basket, she'd be careful where she set it down. She'd handle it gently, wouldn't she? Instead, her body comes with her, bumps along over these dusty roads. She worries, and she hates that. Why can't she learn to drive a stick shift without wondering if it's bad for the baby? She should've been able to frolic a while before she turned into an incubator. Why does anybody ever do this willingly?

"C'mon. Once more," Clay coaxes.

She pushes the clutch in with her left foot. Turns the key in the ignition and feels the motor chug to life. She shuts her eyes and concentrates on moving her feet in opposite directions, not too fast, no sudden shifts, and the truck eases forward. Her eyes fly open. "We're moving. We're moving," she shouts.

"Wahoo!" Clay yells. They both laugh, and she keeps the truck surging forward with only a few jolts.

"Wait a minute," she says. "Where should I go?" They're rolling over prairie. There's not a road in sight.

"Anywhere, silly. It don't matter."

She turns and drives. Makes a big square. She's moving, and it's fun.

"Okay. How do I stop?"

"Put your foot on the clutch. Now the brake."

Somehow she manages to bring the hulk in for its landing. She stops smoothly, and the truck purrs away, idling happily there in Toby's pasture while the sun dims in the west.

"Next time I'll show you how to get out of first gear," Clay says.

Lila grins. She feels like a grown-up, sitting here beside Clay, mastering a skill. The sun glints off the hood of the pickup. She turns the engine off, and there's nothing but grass and quiet for miles.

"Can I ask you something?" Clay says. He props his left arm across the seat back, turns toward her.

"Yeah, sure," she says. Anything, anything.

"Did you . . . did you love the guy?"

She turns from Clay's face and looks out over the empty prairie. "No. Not really. I guess I thought I did."

"But it wasn't rape or anything?"

Shocked, she looks at Clay's face. Worried. He looks so worried. "God, no," she says.

"Okay then." He nods, takes his arm down from the seat back, turns to face the windshield. He slouches down, his long legs bent, half closes his eyes.

While he's not looking at her, she starts talking. "We were dating. He was just a kid. Like me. Homecoming was coming up. I thought something might happen. So I went to Planned Parenthood and got on the pill. Because I didn't trust condoms. Isn't that a joke?"

He says nothing. She loves that about him.

"We didn't use a condom. Neither of us had ever done it before. We had sex three times, and then he dumped me. I didn't care that much. I didn't notice that my period was late. I'm not that regular. Besides, I wasn't worried, you know? And then by the time I figured it out, I didn't know what to do. I just pretended it never happened. Dumb, huh?"

"No, uh-uh. I've felt like that."

"Yeah, well . . ."

He sits quiet with her. She leans her head back, closes her eyes, waits for her breathing to steady. Then she goes on.

"I'd had a sore throat. Mom called the doctor, who phoned in a prescription for me. Because I get strep throat like once a year.

Hey! I'll bet you don't know that antibiotics can make birth control pills not work."

"No shit?"

"I looked it up later on the Internet."

She's laughing now. Her shoulders shake with it, her hand over her mouth. "Isn't that funny? My mom got me pregnant. I could get on *Oprah*." Laughing, laughing, and tears squeeze out the corners of her eyes, and she feels Clay's hand on her shoulder, then on the back of her head. He's patting her, his hand quieting her, his voice purring softly.

"C'mon now."

"I'm always so fucking responsible, you know?" She spurts this out, hiccuping between sobs. She blows her nose into her hand and flings the snot out the window, wipes her palm on her jeans. His hand is still on the back of her head, and then she turns to look at him, and they both laugh, a real laugh, breaking the tension. Clay gives her head a small thump and retreats back to his side of the cab. She feels spent, but good. God, it felt good to tell that to somebody.

They sit for a while, letting the air settle. A meadowlark's voice calls to them. Not twenty feet from the pickup, a prairie dog rests on the porch of his house.

"Want to see something?" Clay asks. His hand rests on the door latch of the pickup.

"I guess." Lila shrugs. There's not much out here, windmills and grass, dirt blowing because they need rain.

She moves as quickly as she can, an eye out for rattlers. Clay has scrambled to the top of a bluff. He's waiting for her, hands on hips. She places her feet carefully, struggling not to topple backward. Her weight is in all the wrong places. If she fell down, she'd be a turtle on its back. Clay scrambles back down the grassy slope to give her a hand. She stretches up to reach his fingers. He tugs her up over a rocky knoll. He keeps her hand in his while they move down the other side of the bluff. About halfway down, she lifts her eyes from the grass in front of her and sees a pattern of rocks in the draw at the bottom. It's a small protected place, two bluffs forming a wide V, some scrub brush and sage sprouting up in the hollow. At the bottom, laid out in a spiral, a path of stones.

Lila stops to ease her back, keeping Clay's hand for support. Her footing is precarious in her high-topped tennies on the slope of the hill. "What is it?" she asks.

"It's a prayer wheel. Or mandala. Whatever you want to call it."

"Out here?"

"Unless we're dreaming."

By now they've reached the bottom of the draw. Several of the rocks have been washed over by sand, some are overgrown with grass. The path is more discernible from above than it is close up. It's clear that the stones have been here a while.

"How'd you find this place?" Lila asks.

"Out riding fence. Walter hired me one summer."

"This is part of Toby's land, isn't it? I mean, the part she doesn't lease to Royce."

"Yeah. We're not that far from George's house, maybe mile, mile and a half."

"Who made it?"

"Toby and George. Long time ago. I asked Walter, and that's what he said. Oh, that's some of Toby and George's foolery, something like that."

"Did you ask Toby?"

"No. I never did." Clay shrugs. He takes off his Go Big Red cap, holds it in one hand, and scratches at his scalp. He smoothes his hair with his left hand, front to back, before fitting the cap back on. "Seemed private, somehow."

Lila looks away. She angles her head to listen. The air buzzes with insects, electric but also still. There's a calm here. She figures it's the way the wheel is situated, in this protected draw. She steps between the rows of stones, follows the spiral to its center. There a flat rock rests on another, an invitation to sit. She drops to one knee, braces her hand behind her, and lowers her body.

She can't imagine her grandmother and George toting these stones in here. They would have had to collect them from the far reaches of the ranch or another place entirely. She pictures them rolling the stones down the slopes of the bluffs, the sun naked and harsh, perspiration dripping from their faces. Did they do this for David and Rosemary? She doubts if Clay knows that Luther shot David. She thinks about telling him, but decides she's told enough for one day. Besides, like Clay said, it's private.

Clay walks out to join Lila in the middle of the circle. He doesn't cross over the path. Instead he walks around the spiral, his boots kicking up dirt. He squats on his heels and looks in her face.

"Pretty here, isn't it?"

"Yeah. It is."

Clay shifts his weight, sits on his butt with his knees bent in front of him. He chews a blade of grass between his teeth. His baseball cap doesn't go with the boots. Lila smiles, thinking here's a boy trying to decide what he wants to be when he grows up.

"Lila. I'm going to tell you something."

He's not looking at her. His eyes are focused on the sky, his arms locked around his knees. The bottoms of his jeans are starred with sandburs. She watches his face and doesn't speak.

"Alicia and me. Alicia and me, we . . . well, it's more serious than you think."

She waits him out.

"Last April we went to Mexico together. She told Randy she was going to visit a cousin in San Antonio. She left Amber with him and we flew to San Antonio, and then we went to Mexico. We're going to get married."

"Soon as she leaves Randy." Lila knows her voice sounds hard. She can't help it.

"It's complicated." Clay bites on his grass, looks away across the hills.

"At least you got that right."

"I'm telling you because I'll explode if I don't tell somebody. I figure you can keep a secret."

Lila lays her hand on Clay's arm. She's silent for a long time.

"So what are you thinking?" Clay asks. He looks straight at her, asking for the truth. She expects him to look behind her to check for crossed fingers, the way they did when they were kids.

"Remember when we used to swing from that rope rigged out in the barn?" she asks him.

"Yeah. You were always scared."

"You'd lift me up. Hold on now, you'd say. Hold on. Don't let go. I'll catch you, so you won't fall."

"Is there a point to this?"

"You did, too. You caught me every time." She keeps her gaze steady on his face. She can't catch him. Just so he knows that.

Clay looks away. Shy. Or embarrassed. "Well, it was easy then."

Toby

The house is in a residential neighborhood of Scottsbluff, the front lawn decked out with painted cutouts of Dutch children in wooden shoes, their hair in blond braids, chubby dimpled hands clutching tulips. There's a deer, too, ceramic and painted a spotted brown, a timid fawn poised for flight. Toby wonders if there's a plastic predator lurking in the bushes, but decides that would be going a bit too far, especially for a place called Serenity House.

Toby and Gertie walk Howard between them, though he's not agitated. On the way up the walk, he stops and cups a geranium in his hand, then lifts his face to the sun. "I love red flowers," he says.

Toby looks over Howard's head at Gertie, whose hands are clasped tight around her black shiny pocketbook, fake patent leather. She's the one who looks terrified, even though she and Toby have checked this place out, heard nothing but good reports about it. The nursing home in Elmyra doesn't want Howard anymore. He wanders, and they can't keep track of him. Not only do they have to drag him out of the bed of the Stewart woman, but he somehow escaped the nursing home and meandered downtown. One of the candy stripers found him gazing into the window of what used to be the Rainbow Cafe, his fingers playing over the plate glass. The girl said he was humming something, maybe "The Tennessee Waltz," which she recognized because her grandpa plays in an old-timers' band. Howard seemed perfectly content. She brought him back without incident, but next time he could drift out onto the highway, get struck by one of the semis passing through. They won't take responsibility.

There are wooden railings on the front steps of Serenity House. Three people won't fit abreast, so Toby drops behind.

Gertie has one hand on the railing, the other on Howard's elbow. She needs help getting up the stairs, and he looks the part of the gallant gentleman. Climbing pink roses flank the steps on either side.

"Is this Maddie's house?" Howard asks.

"No, Howard. Maddie lives in Denver. You know that." Gertie's face snaps shut. Nothing readable there, but Toby knows better. Maddie is Gertie and Howard's daughter, Madeline Grace, and she's been gone for years. She calls Gertie once a week, but she doesn't come home. That's the way it is with some of the young people who grow up out here. They shake the dust off their feet, the advice Jesus gave to his disciples, and they don't look back. Maddie. Nola Jean. It's like one glance toward the past and they might turn into a pillar of salt. God, Toby thinks, why is she stuck in all these old Bible metaphors?

Toby reaches around Gertie and rings the doorbell. The house is painted bright yellow with teal and lilac trim, a giant Easter egg dolled up for the Resurrection. They learned on the previous visit that the doors have to be kept locked, even though this door opens onto a big screened front porch. "What if there's a fire?" Gertie had asked. "How will you get them all out?"

Standing on the step waiting for Mrs. Lang to open the door, Toby hears laughter mixed with the light tinkling sounds of a wind chime. Through the screen she sees one of the patients sitting on a porch swing. Fake ivy climbs up the chains attaching the wicker swing to the ceiling. There's a wire birdcage on a stand in the corner, crowded with fake peonies. Maybe, Toby thinks, the residents of Serenity House can't tell the difference between real and artificial. Maybe Howard's world is like a postcard Nola Jean once sent from Paris of a huge red lobster lying on a sofa. How strange, to imagine ordinary objects turned into something unfamiliar. The world could be a playland, magical, or it could be terrifying, just enough adult sensibility left to render it all slightly menacing.

"Well now, this must be Howard," Mrs. Lang says on opening the door. She smiles straight at Howard, reaches out a hand. Howard looks up, eyes shining, like he's in kindergarten and he's got a pretty teacher. Toby knows this will be hard for Gertie, seeing Howard walk willingly into the arms of another woman. Mrs. Lang is in her fifties, Toby'd guess. Bottle blond, pretty in a down-home way, plump. She's got an air of the little brown hen about her, as though she'd like nothing better than to fluff your pillows and lay her cool fingers on your fevered brow. Toby knows there's a shrewd businesswoman behind her calm and friendly demeanor. She's making money here, but the way she's doing it leaves room for thinking she's part saint, too. This house is a home for Alzheimer's patients, and she handles eleven of them. The whole house has been remodeled to accommodate their needs. She keeps a staff of nurses, a cook, and a doctor on call. Her husband serves as the handyman, probably a forced early retirement. They don't live here. No one actually lives here, only the patients, and they're just stopping by on their transition from this world to whatever lies beyond it.

Toby has had to work hard to talk Gertie into this possibility. Gertie wanted to try moving Howard home with her, back to their house in town, but Toby knew that spelled disaster. Gertie can hardly take care of herself. How would she manage Howard's nighttime meandering? What would she do, lock him in a room? Gertie herself would be as much a prisoner as Howard. Scottsbluff is a long drive from the ranch; that complicates things. But there's no place like this in Elmyra. Toby has assured Gertie she'll bring her to visit Howard at least once a week.

They'll make a day of it, have lunch out, maybe take in a movie, although movies aren't much fun for Gertie because of her eyes. She doesn't like modern films anyway, the language raw and offensive to her.

Toby watches now while Mrs. Lang skillfully coaxes Howard into the ways of the house. There are two other men here, all the rest women. That figures, since men die younger. One of the nurses, Nancy, has taken Howard and moved down the hall to show him his room. It's already been explained to them that Howard will help make his own bed, be given chores that make him feel he is a part of a family. He'll eat meals with the others at a real table.

Mrs. Lang turns toward them. She holds her hands pressed together below her breasts. She looks like an opera diva that Toby once saw on television. Or a prim teacher who won't brook any nonsense. "I think he'll be just fine," she says.

Toby knows this is their signal to leave. Mrs. Lang has explained that the residents adjust better if they leave their old attachments behind. Family is not allowed to visit for a month. Not allowed. Gertie has bristled at this, and Toby doesn't blame her. First you have to let your children go, one way or another. Gertie lost one to the city and death swallowed up the other. Now she's being asked to let her husband go after fifty-five years of marriage. She's supposed to simply walk away and let him form another family. Let him forget about her. That would take a kind of generosity that Toby doesn't think Gertie is capable of. Still, what choice does she have?

Toby watches Gertie looking over Mrs. Lang. Gertie's eyes are narrowed, an expression the uninitiated might associate with her vision problems, but Toby knows better. From the looks of her so does Mrs. Lang. She doesn't argue. She doesn't press

Gertie to leave. She doesn't invite them into the kitchen for coffee, either. She stands there with her hands folded and waits.

Toby glances around the room, at the upright piano against one peach-colored wall, the sunny furnishings, the collection of rockers. Howard could do a lot worse. There don't seem to be any residents around; they must all be in their rooms, taking an afternoon nap. Except for the woman on the front porch. Toby glances through the doorway at her, sees her sitting bolt upright on the porch swing. She's wearing a jaunty straw hat, slightly askew. She's striking, even though she's old: eyes a clear blue, hair silver and curly. She's wearing a printed summer dress, something pastel and floral, pink satin ballet slippers on her feet. Her toes are pressed to the floor to keep the swing moving. She's humming a melody vaguely familiar, something classical. While she hums, her fingers work up and down the edge of a light pink shawl that is wrapped around her shoulders and spilling over her arms. If Toby remembers correctly from their first visit here, she's a former music teacher.

When the silence has stretched long enough, Toby puts her hand on Gertie's arm. "C'mon now, Gertie. We got to get home."

"I want to say good-bye." Gertie says this to Toby under her breath, as if she doesn't want the mean Mrs. Lang to hear her. But of course Mrs. Lang does. She's standing only two feet away.

"That's not a good idea," Mrs. Lang says. She says it kindly, in her best Mother Teresa voice. "It will only upset him."

Toby bends and talks low into Gertie's ear. "Now Gertie, we've been all over this. C'mon now."

But Gertie will not budge. She's turned into concrete. She will not sit or speak or move. Toby looks at Mrs. Lang.

"Could she say good-bye?" Toby asks. She's not sure whose side she's on here, but she knows Gertie.

"I want to see his room," Gertie says.

Mrs. Lang seems to weigh her options. Gertie stands with her pocketbook clasped straight in front of her. Toby has to smile in spite of herself. Gertie's not letting Mrs. Lang forget who's paying for this outrageous venture.

Eventually Mrs. Lang turns on her heel without another word, and Gertie and Toby follow her back into the dormitory part of the house. Howard's room is third on the right, and he's already sitting on his bed. Nancy is hanging his few articles of clothing in the closet. She's maybe thirty, thirty-five, short and round, her movements quiet and efficient. She's wearing a gold cross on a slender chain around her neck, and her upper arms, where the sleeves edge up when she stretches to reach the closet rod, are purple and mottled like mishandled pears. She catches Toby looking at her and flushes, and with that Toby knows the whole story on Nancy – that cross and those bruises. "Unpacked already," Toby says, trying to throw Nancy a compliment, hoping it's not too transparent.

Howard's pictures of home are displayed atop a dresser that's been salvaged from a garage or basement, cheerily painted in green and yellow. There's a rocking chair in one corner, a green afghan tossed across the back. The walls are painted a soft sage, white curtains at the windows. Landscapes on the walls. One picture of Jesus standing at the door and knocking, the kind you find at K-Mart or Wal-Mart. The room feels airy and pleasant, and Howard sits on the foot of his bed grinning.

Gertie moves in and sits on the bed beside him. Suddenly Toby feels embarrassed to be looking on. She steps out into the hall. Mrs. Lang and Nancy both follow her. They confer for a moment, talking over details of the day. Mrs. Lang tells Nancy to go on to another room, and then she waits with Toby.

"It's hard for families, I know," she says to Toby.

Toby nods. She's finding it difficult to speak because she can see what's happening in Howard's room. Gertie has her arms around him and is rocking him on the foot of the bed. She pats him a few times. Then she holds her hand up to his cheek. She stands then and Howard lies down on the bed. Gertie unties his shoes and slips them off. She lifts the afghan off the rocker. It's summer, but this house is blessedly air-conditioned. She lays the afghan over Howard, then tucks it around his feet. She stoops and kisses him on the cheek. When Howard has closed his eyes, she turns and walks away.

"He'll sleep now," she says to Mrs. Lang.

Mrs. Lang smiles. She's gracious in defeat. "You can call any time to check on him."

Gertie nods. She marches forward, past the piano, past the frail and lovely woman humming and swinging on the front porch. When they are on their way down the walk, she turns to Toby, her nearly sightless eyes shimmering with tears. "They put him in a green room," she says. "Howard hates green."

Gertie

This is it, then. This is the next in a long line of testings. Gertie has had to suffer more than most, she knows that. The Bible says God will not tempt you beyond what you are able to withstand, but she's come close to breaking several times. When her mother died, that was bad. She was better prepared when Luther crossed over, he'd been in that wheelchair for years, and by then he was an old man. Still, nothing prepared her for Grady's death, her only son, her boy, the pride of their lives, their insurance for the future. Somebody pulled a dark shade on a window and left it there.

She sits in that car while Toby drives home and can say nothing. She's never before felt this abandoned. It will upset him, Mrs. Lang said, and she had to work hard not to shout, Him! What about me?

All her life she's taken a back seat to other people's suffering. When their mother died people felt sorry for Toby. Always Toby. George hovered over Toby like she was a china doll. Even Howard felt sorry for Toby, brought her ribbons from town. When Grady died it was his widow, that Wanda, parading around, getting drunk in every bar in three counties, Clay having to drag her home and put her to bed. Besmirching Grady's memory with that kind of carrying on.

She knows this about Howard's sickness. He's not the one suffering from it. It's costing her a fortune to put him in that place. Where they lock him up. Where they won't let her see him, as if he's a prisoner, or she is. What could she do to hurt him? Why should remembering her hurt him? She has to remember him, her old Howard, her proud, independent, Republican-voting, principled, Bible-class-teaching Howard, and measure him against what he has become, a sniveling wreck who crept into the bed of that Stewart woman.

Why should she have to go through this alone? He has that Stewart woman, now that Mrs. Lang, nurse Nancy, a cook, that fluffy music teacher on the porch swing, and who does she have? Why is this happening to her?

"Gertie, do you want to stop in Elmyra for anything?"

She hears Toby's voice coming at her. She shakes her head. No use. No use in anything. She'd like to stop at the cemetery in Perkins and throw herself down on Grady's grave. She'd like to weep and wail, kick her feet, punish the earth until somebody gives her some answers. She'd like to walk in the door of Our Savior's Lutheran Church, storm up to the altar, and raise her fist. What are you doing, you lazy son of a bitch, she'd like to say. Let the minister hear her, she'd have a few choice words for him, too. He ought to be arrested for bearing false witness. Throw him in jail, throw away the key. Where is grace? Where is it, you lying bunch of putrid gray sepulchres?

Next she'd like to go back to her old farm. She'd pour gasoline on the place and burn it to the ground. Especially that big old house that Wanda made them leave. She'd make sure Clay wasn't home, but she wouldn't care if that Pickford boy got burned down with it. Burn it all to hell, burn it, burn it.

"Gertie, Gertie." She hears Toby's voice from a far distance. She jerks when she feels Toby's hand on her arm. She sees the look of concern on her stupid sister's face, as if Gertie doesn't know what truly lies in Toby's heart. She fishes a handkerchief out of her pocketbook, wipes her face with it.

When Grady died Howard had taken a crowbar to the machine shed. She found him out there, and she put her hands on the boards and ripped them off, her palms and fingers bleeding and raw, and still they worked until nightfall, tearing that old building down, and she can't remember when anything has felt that good. She needs, she needs, oh God, she needs a cleansing. She needs a furnace.

Shadrach, Meshach, and Abednego. They may have walked on ashes, but they knew nothing of the real burning.

Lila

The office of the *Elmyra Newsblade* is on Main Street, halfway down the block from the Gambles store where Lila shopped with her grandmother a few weeks ago. She walks past a video rental place, then a boarded-up storefront. In a vacant lot a wrought iron bench sits next to a tractor tire filled with red and white petunias, somebody's idea of a wayside park. The wooden door to the newspaper office has a glass pane on top, the letters *Elmy News* legible, but the right halves of the words strangely smudged, as if the paint job had been botched from the beginning and never fixed. Figures, Lila thinks.

She's been sent here by Mrs. Hewitt, the town librarian, a skinny woman with wire-rimmed glasses and a voice like a rusty hinge. Lila tried the library first, a new building located where the creamery used to be. Lila knows that useless fact because Mrs. Hewitt told her, along with details about the Oregon Trail and Mormon Trail and grasshopper plagues and the blizzard of 1885. Mrs. Hewitt fished to find out why Lila was interested in newspapers from 1948. Lila told her nothing, but she had to endure a litany of town history before Mrs. Hewitt got around to explaining that the library burned down in 1959, when the mayor's wife dropped a smoldering cigarette behind the magazine rack. For years the library had been a makeshift bunch of shelves crammed into one corner of the Legion Hall until the town finally passed a tax levy to erect a new building on Main Street. Lila managed to escape before she had to tour the entire library, although it wouldn't have taken long: a table with two computers, a kiddie section with circled chairs, adult shelves, a rolling cart with best sellers – Danielle Steele, Robert Ludlum, the newest Harry Potter. When Lila stood her ground and smiled without coughing up information, Mrs. Hewitt gave her the clue: Try the newspaper office.

Now Lila pushes open the door to the *Newsblade* office. She stands in front of a long counter topped with mottled brown linoleum, chipped and flaking away. Behind the counter a gray metal desk sits buried under a mess of papers. Lime, orange, and yellow Post-its cling to the wall at various angels. Lila isn't close enough to read most of them, but she can make out two: "Get the dirt from Sylvia" – another just below it, "Get the dirt on Sylvia." The sticky floor, beige-flecked tile with dark stains, grabs at the soles of her red high-tops. The air smells of chemicals. An enormous cobweb stretches across the right-hand corner of the room, flies dangling from it, their iridescent bodies glinting blue-black in the sun. There's an old-fashioned bell sitting on the counter; Lila presses the button, but the bell doesn't ding. To the right, under the cobweb, a door leads into the print shop. It's ajar and Lila hears voices. She's trying to decide what to do, how to sing out and make her presence known, when a sandy-haired boy steps through the door. He's tall and lanky, about her age. He's wearing glasses and a tattered Grateful Dead T-shirt, floppy blue jeans, athletic shoes. He looks like a regular kid, not like the cowpunchers Lila's been hanging around with this summer.

"Yeah?" he says. He gets one glance at her and looks away. He stumbles behind the counter, kicks into the trash can. He's so nervous that Lila decides to cut him some slack.

"You get used to it," she says quietly.

He looks at her face. He's got nice eyes, brown and deep. A little acne, not too bad. His teeth are white, though jumbled. He's cute, but he needs more weight on him. "Something you want?" he says.

She tells him what she's looking for, newspapers from 1948. He says he'll have to see, they've got a bunch of files stored in the basement. She waits, standing at the counter until he comes back with a manila folder, newspapers spilling out of it.

"You'll have to look at them here," he says.

She takes the file he slides across the counter at her. She opens it, leafs through the dates at the top. The boy hasn't moved. He's watching her.

"If you want you can come in the back room and sit at a desk. If you want, is all." He shrugs. His shoulders are bony but wide.

"Okay," she says.

He shows her into a small office, separated from the press shop by a wall with a huge window in it. He looks down at his hands. They're stained with ink blotches. He turns them over, picks at his fingernails. "You can sit in here as long as you like. My boss is gone to lunch. He won't be back today." He pauses. Pats his hands on his jeans. "Well, I got work to do."

He leaves her then, and she sits down at a metal desk. She goes through the weekly papers, passing over January, February, March, April, and May. The paper is yellowed but still in good condition. Nobody looks through these much, that's for sure. Nowadays, in bigger places, all this would be on microfilm, and all she'd have to do is scroll down a screen. She feels, not for the first time, as if she's stepped into a time warp. That Dead T-shirt the kid is wearing looks old. She wonders if he ever heard of Jerry Garcia. Or if he knows Jerry Garcia died.

Finally she comes to June. She finds the week of June 10 and looks over the front page. Nothing. She flips to the inside and sees a picture of the overturned car. It's not mashed up, just upside down, tires grabbing for the sky. There's a police car on the shoulder in the background, and several people, one in uniform, another in a suit, in various poses around the car. No sign of

David or Toby or their vehicle. The photographer must have ridden out with the ambulance, snapped this photo while they were trying to get Rosemary out from under the car. In the foreground to one side, somebody is bending over Luther, who's laid out on a stretcher. Luther has raised his head, and the photographer has captured his look of bewilderment. Utter dismay. The caption reads "Tragedy on Old Hill Road."

TRAGEDY ON OLD HILL ROAD

Two local people are dead in a tragic series of events that took place on Old Hill Road last Friday, June 10. Sheriff Pete Pankowski said that Luther and Rosemary Bolden had gone after David Bates, age 18, who they believed had kidnapped their daughter, 17-year-old Gwendolyn (known locally as Toby). David was driving a 1938 Chevy and thought to be heading toward South Dakota, where he had relatives. Luther Bolden, local owner of the Bluestem Ranch, took up the pursuit in his 1947 Buick. Apparently, Mr. Bolden pulled his car alongside the young man and threatened him with a shotgun. What happened next is not certain, but the gun discharged, hitting David Bates in the face. Mr. Bates then lost control of his car, which swerved into the Boldens', knocking them into the ditch. Both Rosemary and Luther Bolden were thrown from their car, but in a strange twist of fate, the car landed on top of Rosemary. Toby Bolden managed to bring David Bates's car to a stop.

The first person on the scene was George Bates, David's brother, who had followed behind Luther in his truck, hoping, George said, "to prevent Luther from going off half-cocked." George drove to the nearest ranch, the Hempsteaders', twenty-five miles away, to call for help. When the ambulance arrived Rosemary Bolden and David Bates were both pronounced dead. Luther Bolden was taken to the Elmyra Hospital with two broken legs. Toby Bolden was ap-

parently unharmed. She is resting at home and has refused to comment.

Sheriff Pankowski says no charges will be filed in the shooting death of David Bates, since Mr. Bolden has sworn that he only meant to frighten the boy. "I'm not saying he used good judgment," the sheriff said, "but it's understandable that a father wants to protect his daughter. It's just too bad, all around."

Services for Rosemary Bolden will be held at Our Savior's Lutheran Church in Perkins on June 15, 2:00 p.m., Rev. Fenton Smith presiding. David Bates's memorial will be held privately. Both will be interred in the family cemetery on the Bluestem Ranch, where the Bates family has lived as hired help for the past nine years.

Thought to be kidnapped! Lila's hardly aware that she has banged her fist on the metal desk more than once, causing the in-basket to topple and a fan of papers to cascade to the floor. She's down on her hands and knees when she looks up to see the boy standing white-faced in the doorway.

"I'm sorry," she says. "I knocked these off."

"Get up," the kid barks. She's taken aback at his tone.

"I said I was sorry," she says, hauling herself to her feet.

"Sit down." He stoops and makes quick work of picking up the papers. While stabbing here and there with his long arm, he goes on talking, not looking at her. "Jeez. I thought you had fainted or something. I looked up, and you were gone. I got five little brothers and sisters. My mom's been pregnant half my life, so I know you're not supposed to be grubbing around on the floor."

By now Lila has sat down. The kid flops the pile of papers back in the in-basket, catches the whole lopsided tower before it falls on the floor again.

"That's an old trick," Lila says. "Your mom's just getting you to do the slop work."

"Did you find what you're after?" he asks.

Casually she lays her arm across the newspaper article, decides to change the subject before he gets any more curious. "Where'd you get that T-shirt?" she asks.

He runs his hand over his chest. "It was my grandma's." Then he cracks a grin. "She was at Woodstock."

"No kidding. Your grandmother!" Lila tries to picture Toby at Woodstock. No way.

"She died last year."

Lila's not sure what to say. He's got the papers under control now.

"I'm Lila," she says. She closes the June 10 issue of the *Newsblade*, folds it in half, stuffs it back in the folder.

"Owen. I work here. Well, you know that."

"My dad's a musician." Why is she talking to this kid anyway? "He's a big fan of Jerry Garcia."

"Yeah," Owen says.

She has no idea what he means by that. She swivels the chair back and forth, trying to decide if she should leave. She's probably found all there is to find here.

"Where you from?" Owen asks. He leans on the desk, picks up a paperclip, spins it in his fingers. Lila waits for it to drop, and it does. He lets it go, picks up another.

"Minneapolis," she says.

"Uh-huh," he says, on his third paper clip.

When he drops it, she tries not to notice. "I'm visiting my grandmother for the summer. Toby Jenkins."

"Oh, yeah. On the Bluestem Ranch. I know that place."

"You do?"

"We did a story once. On that house. It's got a funny name."

"The Alhambra. It's named after a Spanish palace."

"Yeah. Your grandma was great."

"Oh?"

"I mean, she's a character. Like out of a book. Willa Cather or something."

Lila raises her eyebrows. "You read Willa Cather?"

Owen shrugs. Something closes up in him. "Did you get what you needed?" He nods at the pile of newspapers.

"I guess. But it's full of lies." She's not sure why she tells him this, but instantly she wishes she hadn't.

"Yeah." He grins at her.

"You think that's funny?"

"No. It's just . . ." Owen scratches his eyebrow, pulls at his lip, his hands constantly in motion.

"Just what?"

"A really long time ago."

"You know what? You're right." Lila scrambles to her feet and grabs her backpack off the floor. She stuffs her notes into it.

"I mean . . ."

She turns on him. "It's not a big deal, okay? It's ancient history."

She lets the door slam on her way out. Who cares about any of this? Luther Bolden was a murdering bastard, so what? What's it got to do with her? Big fat nothing. She's not even related to him, not by blood. She's halfway down the block before she realizes she is walking in the wrong direction and retraces her steps. When she crosses in front of the *Elmyra Newsblade* office, she makes a point not to glance inside.

George

He keeps vigil. He watches her. This has been his role since the day David died from a shotgun shell in the face.

He follows her on a summer morning. She has asked him to saddle Cream, her favorite of the pair of geldings. He prepares the horse and holds the reins for her as she mounts. She has circles under her eyes, and her breathing is heavy. She's not sleeping. She shouldn't ride alone.

She turns from him and walks the horse away from the barn. He knows where she will go. He lets her get ahead, out of sight over a small knoll, and then sets out on foot. He knows her route and avoids coming into her view.

He crouches when he reaches the top of the butte, creeps forward on his hands and knees. He feels like a spy but tells himself he's respecting her privacy. He lifts his head and looks down into the draw. Cream stands patiently, the reins dropped to the ground. She's a good rider. He does not have to worry that she will be thrown. She has entered the spiral of stones. She's seated on the slab at the center, facing east, the way he has taught her, to greet the morning sun. He thinks this is a hopeful sign, that she is facing east, the direction of beginnings.

He watches her and waits. He knows that she still prays to the Lutheran God, even though she's been mad at him most of her life. He himself has kept his mother's rosary, burns incense, thrills to the tones of a Gregorian chant, although the content, for him, is largely hollow. She recites the Twenty-third Psalm, the one about shepherds and goodness and mercy. George likes that one and thinks that it can do no harm.

He likes to think he has protected her. Thrown his mantle over her. But he knows she has saved him. If not for her, he would have killed Luther. Not the day of the accident, but a thousand times afterward, when he thundered from that wheelchair. The sight of him curdling George's insides.

She taught him. He watched her turn from her anger. He tried to throw his hatred into the passing streams of life, but as long as Luther leveled his gaze at him from that wheelchair, he lived with a seething snake inside. He carried Luther up those stairs, wrapped his arms around his back and legs, cradled him as a man would his beloved. He laid him on his bed, and Luther looked at him with knowing eyes. There were no secrets between them.

Once he had stood over Luther with his shotgun loaded. Luther had been home from the hospital two days, David's death still fresh, the burning incense from his burial sharp in George's nostrils. George waited until Toby had gone out to the garden, and then he stole into the house. Up the stairs. Stood over Luther, who was pathetically propped up in his bed, mouth sagging, drool pooling on the chenille bedspread. Luther looked at him without surprise. A crooked grin split his features into the grimace of a gargoyle.

"Well, well," Luther said, his voice croaking from parched lips. "It's about time."

George raised the gun to his shoulder, sighted down the barrel at the white space between Luther's eyes. His finger restless on the trigger. He took a breath, stilled himself to squeeze, when he heard Toby's voice.

"Don't do it, George."

She stood in the doorway. He did not turn his head to look at her. He heard her voice, and she was young to see her father die. Her mother and David gone. He hesitated. And then she gave him the reason.

"Don't you know that's just what he wants you to do?"

He lowered the barrel and looked into Luther's eyes, and he saw clearly the path of his revenge. He would not lift a hand against him. But neither would he forget. He would burn incense and turn his face to the east, ask for deliverance from the snake that hissed inside him, and eventually he would not boil with hatred in Luther's sight. But he would not forget.

He watches Toby with the morning sun on her face. She turns her head then, and he lowers himself from her view. Although he is sure that he is hidden from her sight, he is not surprised to hear her voice.

"C'mon out, George. You're too old to be playing cowboys and Indians."

He stands and dusts his hands off on his jeans. His silver buckle glints in the sun. He makes his way cautiously down the slope toward her. He enters the prayer circle and follows the path of stones. When he comes to her in the center, she motions him to sit, and he does. A long silence stretches between them, a comfort they have developed over the years. He waits for her to voice what is troubling her.

"We're going to lose this place, George."

It's the land, then. He had thought it was the girl. Perhaps both.

"Malcolm Lord?"

"He says we have until September. Then he's foreclosing. I can't pay the taxes."

He has known this was coming, but did not know it would be this soon. He will have to act quickly.

"Western Cattle wants to buy. You know Nola Jean has no interest in this place. I've always known I'd have to sell at some point. But I hate to lose the ranch to some conglomerate. It'll ruin Royce and Julia, too."

"Something might happen."

"An act of God?" She is teasing him, her voice lilting. They've seen too much to hope for miracles.

"Something might happen."

She quiets then. He is pleased to see that. He suspects that she does not believe him, but she rests in the comfort of his voice.

"The girl is asking questions," he says.

"Lila?"

"She asked me why David and Rosemary died on the same day."

Toby looks away. Her hand brushes at imaginary dirt on her knee. He watches the hand, and when it lies still, he goes on. "I told her."

"All of it?"

She looks at him. Her face has gone softer and wrinkled, more beautiful with age. She is worn like fine leather. He'd like to tell her these things. He'd like to tell her of his pride in her life, her strength.

"Not quite all," he says.

She sits a moment longer. Then her voice trails up from a deep well.

"David and me . . . it could all have been so different."

He says nothing.

"Funny, don't you think?" she goes on. "Lila's here for the summer, and she's curious. Nola Jean never asked."

"Nola Jean never pitched her tent here."

Something flashes across her face. Perhaps it is pain. It is fleeting, and then the knowing of the truth settles her. This, he understands, is Toby's great secret. This is how she has borne the sorrows of her life. She does not bar the gate against the truth.

"It was the gravestones," Toby says. "Lila saw the dates. She asked me about them the first week she was here. I thought you should be the one to tell her."

The sun is higher overhead now, casting their shadows intense and small. George ponders this, the way he does all things. He believes there is great might in small things – the ant, the bee, a woman's touch, a man's heart. His god is very, very small, as small as the molecules of air that permeate everything.

"She will ask more," he says.

"Why would she?"

"She will not be content."

He waits for her to understand. She touches her right hand to the collar of her shirt, smoothes the edge between her thumb and fingers, the way a baby worries a blanket. "You think we should tell her."

"It might help," he says.

She takes a deep breath. Her hands are quiet now. "Penny's got a couple in mind. She's got contacts from medical school. She says there's somebody in Colorado. Good people."

"Has she talked to the girl?"

Toby shakes her head. "Not yet. Maybe at Lila's next appointment."

"She could keep the child," George says.

"Her mind's made up."

"You could help her."

"I want her to look back and know she decided for herself."

George looks, then, into the future. It is not long. Now his life stretches more behind him, and the future is a path that disappears quickly over the hill. He knows only how to put his feet on the straight path. "It will be all right," he tells Toby.

"What shall I do?"

"Wait," he says. "The future will come to you."

He stands then. He leaves her in the circle of stones. He does not look back and sets his feet toward home. He has work to do.

Lila

Lila tears open the letter from Owen. Toby handed it to her when they settled at the kitchen table for supper, and she waited to open it in her room. It contains several pages of photocopies. A lime Post-it note stuck to the top page reads: *Thought you might like these. Owen.* Nosy brat, isn't he? She sits still, trying to decide if she's irritated or mad. She's surprised to discover that she's neither. She knows this is an apology, a white flag waving for a truce. She smiles and runs her finger over Owen's name. Why did she walk out on him like that?

The top copy is the article that she read in the *Newsblade* office. He didn't have to be much of a sleuth to put that together. She's touched, though, that he went to the trouble to look up the obituaries.

Rosemary Katherine Bolden died Friday, June 10, at age 47. She was born May 12, 1901, in Kingsfield, Ohio, and christened Rosemary Katherine Leary. She married Luther Bolden in 1919. Their union produced three children. Luther and Rosemary resided from 1919 until the present on the Bluestem Ranch northwest of Perkins.

Rosemary was an active member of the Mary and Martha Circle at Our Savior's Lutheran Church in Perkins. She will be remem-

bered as a gracious and lovely hostess at the numerous parties held in the Boldens' spacious ranch home.

Rosemary is preceded in death by her parents, John and Alice Leary. Her brother, Norman, was a casualty of World War I. She is survived by her husband, Luther, and three children, John, Gertrude (Mrs. Howard Hoffman), and Gwendolyn.

Services will be held at Our Savior's Lutheran Church in Perkins, June 15, 2:00 p.m., Rev. Fenton Smith presiding. Interment will be in the Bluestem Ranch family cemetery.

David Bates, age 18, died of a gunshot wound Friday, June 10. David was born February 10, 1930. He lived on the Bluestem Ranch with his brother, George Bates, hired hand at the ranch since 1939.

David was a recent graduate of Elmyra High School, where he played football. He was known to be a good boy who worked hard.

David's memorial will be a private service held at the Bluestem Ranch and presided over by his uncle, Fred Billings, from South Dakota. Interment will be in the Bolden family cemetery.

When her grandmother calls her to the phone, Lila slides the clippings beneath the pillow on her bed. She trots down the stairs. Maybe this is Owen calling. Maybe he'll ask her to a movie. Like she's a regular girl. He's geeky, but sweet. It would get her out of the house. He knows better than to expect much. And she could use a friend her own age. She's tired of living in an old folks' home.

She's breathless when she picks up the receiver. She glances toward the living room, where Gertie sits in front of the television. Toby is at the kitchen table reading. You'd think she'd know a person needs a little privacy. Lila turns her back toward Toby and speaks into the receiver. "Hello?"

"Hi, darling."

"Oh . . . hi, Mom."

"Don't sound so disappointed."

"No, it's just . . . I guess I'm a little tired."

Her mother talks on for several minutes about nothing – her flight from Paris, the weather. To every general question, Lila answers, Fine. Fine. I'm fine, Mom. She wants off the phone. Her mother's voice doesn't belong here.

"Are you seeing a doctor?" her mother asks, the first real mention of what she calls Lila's "condition."

"Yeah. I'm fine."

"Have you made a decision?"

"About what?" Before she left home, her mother delivered several ultimatums: Lila was to sit and stew in her own juice until she figured out how she expected to finish school, what she planned to do about this unwanted child that she was in no way prepared to care for, yada, yada, yada.

"Put your grandmother on the phone."

"She's not here." Toby's eyebrows go up, but she says nothing.

"She'll try to turn you against me."

Lila sighs. She's heard this theme before. "We don't talk about you, Mom."

"Well. Just don't forget. When you decided to get pregnant . . ."

"I didn't decide to get pregnant."

"You know what I mean. This is not just about you. I have a right to be included in this private loop you and your grandmother have formed."

"You sent me out here."

Pause. Then a softer tone. "I thought we could use some space."

"Mom, I'm fine. G'bye."

Lila hangs the phone up gently, her mother's voice still coming through the line. She stands a moment, not sure what to say or do. She turns toward Toby, who rises from her chair and rests her fists on the table edge.

"I think," Toby says, "it's time for ice cream."

She pushes Lila gently down in the chair. Lila lets her grandmother put a bowl in front of her heaped with chocolate ice cream. She's surprised to discover that she is tired, her body saggy and heavy, her eyelids dragging down. She props her head up with one elbow on the table, spoons two or three bites into her mouth before she risks a look at Toby's face. Toby is busy with her own bowl of ice cream.

"This is never as good as homemade," Toby says.

"I've never had homemade ice cream," Lila says.

Toby points her spoon at her. "Not once, in all those summers you were here?"

Lila shrugs. "If I did, I don't remember."

"We'll have to do something about that."

They eat a few more bites. Lila decides to take a chance. "I'm sorry I lied when she asked to talk to you."

"Are you?"

Lila shifts in her seat. What kind of question is that? "I don't know. I don't even know why I said that."

"Don't you?"

"She knew you were here. You answered the phone, didn't you?"

"Guess I did at that."

Lila slops ice cream on her shirt. These days she can't seem to keep in mind where her body begins and ends. Her belly is a second table. "Did she ask you anything?"

"Anything . . .?"

133

"Like what was I going to do with the baby?"

"No. No, she didn't ask that."

"But she did ask something?"

"No, not really. She said, I hear it's hot. I said, It's been mighty warm. That's about it."

They sit, their spoons clanking against the ceramic bowls.

"How come you and her don't talk?" Lila asks.

Toby pauses between bites. "Don't, or can't. We just never have, that's all."

When she has finished, Lila watches her grandmother spoon up the last bit. Then Toby picks the bowl up and licks it. Lila laughs, and Toby says, "One of the advantages of getting old. People pretty much stop telling you what you can and can't do. You run into other limitations. But you don't have to give a damn what people think."

She stands and runs water over the bowls at the sink. Lila watches her back, the muscles playing under her shirt. Before she goes upstairs she lays her hand on her grandmother's shoulder. "Guess I'll turn in," she says.

Later Lila hears a tap on her door. She knows it's Toby, since this is a habit they've fallen into.

Tonight when Toby comes in Lila's sitting in the rocker instead of lying in bed. She's changed into the old nightgown Toby has found for her. She's tucked Owen's letter away, but she's not quite ready for lights out.

Toby sits on the edge of the bed, their knees almost touching. "Something on your mind?" she asks.

Lila rocks a little longer. Toby waits.

"George told me about David. How Luther shot him."

"I see." Toby lets out a gush of air. Lila can't guess what she's thinking.

"That sucked," Lila says.

"It was a long time ago."

"George says you told him."

Toby looks toward the picture of Rosemary on the dresser. She gets up, walks over, and straightens the frame. Then turns back to Lila. "That morning. We walked down to his house. He was sitting on the porch, and we told him."

"He didn't try to stop you?"

"Nope. He'd already said all he had to say. He knew we were leaving. We only went to tell him that was the day."

"What about Gertie?"

Toby shrugs. "She wouldn't have understood."

"Is that why she's so mad at you?"

Toby stands up straighter, looks hard at Lila. "I don't think of Gertie as being mad at me. She's just . . . Gertie. She doesn't let go of things easily."

"She's horrible to Clay. And his mother. She called her a whore."

"Well. Gertie is her own worst enemy. She doesn't know that yet."

"Yet?"

Toby laughs. She motions to Lila to climb into bed. Lila drags herself up out of the rocker and lies down. Toby tucks the sheet around her, careful not to pull it too tightly across her belly. Before she leaves the room, she puts her hand against Lila's cheek, and Lila closes her eyes. Perhaps, if she doesn't move, Toby will leave her hand there until morning.

Toby

Toby has taken to riding in the mornings. She rides to the far corners of her land. Sometimes she rides fast and hard, her aging hips throbbing hours later, but she loves the feel of the wind in her hair. She rides to the top of Settlers' Hill and out by the old Morton Meadow. She stops under windmills, trickles her hand through the water. She sits her saddle under the shade of a lone cottonweed tree on the marshy land, where every summer there's a blue, blue lake. She's riding over her land the way a lover's hand follows the planes of her beloved's body, so that she will remember, always, when such meetings between them are no longer possible.

She knows that George keeps his eye on her. He no longer sits astride a horse, so sometimes she purposely outruns him. She doesn't want him to know that she's in search of the proper place to die. Some place where she could fake a fall. Some place where the land would claim her as its own.

One morning she rides to the spot where she and David first made love. Two hills nestled together, like a woman's breasts, a large blowout forming a dish of sand in the cleavage. Here she and David lay down and gave themselves to the fierce wanting. He covered her body with his hands, and then his tongue, and she shivered and clung to him and cried his name.

She dismounts Cream, drops the reins to the ground. The beauty of this place is that it is remote, on the far side of her land, away from any roads, prying eyes, away, even, from the cattle, which tend not to drift this far from water. This would be a good place, if she could manage it.

She sits on a nearby clump of grass and pulls off her boots. Her socks. She sets her white toes onto the sparse grass and wiggles them. She stands, works her elastic waistband down over her butt, her thighs. She steps out of her jeans and reaches to the buttons of her shirt. Bra and panties next. When she is naked, she stands with her arms outstretched to the sun and the air.

She removes the blanket from the roll behind her saddle and spreads it on the ground. She takes care to smooth the fringe against the warm sand. She lies down in the middle of the blanket on her back, folds her hands on her abdomen. This, she thinks, is where I would like to wait for the future. If she could fall asleep here and not awaken. If she could pass into the molecules of the sun and the earth, let the hawks and coyotes carry her away.

The problem is, she is seventy-two years old and in cursedly good health. She'd have to be out here for days before exposure would do it, and George would have a posse out looking for her long before that.

The timing will be critical. After Lila's baby, before Western Cattle moves in. There may not be much time. She will have to decide on her method soon. Down a bottle of pills. Fill her stomach with monkshood, grown and harvested in her own garden.

Lying in the sun, she feels her body start to warm. A slight breeze tickles her nipples. She smiles, thinking she hasn't felt that tingly rise for some time. She moves her hand lightly across her breasts, then down over her soft belly to the thinning mound of pubic hair. She places her fingers on the sweet spot and moves in slow, undulating circles. A hawk flies overhead, casting its shadow over her, and she hears a small animal scramble through the brush. She is not afraid. If there are snakes, let them come. What does she have to fear, lying here on her own land with nothing but what is natural and infinite surrounding her? She comes with a long shudder, her mouth falling into a low moan, and when she lies still, she waits for some residual shame. She waits for the critic on her shoulder to denounce her for her foolishness. Instead she is filled with an uncommon glow. Life. Ah, life, she thinks, and a sob tears through her chest. She can't decide if it's too funny for words or sorrowful beyond bearing that she is overcome with the beauty of living while contemplating how to manage her own death.

Lila

Everybody's in town for Camp Clarke Days. Even Gertie has consented to sit in a folding lawn chair by the side of Main Street and wait for the parade. They've got a whole row of chairs staked out: Toby, Gertie, George, John, and Lila.

"Won't people get mad?" Lila asked when she saw the setup. George had toted the chairs to town in the back of his pickup. He must have left the ranch before the sun came up.

"Are you kidding?" Toby said, flopping down in one of the chairs. "Look at us, a bunch of geriatrics and a pregnant kid."

Lila has to admit they make a funny sight, sitting in a row, John and George topped by cowboy hats, Toby's pink straw gardening hat tilted at a rakish angle, Gertie's UVA repellent sun hat snug over her head like a clear plastic lampshade. To keep the peace Lila has agreed to wear a baseball cap although, like everything else in Nebraska, the logo is of the Husker football team.

Lila's glad to have the seat. Her back has been killing her lately. Nobody told her that having a baby makes your back ache. Or that her breasts would swell and wobble like water balloons. Now when she rolls over in bed at night, she has to put her hands under her belly and lift it, as if it is already separate from her.

Sometimes the baby kicks up a rumpus. She puts her hand over a knot, a hard bulge where the baby's foot or hand or head must be. Besides being a headbanger, this baby does the rhumba, makes her whole belly undulate in wide waves. Maybe the baby is musical, like Lila's dad. Wouldn't that be funny?

The street grows crowded. The sun high overhead like a spotlight, eighty-five degrees and sapphire sky. Little kids in tiny shorts and tank tops are perched on the curb. Lila has her eye on a couple of them, one dark-haired, like she was, in a blue gingham sundress, ruffled panties underneath. The girl can't sit still, but every time she stands an older, tow-haired boy pulls her down again. He's looking out for her. The girl rests her hand on his thigh when she sits. Sometimes, for a brief moment, he puts his hand over hers and pats it.

Lila spots Owen across the street in front of the newspaper office, thumbs hooked in his jean pockets. He scans the crowd. When he gets to the row of chairs, she watches a grin crack open his face. She raises her right hand in a small wave. Owen ducks his head toward his feet. He's shy with her. She likes that.

While she's thinking about Owen, she feels a hand thump against her back. Irritated, she turns and looks up into the face of Tim Pickford, the clumsy cowboy from the branding. He's wearing jeans and a plaid short-sleeved shirt, open at the neck. No boots, his feet in tennis shoes. She doesn't remember seeing glasses before, but he's wearing them now, a pair of round wire-rims, the effect somehow comical, a boy dressed up like a professor.

"Hey, Lila." Lila doesn't remember his voice sounding so soft or breathless.

"Hi, Tim."

He squats down, sits on his heels to talk to her. His breath smells boozy, though it's not yet noon. "Seen Clay?" he asks her.

"Not yet. I expect he's here somewhere."

"Heard you been having driving lessons."

Lila leans back to study his face. Has Clay been making fun of her? Yukking it up with his good buddy Tim? His face is blank, unreadable.

"Yeah. Clay's showing me how to drive a stick shift. I've graduated to second gear."

"He says you're doing good."

"It's not rocket science. Everybody drives."

Tim looks away from her, toward the approaching parade. His scruffy beard is gone, and she scans the cut of his jaw, the whiskers he missed in his morning shave.

Down the street Lila can see the parade marshall riding a big bay horse. He's followed by the American Legion Club, a bunch of old men, the middle two carrying a blue banner with yellow fringe. Applause ripples through the crowd.

Above the rising noise, Tim leans in closer. "Going to the picnic?" He looks at her with one raised eyebrow. Neat trick, she thinks. Jack Nicholson.

"I think so." She heard Toby say they'd be making a day of it. Picnic. Then a melodrama at the school. If they aren't too tuckered, an evening rodeo followed by fireworks. They'll get home late but can sleep in the next day. Lila has instructions to whistle if she gets too tired. George's pickup has a covered bed, and they've stuck an old mattress in there. The plan is to take turns grabbing a nap.

"See you later," Tim says. When he stands he puts his hand on Lila's shoulder. She watches him move through the crowd. When she turns back she sees Owen glaring at her from across the street. His right hand shades his eyes. What's his problem? She thinks about flipping him off, but decides he's not worth it. Who is this kid anyway? Just some small-town boy she'll never see again. She turns away, wills herself not to look back.

The parade consists mainly of riders on horseback, various 4-H clubs carrying banners. There's a raggedy band – one bass drum, a couple of snares rolling out a decent cadence. The marchers, dressed in blue jeans and white T-shirts, are led by a majorette in purple uniform, bare legs flashing under a short pleated skirt. After she blows three sharp blasts on a whistle, the band strikes up "Stars and Stripes Forever," off key, the rhythm out of kilter. The crowd loves it. Lots of parading kids, some on bicycles with crepe paper threaded through the wheels, girls walking in pioneer dresses and bonnets, boys in leather vests with tin badges on their chests. Two clowns, one wearing a barrel with suspenders, the other in giant feet and a white pajama suit with red and orange spots, throw candy, and the blue gingham toddler and her brother scramble into the street after caramels and peppermints. Too small to compete, the girl gets shoved aside, and her face puckers with disappointment. The boy leads her back to her seat and dumps candy in her lap. The girl squeals and kicks her shoes, tiny buckled sandals over chunky feet, baby toenails painted red. Lila wants to tuck those feet into her lap, cup them in her palms, kiss the little pads of flesh. She reaches her hand out to the girl, but someone jostles her and she remembers who she is. A stranger.

Soon the highlight of the parade comes by. Royce has hitched up Chip and Dale, his monster Clydesdales, to a Conestoga wagon that he borrowed from the Trail Museum. He and Julia wave from the wagon seat. The crowd cheers when Royce stands and plants one foot on the rump of each horse, balances precariously over the wagon hitch, the reins taut in one hand, hat held high in the other. Julia, who never wears anything but jeans, looks oddly at home in an old-fashioned dress, blue flowers on a white background, a yellow wide-brimmed bonnet. They are followed by a string of antique cars, black and maroon Model Ts, their horns sounding *Ah-ooga*. Behind the whole thing, a couple men with brooms and giant dustpans scoop up horse shit and dump it into rolling plastic garbage bins.

When the crowd starts to dissipate, Lila and her old people sit still. Once the street opens to traffic, George walks a block and a half to where he parked his truck. He drives it around, and with a few grunts and groans but little trouble, George and John stash the lawn chairs in the back of the pickup.

"See you at the picnic," George says.

"Park as close as you can," Toby says. "Lila might need to rest."

"Oh, I already took care of that," George says.

"Used a couple of them homemade highway cones," John says and winks at Lila.

She has no idea what he's talking about, but when Toby threads her big Buick through the traffic, Lila spots George's pickup parked under a tree and in front of it two orange cones with black letters that read *Highway Dept.* Once George spots Toby, he moves the cones and stands in the spot until Toby has shepherded the car into the space. George stashes the cones in the trunk of Toby's car, and they move over to join the crowd lined up for barbecue and corn on the cob. George and John have already unloaded the lawn chairs and set them up under an elm tree. Each one has a sign propped on it with the word *Reserved* and below that a facsimile of the Bolden brand. Lila spots similar chairs dotting the lawn, some with family names, some with brands, but all marked and waiting for the people who've thought ahead.

The park, one square city block, is located six blocks east of Main Street, one block from the high school. Cars line both sides of the street. The whole town must be squeezed onto this little tract of land. Next to the swing sets and monkey bars, there's a covered pavilion where tables are set up with servers behind. All people have to do is file by, pick up a plate, a beverage, and find a spot to sit down. The lunch is free, paid for by the Lions Club.

Gertie and John settle into the chairs. George, Toby, and Lila argue good-naturedly over who should sit and who should stand in line.

"I'm younger than you. And stronger," Lila says.

"Younger, maybe," George drawls.

"Besides, you two can't carry enough food for five."

In the end the three of them move over to the line. While they're standing and waiting for their turn, Lila spots Clay at the far side of the park. He's leaned up against a tree trunk, Alicia standing in front of him. Lila sees Clay's hand shoot out and grab hold of Alicia's wrist. Alicia twists away from him and moves off through the crowd. Lila tries to follow Alicia with her eyes, see if she joins up with her husband and Amber, but she loses sight of her. Clay stands at the tree, looking downcast. Lila is about to ask Toby to hold her place in line when she sees Tim Pickford walk up to Clay. They exchange a few words and move off together. They skirt the crowded park and head toward town. She's wishing she could go with them when she hears George's voice.

"He's trouble," George says.

"Who?" she says. Like she doesn't know.

"Tim Pickford."

That quickly, all the air is let out of her tires. First Clay. Now

George. Everybody thinks they have to warn her about Tim Pickford. What do they think she is, some little kid? Or worse, a girl who can't spot trouble. Because look at her, would she be in this predicament if she made good choices?

She doesn't protest when someone ladles a pile of barbecued pork on her plate. She takes the beans and corn on the cob without a word. She's suddenly exhausted. She'd like to sit in a porch swing, all alone, touch her toe to the floor and gently rock. She takes her plate and styrofoam cup of iced tea and heads back to the family chairs.

She rounds the corner of the public restrooms and nearly runs into Owen. He's planted himself there, obviously waiting for her. She's too tired for him right now.

"What?" she says.

Owen stands his ground. He turns red, but he doesn't move to get out of her way. "Look. I thought you should know. Stay away from Tim Pickford."

Lila shuts her eyes. She'd like to keep them shut, let the dark fold her up. When she looks again, Owen's still standing there.

"Here," she says. She hands him her plate. He takes it to keep beans from spraying his shirt. "You might as well have this too," and she plops her cup of iced tea in the mess of beans.

She turns away quickly, before she can see the hurt in his eyes. She doesn't want to know about it. She can't handle any more grief.

She finds them at Carl's. She stands in the doorway letting her eyes adjust to the dim light. She hears the *pock-pock* of pool balls, smells the clouds of cigarette smoke. At the nearest pool table, a tall man leans over with his arms wrapped around a boy, helping him adjust his pool cue to make a tricky corner shot. Four pool tables, low-slung lights, one long bar with stools, men and boys and not a woman in sight. Clay and Tim are seated at the far end of the bar, their hands wrapped around bottles of Bud.

The bartender spots her, lifts up a hinged portion of the bar, steps through, and walks toward her. He's a heavy man, her dad's age or older, graying hair. He's wearing a white bar apron; if he had a cleaver, he'd make a good butcher. His face is set and grim. He's eyeing her up and down, the belly, the pierced ears and nose, finally the hair. She looks back at him, at his shaking hands, his unpolished boots.

"You looking for somebody?" His voice fits the body, low and coarse. He stops about four feet from her. She wonders if he thinks she's contagious.

"Maybe," she says. "Why?"

"We don't get women and girls in here."

What's he going to do, take her by the arm and throw her out? She's trying to decide if she's up to creating a ruckus when Clay finally spots her. He hustles off the bar stool and moves around the bartender.

"Hey, Spud, this is my cousin." Clay slips his hand under Lila's elbow.

Spud doesn't take his eyes from Lila's face. "What's she doing here?"

Clay reaches up with his free hand and scratches his head. He goes into his good ol' boy act. Lila rolls her eyes. "Lookin' for me, I expect."

"She don't belong here."

"Well, now. Don't you worry about it. I'll look out for her."

With that Clay steers Lila around Spud and toward the bar stools in the back. Spud stares after them. Grumbling under his breath, he goes back to tending bar. Clay sits Lila down on a stool between him and Tim. Spud stands with his back to the three of them and wipes glasses from the back of the bar.

"What's his problem?" Lila says, hooking her thumb toward the bartender.

"Oh, don't mind him. He just don't like women is all. This bar used to have a sign said No Women Allowed. But the mayor made him take it down."

"Don't women come in here?" Lila asks.

Tim and Clay look at each other, screw their faces with comic remembering.

"Once, I guess," Tim says.

"Well, twice. The first time was when Frieda, that's Spud's wife, came in here to tell him she was leaving town with Johnny O'Hara, the owner of the dry cleaners. She said some pretty ugly things in front of Spud's customers. He never could forgive her for that."

Tim nods. "Yeah. Poor guy. She shouldn't have done that."

"Left him, you mean?" Lila asks.

Tim snorts. "Nah. He needed leaving, I reckon. She had to leave, she should've just left quiet."

Lila watches Tim for a moment, his head resting on his arm, eyelids drooping. He doesn't look well. Either that or he's knackered. He's a sorry sight, and she's tempted to reach out and shove him off his stool. The sight of him slavering and loose-jawed makes her want to bang her fist on his knuckles. Prove them wrong, she wants to holler in his face. Help me out here. Instead she turns to Clay.

"You said twice," Lila says.

"Yeah. The second time was last year when the mayor made Spud take the sign down. He brought his wife, Tildy, in here one night. Sat right up to the bar and ordered two whiskey sours."

"That's it?"

"Yeah."

"Pretty much," Tim agrees.

"Why don't the women march on this place?"

Clay sits back on his seat. "What for?"

"Yeah. What would they want to come in here for?" Tim slumps forward on the bar, leans too close to Lila. His eyes are bloodshot.

Lila curls her lips back over her teeth. Her eyes are cold, but Tim doesn't seem to notice. "I see what you mean."

Clay swivels nervously on his stool. He reaches forward and pours the rest of his beer into a glass. "Don't mind Tim," he says.

"You boys always drink in the middle of the day?"

"Well, this here's a holiday," Tim says. He holds his bottle out to Lila. "C'mon. Take a swig."

"No, thanks," Lila says.

Tim pushes the bottle at her. "C'mon. It'll loosen you up a little." Tim nods toward Spud. "He ain't watching. Hell. Buster back there, he's giving snorts to his boy, and that kid ain't but ten years old."

"I can't," Lila says.

Tim reaches around and puts his hand on the back of Lila's head, in the same motion raising the bottle to her lips. She wrenches from his grasp, knocking over Clay's glass with her elbow. Clay scrambles off his stool to avoid the beer pouring off the bar.

"Now look at what you done," Tim says.

"Leave her alone," Clay says. He mops at the front of his pants with a paper napkin.

"Ain't you ashamed of yourself?" Tim rolls himself into Lila.

147

Clay shoots an arm out and grabs Tim. "C'mon, Tim. Let's get you out of here."

Tim scuffles, tries to get his feet firmly under him, but Clay has him by the shoulders and marches him toward the door. "Sorry, Lila," Clay mutters, and leaving Lila seated at the bar, the two men walk outside. Through the dark window, Lila can see them shove each other back and forth until finally Tim crumples. Clay wraps one arm around him and moves away down the sidewalk.

Lila looks up to see Spud staring at her from the other end of the bar. The tall man and his son have stopped shooting pool, both standing with their pool cues resting on the floor. Lila rises and straightens her shirt over her belly. With as much dignity as she can muster, she walks past them. When she nears the front door, she turns her head and speaks to the boy. "Aim lower on the ball," she says. "You'll get more spin on it." The kid smiles, and Lila smiles back.

Standing on the sidewalk outside the bar, Lila finally lets her breath out. Her back is killing her. Her feet hurt, too. She's six blocks from the park, not that far, but the sun has grown hot, ricocheting off the pavement. There's nothing else to do, so she sets out walking.

When Lila reaches the park, she skirts around the outside. Most people have headed over to the school for the melodrama. She looks for the row of chairs, but they're gone. Probably the old people are already seated in the auditorium. The last thing Lila wants to do is hiss at someone in a fake handlebar mustache who leers at Little Nell, then ties her to the tracks. She doesn't want to cheer for the hero either. She doesn't believe in heroes. She doubts that any of these people have ever met a hero, but they can't stop hoping for one. Not her. She's on her own, and she knows it. She's surprised, a little, that no one seems worried about her. It didn't occur to her until she was halfway downtown that she should have told Toby where she was going.

When she gets to George's pickup, she sees that the chairs are folded and stacked against the front bumper. She tries the handle on the door to the truck bed and finds it unlocked. She peeks inside and sees the mattress, covered by a blue flowered sheet, a soft cotton blanket thrown on top. George has opened the ventilating windows, so the air smells clean. A soft light falls in yellow shafts. She thought it would be claustrophobic, but after she has crawled inside, she decides that it's nice. Cozy. Like a cave. It's quiet outside now, since most of the people have moved off.

She lies down. Why didn't anyone come looking for her? What if Tim Pickford, drunk as a skunk, had tried to force her into his car? Her water might have broken. She could have gotten sunstroke. She thinks about the red-toed toddler on the curb, her brother's hand pressing her down. She falls asleep and dreams of playing hide-and-seek. She's little, five or six. There are fields, a corral, a barn. She hides in a good place, behind a pile of hay, and she waits, and she thinks she's outfoxed all of them, found the best hiding place in the world, but they don't come, they don't come, and slowly it dawns on her that no one is looking. They never intended to come and find her. She's alone, and she looks up at the immense sky and listens.

George

When Lila hands her tray to Owen and turns her heaving body toward town, George moves out of his place in line. He takes two steps forward when he feels Toby's arm across his chest, barring his way.

"Let her go," Toby says.

"Where, is the question," George says.

"She needs some space. She won't go far."

George nods his understanding. Toby is right. The girl is young. And she feels crowded. So he will let her go.

He follows her at a distance. He keeps his eye on her as if she is a stray. When training new colts, sometimes he has to trick them this way, let them feel their independence while keeping them from harm. He scans the skies for predators. He tunes his ears to the rustling of the brush.

When the girl disappears inside Carl's, he waits in the shade of the awning across the street. He knows it will not be long. He sees the boys come out first, Clay shoving Tim Pickford, then hauling him off down the street. He sets his mind after them, but does not move his feet. They will keep. Until later.

He watches her when she comes out. Watches her face, young and sad. He does not let her see him watching. He trails her back to the park. He watches her climb into the back of his truck. He chose the blanket himself, with her in mind. Sky blue, to remind her that the sky is big and open. Full of possibility.

He unfolds one of the chairs and sits by the rear wheel of the truck. He wants to keep the door in sight. He has missed his dinner, but does not mind. He smiles, thinking of Toby herding Gertie and John to the melodrama. He folds his hands in his lap, and he waits.

Toby

Toby sits through the melodrama, working hard to keep from standing up and walking out. She's always hated these things. Stupid. Some silly woman falling for a line of demeaning flattery from an obviously wicked man. When Little Nell gets tied to the tracks, Toby hopes the train will run over her. Just this once. Let the crowd respond to that. Trains run over women who allow themselves to be victims. The hero would be down at the bar playing poker with his buddies, too late to stop the rolling engine. Let him deal with grief. Now there would be a story.

She glances at Gertie and John, seated on either side of her. John's head nods on his chest. Gertie's eyes are open, but she's so still that Toby thinks she's all but asleep too. She lets her mind wander over to Lila, that Pickford boy, and Clay. She wonders what hold Tim Pickford has on Clay, why Clay puts up with him.

She knows that Lila feels hemmed in. Cramped. Her body pressing down on her like a sack full of anvils. A girl that age craves independence. She did. She hated the way Luther bullied her. Too numb, too scared, she hadn't fought for what she wanted. Or even known how to name it. Now with Lila, she's afraid of saying too much, imposing her will and Lila hating her for it down the road.

The crowd suddenly roars to life, booing and hissing, and Toby looks up to see that Malcolm Lord is cast as the villain. He's preening, running his chubby hands over his fake waxed mustache. The audience keeps up the racket, trying to warn Little Nell, who turns a deaf ear.

Still, is that any excuse? With Nola Jean, hadn't Toby opted for the easy way out, waiting for her to ask the obvious questions, and when she didn't, telling herself that her daughter didn't want to know. The past is gone and buried. No amount of digging it up will change what happened. And she knows, though she wishes it were otherwise, that no amount of talk will convince Lila that she's not alone.

Toby's attention snaps back to the play. This Nell is not so easily cowed. Maggie Overstreet, in a blond wig and checkered pinafore, has just slapped the villain's cheek. She's taking a turn around the stage, flexing her muscles. The hero is on the sidelines, twirling his lariat, oblivious to Nell and her plight. She can take care of herself, this Nell. The audience breaks into laughter. But Malcolm sneers behind his hand and leers at Little Nell. The music grows menacing, and Toby, who has sat too long in silence, cups her palms into a megaphone and calls out, "Don't even think about it, Malcolm." Applause, applause, and Malcolm, searching for the owner of the voice, spots Toby in the fourth row of the auditorium. She makes it easy for him by waving her hand in the air. She could swear his beady eyes glow like coals, but give Malcolm credit, he doffs his hat to her and resumes his villain charade, stepping into the role as if he was born to it.

George

The rodeo is in full swing. George and John have hauled the folding chairs to one of the front boxes of the grandstand, the metal bleachers too hard on the back for any of them, including Lila. Over the loudspeaker the announcer's voice crackles, then taped western music between acts, "Tumblin' Tumbleweeds," "Don't Fence Me In," Roy Rogers and Bing Crosby, Hollywood manufactured cowboys, Crosby not even that (didn't he play a priest once?), but nobody cares, the songs old-timey and familiar, the crowd warm and singing along about land and starry skies. Steaming coffee, soda, popcorn, hot dogs striped with yellow mustard, cotton candy stiff and pink on kids' licked fingers. Behind them, on the floor of the grandstand, a constant parade of teenage boys struts back and forth, trolling for girls. Lila, who ought to be one of those girls, sits between Toby and John, her spiked hair up like a thistle, unaware or pretending not to notice when the boys look at her. Toby keeps score on the white program notes, jotting down times for calf ropers, bareback riders. Gertie makes her read the scores every five or ten minutes, and they haggle over whether or not Toby's got them right. John's wedged in the corner, his shoulders hunched, feet flat on the floor. Dust kicks up from the arena along with the smells of manure, hay, animal hides, and the sweat of hard-working men. Once when the pickers are slow to move in to lift a rider off his bucking horse, the black horse careens into the fence just to the right of where they're seated. The crowd surges to its feet, but the horse kicks its white-socked legs, stampedes to the far end of the arena, and the rider, #47 pinned to his yellow shirt back, picks himself up from the ground where he has fallen, waves his mangled hat at the crowd, and limps off. Lila raises her head from Toby's shoulder, where she has hidden it. Behind them, on the first row of bleachers, a child raises her voice into the edgy silence, "Did he break his neck?" Relief erupts in the audience as laughter, the child's comment passed along the stands, and the announcer makes a joke; did she mean the horse or the rider? When the barrel racers come on and George is certain that no one will notice, he slips out of his chair and heads for the exit from the grandstand.

He knows where to find them. Back of the grandstand there's

a low-lying building where the dance will be held. Late, after the rodeo, stiff cowboys and local women and teenagers trying out the adult world will two-step and country dance to a cowboy band. The wooden floor has been coated with pink cleansing powder and swept dry, a few bales of hay piled on the edges to provide seats for the foot-weary between dances. George goes looking among the night dwellers, the young men and few women who hang out in the parking lot, drinking beer from coolers stashed in the backs of pickups, dragging on cigarettes with trembling hands, telling tales until time for the dance to start.

He has not passed far along the line of cars and trucks when he sees Clay's red pickup. There's a full moon, and out here in the parking lot where the only light is from the night sky and one tall lamp on a thirty-foot pole, couples are necking, lying together in the beds of trucks, sucking and moaning and groping. George puts his hand on the rim of the bed of Clay's truck, hauls himself up to the edge, looks over, not knowing what he'll see. There's a blanket, thrown in a heap, but no one lying there. He stands in the dark, waiting for his eyes to adjust. Two or three cars down the row, four young people are squatted on the ground, laughing. He listens, but does not hear either Clay or Tim Pickford.

He turns his head slowly, scanning the surroundings, until over on the edge of the parking lot he spies Tim. He's still wearing the red printed shirt he had on earlier today when Clay ushered him out of Carl's. His glasses glint in the moonlight. Soundlessly, George moves toward him, watching the transaction going on between Tim and the stranger in a tall hat who stands across from him. He sees the stranger slide a small packet into the front pocket of his tight jeans. He's wearing a big silver belt buckle. His hat brim slants down low, hiding his face. George waits while the stranger moves away, until Tim has reached into his back pocket, drawn out a billfold, laid the stranger's money neatly into the compartment that holds bills. When Tim stretches back to shove the billfold once more in his hip pocket, George grabs his arm and wrenches it tightly up his back. The billfold drops to the ground, and George kicks it away while he wraps his other arm around Tim's neck and cranks his head back. He's not strong anymore, but he knows the moves, where to apply pressure so Tim's efforts to free himself cause more pain.

"What the hell?" Tim mutters.

George knows he won't shout. He can't risk it. George speaks into Tim's ear. "You know who this is?"

Tim relaxes slightly. Maybe he feels safe, knowing it's George. Or maybe he doesn't want to break an old man. Either way, it's a mistake. George takes the opportunity to put more pressure on Tim's bent arm.

"Ow. You crazy old man. What do you want?"

"Stay away from Lila."

"Okay. Okay. She don't mean nothing to me."

George fights against the disgust he feels for this creature. He could snap his neck. It would take only an instant. Who would even miss him? Before his thoughts hunt him down, he loosens his hold. Tim scrambles away from him, feels around in the dirt for his billfold.

"You need to get some help, Tim," George says. He tries to say it kindly.

"Mind your own business. I'll charge you with assault, you ever come near me again."

George waits until he's shoved his billfold in his back pocket. "I saw that guy," he says.

"What guy?"

"The one who paid you money."

"So what? He owed me money. No crime against that."

"He paid you for a packet you handed him."

Tim's face changes. One side of his mouth curls up, a feral animal with one leg trapped in a snare. "Old man, you must be seeing things," he says. Tim slips away into the darkness, a creature returning to its lair.

George watches him go, waits a while until his heart slows down and his breathing comes easier. He's way too old to be muscling boys around. He lets himself feel bad about Tim Pickford. He knew Tim's father, a mean son of a bitch if there ever was one. Something got ruined in Tim early on, and George doesn't need much imagination to figure how it happened. But Tim's got his own choices to make. Intent as he is on his own destruction, he could pull a lot of innocent people down with him. The question is: where is Tim getting his product? And how much is Clay already in it?

On his way back to the grandstand, George rounds a corner to thread through a shadowy place between the men's restroom and the holding pens. Back there, in the near dark, two men are shoving each other, their voices loud and cutting through the night air. By the time George gets close, they've exchanged punches, the beefy guy backed up against the fence with blood running from his nose. George lays his hand on the back of the other guy, a tall, stringy kid who's still flailing in anger. "Let him go, Clay," George says. Clay's shoulders stiffen under George's hand, and he says again, "Let him go now." Clay releases the man, who stoops to pick his hat up from the dirt, not taking his eye off Clay. He opens his mouth to utter one last bitter remark, but seeing George's face seems to think better of it. When the man has moved safely off, George turns to Clay. From the looks of him he got the hard end of the fight. George leans him up against the fence, props him with his shoulder while he reaches up to untie the neckerchief knotted around his neck. He licks the end of the bandanna to moisten it, dabs at Clay's bleeding eye. "What's this all about?" George asks.

"Water," Clay mutters.

"That was Randy Wright, wasn't it?"

Clay shoots a look at George. Moans when he feels around inside his mouth with his tongue. "Yeah. That's him."

George looks into the dark where Randy's figure has vanished. He draws his brows together. He knows men who've been shot during a drought. Still, Randy Wright is Alicia's husband, and Alicia isn't happy grazing in her own pasture. "Water, huh?"

Clay's standing on his own two feet now. George moves off a step, leaves his hand on Clay's shoulder to steady him.

"He says my center pivot's lowering the water table. I got my own well. I expect I can do what I want."

George nods. He doesn't take his eyes off Clay's face, watching the way his mouth moves. He wonders if the boy knows he's lying.

"He's mad at the Ditch Board, says they're letting people up the line steal his water."

George is curious now. Wanting to make the connection. "He can't blame you for that."

"Frank's on the board." Frank Trevino. Clay's new stepfather.

George knows the way these things work. The Ditch Board gets pressure from some of the bigger farmers. Maybe a promise or a reminder of a past favor. He doubts that any money has changed hands. Not yet. Not unless the rain holds off for another month. The Ditch Board puts a word in the ear of the ditch rider, and the ditch rider looks the other way while a farmer illegally opens the head gate. Randy Wright's farm is at the end of the line, and that's bad luck for him.

"You felt you had to uphold Frank's honor. That it?"

Clay spits to one side, blood mixed with saliva making a puddle on the ground. "Something like that," he says.

Many words cross his mind. Things he'd like to tell Clay, but he knows from the look of him it won't do a bit of good. He's been bitten, and there's nothing to do now but see where the poison takes him. He steps back and watches Clay straighten his clothes, reset his hat.

"Watch yourself," George says.

Clay nods and moves away. George watches him, envies the walk of a young man, and breathes the night air. Behind him in the grandstand he can hear the crowd roar, and he knows without looking that a man is riding a bull, the hind heels of the mad animal shooting for the moon.

Later, after they have driven back to the ranch and Toby has helped Gertie inside, George joins Lila on the front step. It's long past midnight, but she's got her neck craned up, studying the stars. John waits for him in the pickup, his head low on his chest. George will help him into bed when they reach their house, ease his boots off, let him sleep in his clothes. He steals this moment with Lila, turns his face toward the heavens. The stars are plentiful out here, scattered across the wide sky, not as bright tonight as some nights because the moon is full.

He points to a low star on the horizon. "That one," he says. "That's David." He points out another brilliant star just visible over the roof of the machine shed. "That's Ella. My wife."

158

Lila turns to follow his hand. He wonders how much he should say about star power.

He clears his throat. "When your great-grandmother and David died, I brought Toby out here one night. Choose a star, I said. It will help." He points again at David's star. "She chose that one."

The girl is quiet. He likes that about her. She doesn't chatter and giggle like some young girls he has known.

"What about Rosemary? Does she have a star?"

He puts his hand on the girl's arm and leads her down off the porch. Then he points back over the roof of the house, toward the Big Dipper. He shows her how to guide off the two front stars of the bucket to find the Little Dipper. "That one, the end of the handle. That's Rosemary. Toby wanted her mother to be always visible and easy to find."

"What about Luther? And Walter?"

George clears his throat. "I don't know about them. Toby was older when they died. If she chose stars, I don't know about it. She may have."

The girl wraps her arms around herself. "Does the person have to be dead? Can you choose a star for someone living?"

He smiles. He knows what is in her mind. This is a good thing, then.

"You only choose a star for someone you love. Doesn't matter if they are living or dead. Someone you love who you want to be reminded of."

She stands quiet, and he stands with her. When he is sure she has nothing more to say tonight, he tells her one more thing. "You can't see the stars in the daytime, but they are there. They're always there, but it takes the darkness to reveal them."

She turns to him. Her eyes are focused, intense. He can see that she would be a good student. He tells her what he knows.

"We don't know who we are until the darkness reveals us. That's when we find out."

He places his hand briefly on her shoulder. Then he takes his leave, not needing to look back to know she has lifted her face to the sky and the moon glistens off the planes of her cheekbones.

Lila

Owen doesn't answer the first ring of the bell on the desk in the newspaper office. Lila looks through the doorway, back where the presses are whirling, past the office with the glass window. She spots him, so she dings the bell again. When he still doesn't come, she moves around the counter, stands in the doorway to the back room. Owen's boss, a balding man with a bulbous nose, looks up first.

"Hi, there," he says. "Can we help you?" He sticks his pencil behind one ear, like a TV journalist.

"I'm here to see Owen," she says, her shoulder braced against the door frame, the belly obvious. She reaches up and smoothes her hair at the back of her neck, leaves her hand caught on the nape.

The man looks at Owen, who stands beside him, his face a shade of red she's not seen in a while. The man looks back at her. His tongue hunts a place in the side of his cheek. He stands, closes a file folder. "We can do this later," he says. "Why don't you take a break, Owen?"

The man turns and heads toward the glass office. He sits at his desk, reaches behind him, and swings the door shut. When it doesn't close, he swivels his chair, gives it an extra nudge with his foot. Owen doesn't move. He stands and looks at her across the room. The presses clank, so she raises her voice to reach him.

"Thanks for the clippings," she says.

Owen doesn't answer.

"I wanted to . . . just . . . thanks."

"What do you want?" Owen asks. No smile.

"Nothing, I guess." She turns toward the door. She shouldn't have come. She's halfway out when Owen calls.

"Wait."

She stops, but doesn't turn around.

"Want to . . . uh . . . it's my break time. Want to get something . . . somewhere?"

He's hardly breathing by the end of this speech. Lila doesn't turn around. "Okay," she says.

"Yeah?" He sounds surprised. And pleased.

She turns then, but he's already scurrying back to his desk, calling over his shoulder, "Just a minute." In his haste he knocks the in-basket over, catches it before everything falls to the floor. He sifts through some papers on his desk, comes up with a small manila envelope. He waves it at her, then joins her at the doorway. Outside on the sidewalk, Owen looks up and down the street.

"How about the bakery?" Lila asks, to help him out.

Owen scrunches his face. "Yeah. They got coffee." He doesn't move.

"I don't need coffee," she says, thinking maybe he has no money.

"People talk there," he says. Instantly, she knows what he means. People talk, and people listen. She feels the hair on the back of her neck prickle. What's in that envelope?

"The park?" she asks.

"I don't have that much time. Buzz'll be expecting me back."

"Buzz is your boss's name?"

"Calvin. But everybody calls him Buzz."

He's started walking, and she falls in step beside him.

"We can go back by the old water tower," he says. "Nobody goes there anymore. There's a bench under it."

They walk the two blocks, pass the post office, follow a path between a deserted building with a weather-beaten sign that reads "Blacksmith Shop" from some bygone era and a small, dilapidated house. The grass under the water tower hasn't been cut in a while. They sit on the bench, the tower shading them partially. Lila glances at the windows on the back porch of the house.

"Old man Earlywine lives there. Pay no attention. He can't see much, anyway."

"Owen," Lila says. She turns her knees toward him slightly. "I'm sorry about the picnic."

He watches her face. "I thought you were mad about the clippings."

"About . . . oh, no. I wasn't."

"You didn't think I was spying?"

"No. I'm glad. I mean, that was thoughtful."

"What, then?"

"I don't know. Sometimes things just get to me, you know?"

"Yeah." He looks away. He seems a lot calmer out here, away from the office. "Things get to me, too."

She takes a deep breath. "What's in the envelope?"

Owen turns it over in his hands. "Something I found."

"Is it about Tim Pickford?"

Owen rears back as if she's slapped him. "Gosh, no," he says.

She turns her head away. She doesn't want to hear another

word about Tim Pickford with his boozy breath, his bad reputation. And yet that leaves only the people she cares about.

Owen rubs his foot against the grass. "I looked something up," he says.

"You mean, in the papers?"

"No. At the courthouse."

"Why?"

He shrugs. "Hunch. I wondered, is all." He hands her the manila envelope.

She takes it, expecting it to feel hot or heavy, consequential in a way that it doesn't. She unclasps the bent brass brad, but before she can reach inside Owen puts his hand on hers. "It's about Toby," he says. "Toby and David. So don't look if you don't want to know."

She studies his face. "Too late," she says. Reaching into the envelope, she pulls out a photocopied bit of paper. It looks official, smeared and hard to read.

"What is this?" she asks.

"It's a birth certificate. Look," Owen says. He points at the date: *February 15, 1949. Place of birth: Home. Baby's mother: Gwendolyn Bolden. Baby's father: David Banks, deceased.*

Lila raises her head. She stares at the house with blank windows, the sagging back porch. The elm trees are littered with dead branches, the shingled roof cracked and chipped. From one limb a tire swing hangs from a frayed and rotten rope. Anyone sitting in that swing would land on the ground, thud, the bottom falling away.

She turns to look at Owen and whispers, "Toby was pregnant."

Owen nods.

"That's why she and David tried to run away to get married."

"Maybe. She might not have known." When she stares at him, he tosses his head and shrugs. "I did the math," he says.

Back at the little house, a mangy cat appears on the back stoop. Fat, looking well fed, but its fur matted and clumped, a cat with dreadlocks.

"But what happened to the baby?"

"I don't know. No death certificate. I looked for a notice of adoption, but I didn't see one."

"What was it? Does it say?" Lila turns back to study the small paper.

"A boy."

"Does he have a name?"

"It just says baby boy. They used to allow that, I guess. You didn't have to put a name on the birth certificate."

Lila lays her hand on her enlarged belly. The baby is rolling around, somersaulting and showing off. "She was my age," Lila says.

"Yeah."

Lila feels light-headed, can't get enough air. Her heart pounds in her ears. Why hasn't anybody talked about this? She's positive her mother doesn't know. Is this the family curse, a big fat shameful secret? Like her. Is that what she is to them? She leans back on her hands and tries to gulp some air.

"Take it easy," Owen says.

She hands back the manila folder. Forces a smile.

"Don't you want to keep it?"

"No." She doesn't need a reminder. She's not apt to forget this. And she doesn't want Toby to find out that she knows. "You hang onto it."

"Are you sorry?"

Lila stands, presses her hands against her aching back, arches it to straighten out the muscles. The baby's pressing on her sciatica, so she shakes her left leg to loosen it, get the feeling back. "No. I don't know."

"Well, I better get back," he says.

"Okay."

Owen looks at her, his face knit with concern. She tries to lighten up.

"I think I'll stay here a bit. Toby won't be done at the bank for another half hour."

"You sure?"

"Yeah. I like it here. Thanks."

When Owen has moved away, turned once, and waved to her, she sits again on the bench. She studies the back of that house, the ruined swing, the broken steps. Once it had life in it. Once a mother lived there, and children played on that swing. She hears the laughter, feels chubby hands tugging at the hem of a skirt, a little head nodding on a shoulder. She takes her time inventing the children, one by one, all of them healthy and happy. All of them wanted.

Toby

Standing on the steps to Serenity House with Gertie, Toby hears piano playing and singing from inside. This is their first visit since Howard's lockup. Gertie's so nervous that she hasn't stopped talking since they left home. Toby tuned her out, let her natter on, while she watched the road, took in the progress of passing fields of corn and sugar beets and beans.

A nurse they've not met opens the door. She's young, blond, plump, wearing a nametag that says Sharon, the name surrounded by hand-drawn hearts, pink and glittery. Toby wonders if she could be Mrs. Lang's daughter, or if blond and plump are prerequisites to being hired here.

Sharon smiles and ushers them inside. Once they step onto the porch, Gertie moves past Sharon into the living room. Howard is sitting on the piano bench, next to the dolled-up music teacher. Fingers light and tinkling on the keys, she plays "Sentimental Journey," and Howard sings along. He still has a pleasant baritone voice. He knows all the words. His clothes are clean, his hair combed. His face radiates pleasure. Relieved to see that he is happy, Toby turns to Gertie, but Gertie's lips are white with strain, her fingers locked around the top rim of her pocketbook.

Toby reaches out to put her hand on Gertie's arm. But Gertie is too fast for her, has already marched forward. She jerks on Howard's shoulder.

"Howard," she says.

Howard shrugs, keeps on singing.

Gertie, more insistent this time, calls his name again. Howard stops singing, turns a worried face, leans his body toward the piano-playing music teacher. She's wearing something soft and blue today, ruffles, the blue accenting her silver hair. She keeps on playing, as automatic as a music box. Gertie tugs on Howard's arm, and Howard starts to whimper.

Afraid that Gertie will raise her pocketbook and flail at the ruffly woman in blue, Toby crosses the room, but Sharon moves in ahead of her. She steps in front of Gertie, almost knocking poor Gert off balance. Straight into Howard's face, her hand on his back, Sharon says, "It's all right, Howard." Then Sharon turns to Gertie. "It might be best if you sat over there," she says, indicating a green sofa across the room. She speaks slowly, space between her words, as if English were a foreign language to them. "Why don't you start by observing Howard's day?"

Toby takes Gertie's arm and guides her to the sofa. Before they can sit down, they push aside several crocheted afghans and patchwork pillows that hide the threadbare upholstery. Without ceremony Gertie dumps her pile on the floor. She sits, and Toby sits beside her. Through all this the woman in blue keeps playing "Sentimental Journey" until Toby thinks she will scream. Does this go on night and day?

Having quieted Howard down, Sharon turns to them. She stands square in front of them and delivers a singsong rehearsed speech. "I'm so sorry. I should have explained. This is a regular part of Howard's day. He and Irene have music together twice a day, a half hour before lunch, another half hour before supper. They'd sit there for hours if we let them, but the other residents complain. Howard enjoys it. You can see he does." She points toward the pair on the piano bench, her wrist flopped over, fingers curved, like Vanna White indicating prizes on *Wheel of Fortune*.

"Humph," Gertie grunts. She leans around to follow the line of Sharon's arm, since Sharon blocks her peripheral angle. Toby raises her eyebrows, but Gertie seems content to settle. For now. When Sharon leaves the room to tend to a patient who is caterwauling from the back bedrooms, they watch Howard and the woman in blue move through "Sentimental Journey" two more times. Howard's hand flutters around on the woman's back. She sits stiff as a poker, seemingly oblivious to his touching her. After the second time through, an alarm goes off. The woman in blue jumps to her feet, grabs the alarm clock off the top of the piano, pushes down the button. "That's all for today, class," she tells

Howard. She walks away, back stiff, arms extended and floating, on the toes of her pink ballet slippers.

Howard watches her walk from the room with adoring eyes. Harmless, Toby decides, and rather sweet. But she doubts that Gertie will see it that way. Not sure what to do, she and Gertie sit still. Howard stands. He looks confused for a moment, but soon recovers his intentions and moves toward his bedroom in the back. Toby and Gertie are left sitting by themselves in the living room. They endure a few silent, awkward moments, and then Gertie stands. "Enough of this," she says. "I'm going back there."

"Me, too," Toby says.

She follows Gertie back to the green bedroom. From the doorway they can see Howard sitting in a rocking chair, staring at a painting on the wall of mallard ducks over a bog. He looks up at them, brightens.

Gertie breaks into a smile. "Hello, Howard," she says. She and Toby inch further into the room. Toby sits on the far side of the bed while Gertie moves toward Howard in the chair.

Howard points to the painting. "Look there," he says. "That's them ducks on Crescent Lake. Remember when we went there?"

He says this to Gertie. Toby stirs uncomfortably.

"I left the tractor in the field, and we drove there. Remember that? All them lakes smack in the middle of the Sandhills. Millions of ducks on them. I never saw anything like that before. And you said you hadn't neither."

"We never went to Crescent Lake together, Howard. I haven't been there since I was a girl."

"Never said you did," Howard says. He rocks faster now. His face turned away from Gertie.

Gertie turns to Toby. "He's not making sense," she says.

"Well, Gertie . . ." Toby says. She leaves the line unfinished.

"Not you. Her." Howard points at Toby. His hand shakes with emotion, his voice rising. "You made that picnic. Ham sandwiches."

"What's he talking about?" Gertie asks. She looks more bewildered than Howard. Toby wants to run, far away and fast.

"He doesn't know," Toby says. She whispers it, meant only for Gertie, but the room is small, and for all his other problems there's nothing wrong with Howard's hearing.

"Ham sandwiches. With mustard. And pie."

"Pie?" Gertie asks. She's turned to look at Toby now, something dawning in the back of her eyes.

"Rhubarb pie." Howard sits back, arms crossed. A toddler who won't budge.

"You made rhubarb pie?" Gertie sways. For one terrible moment, Toby thinks she will topple onto the floor, but she lands safely on the edge of the bed.

"Gertie. Gertie, it's not what you think."

"Ham. Mustard. Rhubarb pie. Ham. Mustard. Rhubarb pie." Howard rocks in the chair, reciting his newly made poem, his voice gaining volume.

Gertie turns on him. "Shut up. Stop that right now."

Howard's face crumples. He looks at Toby. "She's mean to me," he says.

"Oh, god," Toby moans.

"Why didn't you come to see me before?" Howard directs this to Toby also.

Gertie's face snaps shut, as tight as the clasp on her pocketbook.

Toby stands. "I'll wait outside," she says.

When she tries to move away, Howard starts yelling. "Don't leave me! She's mean to me. Don't leave me!"

Gertie's face, cold and hard, Toby standing, unable to move, Howard yelling, and finally, merciful god, where has she been? Sharon comes to the door.

"What's going on here?" She sweeps into the room. Kneels down beside Howard. "There, Howard. You're all right." She pats Howard until he quiets. Then she stands and faces the culprits. She looks at them the way a teacher looks at rowdy boys who've spread honey on the girls' desk seats. She's young, way too young to take this attitude with them, but Toby hangs her head.

"I'll wait outside," Toby says again.

"It's too late for that," Gertie says.

Sharon rolls her head from one to the other. Softening her voice, she tries another approach. "Perhaps that's enough for today."

"Where's Irene?" Howard asks. "I want Irene."

Howard has risen from the rocking chair, crossed to his dresser. He's extremely agitated. First he looks in the mirror that hangs above the dresser. Then he opens and shuts the top drawer. Looks again. Opens and shuts another drawer. "Where's Irene?" he mutters under his breath. All this time Sharon tries to convince Gertie to leave. Toby, in agony, waits by the door, unsure whether to bolt or wait for her sister. Gertie sits, as still as stone. Finally Gertie stands. At that moment Howard looks at her, and his face softens.

Gertie walks toward him, and he does not flinch. He seems to welcome her. His face lights, and when she takes his arm, he looks straight into her eyes and asks, "Irene?"

"No, dear. I'm Gertie. Your wife." Toby admires Gertie's fortitude, always has.

"My wife?" Howard asks. He looks at Sharon, and Sharon nods.

"I got a wife?" Howard asks, looking back at Gertie.

"Yes, Howard," Gertie says.

"Who's that?" Howard asks. He points toward the dresser.

Gertie looks at Sharon for clues, but Sharon only shakes her head.

"That man," Howard says. It's clear now that he's pointing at the mirror. "Who is that man? He's always hanging around here."

Toby watches Sharon stifle a laugh. That's how they do it, Toby thinks. That's how they stand it here. Graveside humor. But Gertie is not laughing.

"Never mind, Howard." Gertie says. "You never mind a thing." She pats him once on the arm, tucks her pocketbook under her elbow, sweeps past Sharon and Toby. She's out the door and down the walk, Toby has to move fast to catch up to her. Gertie'd risk falling flat on her face at the curb rather than let Toby touch her.

Once they are in the car, Toby turns to Gertie. She has barely drawn breath to speak when Gertie cuts her off. "Don't you say a goddamn word."

Gertie turns her face to the window, and they ride that way all the way back to the ranch. Two hours of strained silence. They don't stop for lunch. No potty break. Toby drives, and Gertie breathes hard, staring out the window. Toby feels her seething hatred.

When they pull into the yard, Toby pushes a button and locks all the doors. She stops the car and turns to Gertie. Gertie wrestles with her door handle, but there's nothing she can do. She's trapped. Toby feels no pity.

"I'm going to say this once, and by god, you're going to listen. It was the second summer after David and Mother died. Howard took me to Crescent Lake. Nothing happened."

"Let me out."

"We couldn't tell you. You were so damn jealous."

Gertie turns to face her, her head cocked at an angle, her left eye boring down on Toby from a great height. Toby winces. She wills herself to stand up to Gertie's wrath, knows she has it coming.

"Whatever didn't happen that day, it was important to Howard. He remembers one day with you. Fifty-six years with me, and he . . ." Gertie stops. Her chin quivers. She folds in on herself, and Toby thinks absurdly of the Wicked Witch of the West, dissolving, dissolving, and Gertie's breath comes in hard gasps. My god, Toby thinks, she's having a heart attack, and she reaches out to shake Gertie's shoulder, as if that will do any good, as if shaking sense into her will stop this suffering. Gertie wrenches out of Toby's grip. She sniffs hard, once, rubs the back of her hand under her nose, whacks at the window with a hard thump. "Now you let me out of this goddamn car. Let me out." Her voice hysterical and rising, and Toby pushes the button. Gertie opens the door so fast she nearly loses her balance, it's a miracle she doesn't pitch headlong onto the rocks and dirt of the drive. She gets herself out, straightens the hem of her top, climbs the steps, and goes inside the house.

Toby sits behind the wheel of her car, her forehead resting on the steering wheel. Gertie's black patent pocketbook remains on the seat beside her, stiff, upright, the clasp snapped to attention. Toby throws it to the floor, hoping it is scuffed beyond repair and knowing, immediately, that this will be one more thing for which she will have to feel sorry.

Lila

Julia has made chili, and Lila is sitting at the table with her and Royce. They're eating on plastic placemats of scenes from the Black Hills. Mt. Rushmore looms under Lila's blue pottery bowl, and Royce quizzes her to see if she knows the names of the presidents.

"Course," Lila says. "Lincoln, Jefferson, Washington, and . . . is this the one with a nose the size of an office building?"

"Ah. You're stalling." Royce points his spoon at her, the thick chili gravy dripping off into his bowl.

Julia slaps Royce on the shoulder. "Leave her alone."

"Kids today. They don't know history."

"Yeah," Lila says, grinning. "Like Mt. Rushmore is history."

"I'm just saying . . ."

"Roosevelt. The fourth guy is Roosevelt," Lila says.

"Bingo," Royce says. "Advance to the head of the class."

"Wasn't he the guy in the wheelchair?"

Royce groans, missing Lila's sideways look at Julia. Royce takes off, heedless, expounding on the faults of education today, covering World War II and FDR with a few facts about Churchill thrown in and winding up with Teddy Roosevelt's contribution to U.S. history through the set-aside of national parks. Lila watches him, feeling floaty, rising on hope. She's thinking that he'll make a great dad.

She's come to ask Royce and Julia to take her baby. She drove Toby's Buick here by herself. Yesterday, while Toby and Gertie were gone visiting Howard, she prowled the house, restless, unable to get Owen's revelation out of her mind, eager to get this over with. It's Sunday, and she knew Julia would be stealing time in the afternoon away from the herds. She wanted to talk to Julia while they were alone, but she's been kept busy, gathering peppers from the garden, rinsing beans, mincing onions. Julia said she knew chili was a fool thing to eat in the middle of summer, but she had a hankering for it. Lila took this mention of craving as a good sign, some simpatico urge, like men who experience labor pains. She's been reading about this stuff, on the Internet and in tracts she picks up in Dr. Penny's office.

Now they sit, the three of them, under the copper lantern chandelier, spooning up beans and beef in a thick soupy mixture that bites Lila's tongue. Royce's hair is wet, slicked back from the shower he took right before supper. Julia's face shines hot and red from the stove and the chili peppers. Country music whines in the background, Patsy Cline asking "Have You Ever Been Lonely," interspersed with market reports in response to which Royce occasionally halts and turns a listening ear. It's been a year of dry weather, a year to worry about the markets.

"How about the Needles?" Royce asks. "You ever seen them?" He lifts his bowl and points to the scene on his placemat. Sure enough, narrow spikes of rock with eyes cut straight through them. While his bowl is held high, Julia takes it from him and walks to the stove to ladle in a second helping.

"Nope," Lila says. "Never been to the Black Hills."

"You should go," Julia says. She sets Royce's bowl in front of him. Lila notices the hand that lingers on Royce's shoulder. Another good sign.

"Get Toby and George to take you up there. Hell, it ain't but a half-day's drive, not even that. Everybody ought to see the Black Hills before they're twenty. You're not twenty, are you?"

Lila rolls her eyes. He knows she's a kid.

"Well, then. There's time yet. But it's going by fast. We could take you if it wasn't summer."

Julia refills her own bowl. When she lifts it, Lila sees that Julia's placemat is a wide, open meadow with buffalo grazing. Julia offers her seconds of the chili, but Lila waves her away. She's barely touched her food. When Julia sits, she raises her eyebrows at Lila. They have a small conspiracy going, both of them loving Royce and thinking he's silly at the same time. He's a man of many moods, Lila has learned. He can sit in thick silence, content to share your company under the stars. He might take off his hat and use it to whack a stubborn horse, curse a streak to make even a city kid squirm. Now he's in his teacher mode, and when he gets going like this, there's nothing to do but ride it out.

"Be sure they take you up to Spearfish Canyon. Don't go to that passion play, that's a big rip-off. But there's some real pretty falls there. They had a flood in that canyon once, remember that, Julia? Killed a lot of people."

"You're thinking of the Big Thompson Canyon in Colorado."

"I am not thinking of the Big Thompson. No, sir. It was Spearfish Canyon. So don't stay in the canyon if they're predicting heavy rain. And I'll tell you what else. Skip that town of Keystone at the foot of Mt. Rushmore. That's nothing but a bunch of tourist traps. And you probably can't go through Wind Cave in your condition. Which is too bad, because Wind Cave is something to see."

There it is. Her opening. Her condition. But before Lila can vault into the conversation, Royce has launched past Wind Cave into advice about feeding the burros and not feeding the prairie dogs. Or the other way around. Lila has stopped listening to the exact words, although she loves the sound of his voice rising and falling, the teasing tone of it, the laughter hiding under the words.

Lila bites down on her lip, turns her spoon over in the bowl,

175

not sure how to begin. Royce and Julia have an easy rhythm together, not like Lila's parents when they were still married. Her parents bickered constantly, trying to cast each other as the one at fault. Around them she'd shrunk until she got small enough to slip through a keyhole. She could disappear from a room, and they wouldn't even notice.

"You feeling all right?" Julia asks. Her face full of concern.

"Yeah. Not that hungry, I guess."

"Don't you like chili?" Royce asks between mouthfuls.

"I could get you something else. Cheese. Peanut butter sandwich?" Julia says. "Maybe all this spice is too much for you."

"No. No, I like it," Lila lies. She doesn't like it, never has, but even if she did she has no appetite tonight.

"Get them to stop at Fort Robinson, too. It's more or less on the way. That's where the U.S. Army killed Crazy Horse."

"Royce, stop going on. Let the child eat."

"They tried to lock him up. Coaxed him in to surrender because his people were starving. He protested, and they knifed him. They trained canine troops at Fort Robinson during World War II. That must have been a sight."

The whole meal passes by, skating on Royce's travelogue. Lila wishes they would ask her things. If they asked about her doctor visits, she could tell them she's worried about what to do with this baby. And then maybe they'd offer, Why not leave it with us? She would act surprised, like she hadn't thought of that, but only for a minute. She wouldn't want them to think that she had doubts. Not too eager either. She'd like them to think it was their idea, so the baby would feel wanted.

They don't ask. She's been driving over once a week for seven weeks, and they never ask. People out here don't meddle, her grandmother says. You learn to read signals. Out here tenderness is a code that needs unraveling, the clues in a teasing tone or Julia's eyes lingering on the muscles under Royce's shirt. She can't just blurt out, I want you to raise my baby. They'd shy, like calves when you step too close.

"Did you have brothers and sisters?" She keeps her voice neutral. Just information, that's all.

Julia looks at Royce and he at her.

"She's talking to you," Royce says.

"I meant both of you," Lila says.

"Yeah, I did," Royce says. Then he lifts his coffee cup to his lips. He's passed Go now. He's rounded the bend on Mt. Rushmore and Crazy Horse, headed into territory marked personal, and he's got nothing to say.

"Two older brothers," Julia says.

Lila waits, but they offer nothing more.

"Royce, did you have brothers or sisters?"

He stops mid-swallow. "Both."

"Older or younger?" she prods.

"Both, I guess."

"Who's the oldest, your brother or sister?"

"Sister."

With that settled, Royce leans back in his chair and sets his coffee cup on the table. He plays with his mustache and smiles at Julia.

"Well," Royce says. "I think I'll take a ride down to Burns Meadow before the sun goes down. Got a heifer looking poorly."

Royce slams the screen door. Not until he's gone does it occur to Lila that Julia might have wanted to go with him. Julia has risen from the table, grabbed up the supper dishes, and is washing them in the sink, stacking them in a drainer.

Lila picks up the yellow plaid towel that is crammed over the door to the oven. She takes one of the bowls to rub it dry.

"Leave them be," Julia says.

Lila replaces the cloth, swings her arms in front of her big belly. She knows she ought to go, but this is her one chance. Now, while Royce is out of the house.

"Did you ever think about having kids?" She says this to Julia's back. Lila leans against the front of the stove and watches the back of Julia's head.

"Thought about it," Julia says.

Lila takes a big breath. "I'd like you to have this one."

She wonders at first if Julia has heard her. She waits, and Julia finishes with the last bowl, runs rinse water down the drain, wipes her hands on the seat of her jeans. Then Julia turns and faces her. "Let's sit, shall we?"

Julia ushers Lila into the living room. Lila sits on the cowhide loveseat, crams her hands under her thighs so she won't bite her nails. Julia sits opposite her in the old rocking chair.

"Now, what's this about?" Julia asks.

Lila tries to look at Julia, but the closest she can fix her eyes is to the right of Julia's ear, on out the window, over the heads of the cacti in the bay. All the air in the room has been kidnapped.

"Well, you and Royce, you got this place. And you need some-body to help you with it someday. And you seem like good people. And I'd like my baby to know what it's like out here, with the big sky. And stars. And you're close to Toby." Her voice comes out ragged as a serrated knife blade.

Julia sighs. The whisper of a deflating balloon. Lila steals a look at her face. She's not angry. She seems tired. And oddly sad.

"Is that what you've been thinking all this time? That you could just offer us your baby, and we'd take it in?"

Lila shifts in her seat. She's afraid she'll start crying. "You have those boys come from the Boys' Ranch. You know. Those city kids. I watched you with them. You're real patient, and they like it here."

"Sure. We have kids come once or twice a summer. They learn to work, and we teach them a thing or two. But that doesn't mean we want a baby. What would Royce and I do with a toddler? Who'd take care of it when we're out on the range?"

"Toby's nearby."

"And you think Toby'd like to babysit at her age?"

"She likes kids." A defiant tone has sneaked into Lila's voice. She doesn't want to beg. She didn't think it would be like this. She thought Julia might be a little shocked at first, but that she'd say she'd think about it. Talk it over with Royce.

"Look, Lila. You got yourself in some trouble. It happens all the time. You're going to forget about this baby and move on with your life. Royce and me . . . we got no room for a kid in our lives."

Lila's on her feet, though none too steady. She's shown up for the party late, the only kid in costume, green face paint and clown shoes amid tuxedos and prom dresses.

"I gotta go," she says. She's out the screen door, hurrying to her car, Julia hollering after her, "I'm sorry." Lila dodges the words, lets them sail by, the echo of Julia's sorrys sweeping across the empty prairie.

Toby's waiting for her when she gets there, standing on the porch, arms crossed, watching her drive up the lane. Julia's called her no doubt. Otherwise Toby'd be sitting in the chair, her whiskey mug propped on the railing.

Lila brakes the car and turns the ignition off. She hangs her head a moment. She stopped along the way and cried until she got the tears all out of her. There's nothing left now, just a dry lonely spot too deep for telling. She can't wait to get up to her room. She wants to get behind the closed door, peel off the jeans with the elastic that cuts into her skin. She wants to talk to Rosemary, the woman of the sad eyes. The North Star. The constant in her life.

She stops at the bottom of the steps and looks up at her grandmother. "She called," Lila says. She's glad that her voice is steady.

Toby nods. Says nothing. Perfect.

Lila slides on past her grandmother. She has her hand on the handle of the screen door, thinks she's almost made it, when Toby decides to speak.

"Penny, Dr. Sadler, she has some other options," Toby says. Her voice lands gentle.

Lila snorts. "That's just great." She can't risk looking at Toby. Instead she stares inside the house, straight at Gertie, who's slumped over in her chair, asleep in front of the television, her mouth gaping open, a thin stream of drool dangling from her lip.

"There are people who want babies," Toby says. "Who can't have them, but would make wonderful parents. Someone will be thrilled to raise this child."

Lila turns. There's David's star, beaming away over Toby's shoulder. Funny. Everything in life is funny.

"Why can't I raise it?"

Toby moves toward her. "Well, you can, honey. Do you want to?"

Lila shrinks back, and Toby stops, her hand poised in midair. Lila watches the hand drift to Toby's chest, then trail down along her side like a paper airplane dropped and floating. She hates

Julia. And Royce. She hates Gertie and her slobbering mouth. She hates the sun angled down and the flat bawling of the calves. She hates this house of shame and secrets. Her mouth contorts with the effort to speak. She chokes but gets the words out. "She said I'd forget about this baby."

Toby makes a strangled sound. She inhales, a slow deep breath, and then in a voice Lila strains to hear says, "Well, she's dead wrong about that."

Lila leaves her grandmother standing there. She crosses in front of Gertie, punches the off button on the television as she goes by. She thumps up to her room, shuts the door, and sinks to the floor with her back against it before she lets the sob escape from her throat and float outside to ride the night air with the call of the mourning doves.

Gertie

They think she's deaf and dumb. They think she doesn't know what's going on. She does not flinch when the girl punches the television off. She does not open her eyes. She waits to see if Toby will come inside, shake her shoulder, tell her to go to bed. She waits, and when Toby doesn't come, she risks a lifting of an eyelid. Then shifts her weight forward. Wobbles to her feet. Treads upstairs. She washes up and lowers herself heavily into bed.

She wonders that she doesn't feel elated. Here, finally, the judgment of God, the grapes of wrath settling on the next generation. She should feel some satisfaction.

Gertie rolls first to one side then the other. She cannot get comfortable. This bed is not her friend. She thinks she will get up, sit in the rocking chair, watch the sun rise, but she is too tired to move. Her bones ache.

Howard chose her. He picked her out, even though Toby was prettier. Toby was young then, and Howard home from the war. He didn't look at Toby. Not then. Not until later, after David died, and Howard felt sorry for her.

Gertie twists in the bed, the sheet wrapping around her like a shroud. She struggles to free herself, to get the picture of that awful day out of her mind. Rosemary and David had been dead four years. It was Luther's birthday, and they gathered at the Alhambra for a summer picnic. Gertie dressed herself up for it, not for Luther but for Howard. Wanting him to notice her. A new dress she'd made herself, a blue shirtwaist with box-pleated skirt. Her hair done up in the new way, set on brush rollers that punished her scalp through the night. Howard had Mattie and Grady, two and five years old, dancing under the pump, the cold water splashing on the rocks and on their bare feet. John and George cranked the ice cream freezer. Up on the porch, Toby sat in a chair, her bare feet propped on the railing, looking down on the scene like a queen, like the Jezebel she was.

Gertie walked her father in his wheelchair. Pushed him this way and that in the yard. He didn't want the sun in his eyes. He wanted to look out on the cottonwoods. Nothing pleased him. She got mad, parked him, set the brake. She would have walked off, left him sitting in the sun to bake, but he put out a hand and stopped her. Grabbed her wrist. Look at them, he said to her. Then he nodded toward Howard, standing at the pump, flipping water up at Toby. Toby laughing and Howard grinning at her. Him too old for her, not quite old enough to be her father, but still. Cupping the water in his hands, the droplets flung in a silver arc, her hand lifted to shield her face. And Luther said, Look at them, and she did. And when she looked back at her father, he raised his eyebrows at her. As if to say, It can't be helped. See, even your own husband likes her more than you.

She stumbled away from Luther then. The rest of the day she felt numb, the shock, the humiliation of others knowing. And that night she'd put her hand on Howard's thigh. Moved it close. He sighed, heavy and deep, and once again turned his back to her. He was through with her in that way.

She learned, after a while, to put her hand between her own legs. To lie still in the white mornings and bring her body to a shudder, the release followed immediately by shame, the words of penance forming on her lips even while the orgasm wrenched her.

Toby married Walter, and it didn't make a bit of difference. Still Howard did not turn to her in the night. Luther died, and they buried him, and Howard held her and patted her shoulder, but he might have done as much for his sister. She doubted now that he had ever laid a hand on Toby. He was a man of principle, not duplicity. It was his damned honor, wasn't it, that kept him from turning to her, his wife, when his heart lived elsewhere. Men are such fools. Such romantics. She would have taken the empty husks, if he had seen fit to toss them her way.

After, long after, when her desires had smoldered and finally gone out, she found comfort in Howard's presence. She liked the touch of his whiskers against her cheek when he left her to go out to the barns. She cooked for him and smiled when he sopped up double portions of gravy with her home-baked bread. Their life took on an ease, a rhythm of familiarity, and she rested in it.

Gertie stares into the dark now, in the unlit room of Toby's house. She takes hold of her mind and yanks it away from these thoughts. Grits her teeth against the pain. She won't think of Howard and the stolen picnic. Instead she roams through the Bible verses she has memorized, snatches floating up, *a virtuous woman is the crown of her husband.*

She has no patience with the women who are victims in the Bible: Jepthah's daughter, Dinah, David's sister, Tamar, the dismembered concubine. She knows what kind of women they were. She knows the texts were written to punish women with wanton lust. She has waited all her life for Toby's punishment to rain down. She pictures the girl, Lila, with her big belly stretched under a red knit shirt. Metal in her face. Hair spiked on end. She pictures the girl, Lila, sitting in the row of chairs at the Camp Clarke Days parade. That girl, Lila, hiding her face from the horse that slammed into the fence at the rodeo. Day after day she has sat across the table from that girl, Lila, blue eyes intense.

Perhaps tomorrow she will feel the exaltation she has every right to feel. Tonight, tired of chasing sleep, she sits up, her feet on the rug. She feels her way to the rocking chair, reaches down and picks up her knitting. Her hands glide along the needles until she finds her place, the yellow variegated yarn flowing in a wavy shell pattern. She works on this project only at night or in the secret recess of her room. A blanket for the innocent, yet to be born.

Toby

Monday morning, and Toby waits on the front porch for Lila. She holds a bit of knitting in her hands but can't concentrate on the stitch, a complicated fisherman's pattern. She's trying to decide if she should go up to Lila's room, wrest her out of bed. Last night she stood in the hall, her hand pressed flat against Lila's door. Finally she turned away and spent a sleepless night. She got up as soon as the sun appeared, grateful for morning. She's been on this porch for hours.

When Lila doesn't appear for lunch, Toby can't stand the wait any longer. She climbs the stairs and taps on Lila's door. "Lila? Can I come in?"

When Lila doesn't answer, she puts her hand on the knob and cracks open the door. She can see Lila on the bed, asleep. She has Rosemary's old picture cradled across her chest, her mouth slack. Though it's too hot for a blanket, Toby fights the urge to tuck something around her. She looks young and vulnerable lying there, her feet bare, toenails painted dark blue, as if she's struck every one of them with a hammer.

She enters the room and sits on the edge of Lila's bed. She speaks barely above a whisper. "Are you awake?"

Lila rouses. Rosemary's picture slides off her body, and Toby picks it up, stands, and places it on the dresser. She turns her back to Lila, waits until she thinks Lila has had time to compose herself, yank her shirt down over her stretched belly. Then she turns and sits in the rocking chair. Lila sits propped up in the bed, her head against the wall behind her. She's wearing the T-shirt and jeans she had on when she came in last night. Her face looks puffy, her eyes dim and disoriented. For a minute Toby wonders if she's taken something, but she dismisses the thought. Tears, she decides.

"You don't have to talk to me," Toby says. She shakes her head, wondering why, at this age, she thinks only of stupid things to say.

Toby stands and steps to the window. The sun, high above the clouds, casts shadows on the hills. She looks out on her land, the face of it subject to the sun and the clouds by day, the stars and moon by night, and thinks, as she often does, that nobody owns the sky. The thought calms her, and she settles within herself. Through the night she's been planning to tell Lila something she has rarely spoken of to anyone.

"I was pregnant when David died," she says.

Lila doesn't respond. No sharp intake of breath. Toby's surprised, but then young girls today have seen so much. Without turning, she breathes deeply and goes on.

"I didn't know it, the day we tried to elope. I found out later. By then I was too shocked, I guess, to think straight. So I let Luther bully me into giving him up."

Toby stops and bites her lip. She didn't want it to sound like that. Luther ordered and she complied, too exhausted to care. That is the truth. But she doesn't want Lila to think she means any judgment pertaining to her.

"It's just . . . times were different then." She doesn't know what else she can say. She's not good at this, no practice at it. She forces herself to go on talking. "But the baby was born, a boy. He was taken to relatives of Ella's in North Dakota. They seemed glad for it. And for a while they sent pictures. I sent him a card on his birthday."

Toby's fingers saw up and down on the edge of the curtain. She's tuned to Lila's silence, waiting for a rustle or a murmur, something that would give her permission to turn around. Feeling like a damn fool who can't wait for a coyote to reveal himself, she plunges ahead into the thicket. She doesn't want to scare Lila away, but she's afraid if she stops she won't get started again.

"George saw him from time to time. He'd go on up there and visit. He'd tell me stories, how Paul liked Elvis Presley, how he could draw a horse that seemed to trot off the page. I picked out

186

his name, Paul. He was like a character in a favorite book, someone I knew well but had never met.

"Then, when Paul was twelve years old, he got sick. Leukemia. People died from it back then. His folks wrote and asked me to come. And so I went to see him. They were all in a bad way. So I stayed on and took care of things. Until Paul died.

"At night, after Paul was asleep, I'd sit with his folks on the porch, and we'd watch fireflies and listen to the night sounds. He died early in the morning, on a Sunday in October. The cold came early that year. We thought it might snow before he was put in the ground."

Toby stops talking. She's thinking how small Paul had looked in the bed at the last, his face sunken behind dark eyes. She'd stopped looking for signs of David in him by then. She'd found David in Paul's stillness, the way he held her gaze when she came into the room. He would have become a fine man.

She waits a few moments, then turns. She moves over by Lila's bed, but Lila doesn't look at her. She's leaning against the wall, her face wet. She's not hiding the tears, they just run down and over her still lips. Toby doesn't know if she is crying for her or for Paul or for herself. Maybe the whole ruined world. She thinks about scooping the girl in her arms, but something stops her. Some old reserve. She will wonder later if she should have grabbed her up while she had the chance, but now she settles for softly laying her hand on Lila's head as if to say, There, there, and then she slips out the door.

Lila

The monument to Crazy Horse at Fort Robinson stands on ground covered by dry prairie grass. Lila curls her toes up, her shoes dangling from her hand. The parched grass pricks her feet, but it's way too hot for high-tops. Clay and Tim Pickford dropped her off here, at the central square twenty feet off the main road, while they went to park the pickup in the lot. The pyramid monument is made of smooth rounded pink stones, a bronze plaque commemorating the day Crazy Horse died. There's an identical monument on the north side of the square, that one dedicated to the man who founded this place. Lila's not interested in him.

Dropping her shoes, she places her hands on the stones. The sun beats down, the baked granite hot enough to burn her skin. She pulls back with a small yelp, blows on her fingers, then places them down again, this time leaving them until they adjust to the temperature. She'd like to lean her face against the stones, but the angle is difficult. She turns sideways to get her big belly out of the way, leans in, puts one cheek against the warm surface. She listens. She wants Crazy Horse to tell her what to do with her baby.

She hears the boys – she thinks of them as boys, though they are older than her – whooping it up as they walk from the parking lot, past a hedged area she will later learn shields a tennis court, on up the steps of the main lodge. They are calling to her now, Lila, Lila. She hears them through a curtain, her ears straining toward the silence of the stones and the whisper of Chief Crazy Horse.

Soon they will leave her. Go ahead without her. Go inside and have some lunch. Sign up for a Jeep ride. They couldn't stop talking about that on the way up here, the bumps and thrills, not remembering or stopping to think that she can't risk a bumpy ride. Can't ride horseback either. She's annoyed that Clay has brought Tim along. He'd said nothing about Tim late last night when she'd finally decided to call him. Going to Fort Robinson tomorrow, he'd said. Want to come along? She'd lain awake, picturing how she would tell Clay everything, how he would help her decide what to do. She cried half the night for Toby and her lost baby, another sad story she can't use. She didn't know what to say to Toby or how she could say anything at all without betraying that she'd been snooping into her life. Now she only wants the boys to go on without her. She wants to take her time, poke around in the museums, look for clues, sit on the verandah of the officers' quarters. She wants to walk along the stream, listen for the creak of ancient wagons. Let them go. Please go.

At last they stop shouting her name. Lila smiles faintly, her eyes still closed. She has outwitted them. Sealed them out of her cocoon of heat. Nothing exists but her and Crazy Horse's silence. She could sleep here, standing up, the way a horse does. She could sleep here and turn into stone, meld with the monument. Nouveau art. Live girl frozen to monument in the heat of summer. Some headline. Owen Cunningham could write about her.

The tug on her arm comes as a surprise. Jolts her. She nearly topples over, but he reaches his other arm around her to steady her. "C'mon. Clay's saving a table for us."

She lets Tim Pickford lead her by the arm. She leans back, making him drag her, she's seen horses do this in the corral, their resistance stronger than hers. She climbs the wooden steps of the lodge. She tries to get her mind here, with her body, Tim's hand on her arm like a clamped vise. She jerks away from him as they come through the double doors into the front hall. A small tourist shop opens on their right, offering T-shirts showing buffalo and bright-colored birds, a few baseball caps, western string ties with fake turquoise slides. On their left, beyond a stone fireplace, through the entrance into the dining room, Clay sits at a square table near a window. There are a few other tourists, not many, this place being off the beaten track and not in its heyday anymore. An older couple, both overweight and wearing shorts, sit near the door. A family, two little kids, boy and girl, have left their seats. The dad hands money over the counter while the children take turns bopping each other and crying out in tired, whiny voices; the mother sighs in defeat, holds her fingers to her forehead as if to soothe a splitting headache. The all-American family on vacation. The room is spare, wood floor, a mounted buffalo head on the back side of the fireplace. Clay looks up and smiles. His feet are in boots today, playing the part of the cowboy. One toe taps up and down with nervous energy. After Lila sits, Clay turns his head toward the window.

"Want some lunch?" Tim asks.

She's not hungry. She's supposed to eat. There's almost nothing on the menu except hamburgers and buffalo burgers.

"Yeah. Some coleslaw, I guess."

"That's it?"

"You got a problem with that?"

"Ain't you supposed to be eating for two?"

Tim Pickford shoots his shiteater's grin at her. How could she once have thought he was cute?

Clay is still watching out the window when his face opens up. "She's here," he says. He collects both his feet under him, stands, smoothes his hair with his hand. "I'll be right back."

Shit, Lila thinks. She knows before Clay returns who he'll have with him. She knows now why Tim was brought along. To keep her occupied and out of the way.

"You going to order that slaw or not?" she asks.

"Yeah, sure," Tim says. He nods at the waiter, a young man who's nervously standing on the sidelines. The kid looks like he's about fifteen, wearing blue jeans and a vest, a long-sleeved white shirt. Lila guesses he's dressed in somebody's idea of an old-timey saloon getup, except they forgot the garters on the sleeves. If he was a girl, he'd be wearing a low-cut dress, maybe even off the shoulders, a thin velvet ribbon tied around his neck.

"I'll have a hamburger and fries and a Coke. She wants coleslaw. Nothing but coleslaw." Tim screws his face up at the kid, inviting him to go along on his aren't-women-crazy trip, but the kid looks straight at Lila.

"Anything to drink?" the kid asks. He doesn't blink or look away.

"Just water." She rewards him with her best smile, and he grins back.

After the kid has moved away, gone to report their order to the kitchen, Tim speaks. "Ain't that just peachy?"

"What're you talking about?"

"You and him. That kid. Making googly eyes at each other. He's probably never seen a knocked-up chick before."

Before she can respond, while she's still wishing she had her water so she could throw it in his face, Clay comes in, holding Alicia's hand.

"Look who I found," he says. Alicia's wearing pink shorts and a pink T-shirt with hearts rippling across the front. Her hair tied up behind, she looks young and fresh and pretty. Lila hates her.

"What a surprise," Lila says.

Clay has pulled out the fourth chair for Alicia. She sits, turns to Tim, and smiles. "Hey, Tim," she says.

"Howdy," he says.

Clay sits and looks from Alicia to Lila. To Lila he says, "Alicia had a free afternoon. Randy's taking Amber into town to go swimming."

Lila waves her hand. "Save it." She doesn't need to hear his excuses. Clay looks at her like he's begging her to understand. She turns away.

The waiter comes back and Clay and Alicia both order buffalo burgers, fries for Clay, salad for Alicia, iced tea. Lila studies Alicia, checks out her carefully applied mascara, the lip gloss, the little fake diamonds glistening in the lobes of her ears. She doesn't look like a farmer's wife, but then that's the point.

"Ever tasted buffalo?" Clay asks. He's looking at Lila. Attempting a civil conversation.

"Nope."

"It's good."

"Healthy, too," Alicia adds.

"That's right," Clay says. He beams at Alicia, like she's his prize student. "Less fat than beef."

"I heard that they slaughter a buffalo a day up here to feed all the tourists," Tim says.

Lila gazes around at the empty room. The older couple must have slipped out. "Doesn't look like they'll be needing much meat today. You better hope your meat's been frozen."

Clay leans forward. "Maybe they get the meat from Kenny Loggett's outfit."

At that he and Tim Pickford start to laugh. Lila looks at Alicia, who appears as clueless as she is. She's determined not to ask. But Alicia pipes up, right on cue.

"Kenny Loggett? Who's he?" she asks, her eyes all big and doelike.

"He's a washed-up rancher, up in the high country by Valentine. Drunk most the time," Tim says.

"He makes his money off city slickers from back east. He charges them big bucks to come and hang out on his ranch for the weekend," Clay says.

"Upwards of two thousand dollars a head, I heard," Tim says.

"Puts them up in an old bunkhouse he converted, little whirlpool out under the stars. Got an old Indian, Gus Rappaport, he parades for local color. Then he and Gus drive these guys around in the back of a pickup until they spot themselves a big bull buffalo. They shoot the big guy off the back of the truck, leave him lying in the dirt, go back and have a hearty breakfast of spuds and eggs and bacon. Then Kenny and Gus dress it out, ship it off to restaurants in Omaha, maybe here, for all I know. The cowboys spend the rest of the weekend drinking. Everybody goes home happy."

"You forgot the picture-taking part," Tim says.

"Oh yeah. Before they climb back on the truck, old Gus takes a trophy picture of the shooter with his game. Sometimes they want the head for mounting. Kenny takes care of that, too. For a fee, of course."

"That's awful," Alicia says.

Lila hates being on the same side as Alicia, but she can't get the picture out of her head. Drunk accountants shooting buffalo from the back end of a pickup. "Is that legal?" she asks.

Tim shrugs. "They don't need a license."

"They're not hunting," Clay adds. "It's more like a dude ranch."

"That's disgusting," Lila says.

"Why?" Tim says. "He's just enterprising, that's all. People around here are always talking about diversifying, that's what Kenny's doing. What's the difference if he raises buffalo to slaughter or lets some drunk cowboy shoot one? Either way the buffalo's dead. This way Kenny gets a few dollars in his pocket, gets to keep his land."

This is a big speech for Tim. By the end he's twirling his glass of iced tea, sloshing the liquid over the sides. Clay's studying Alicia's fingers, taking a course in braille, when the waiter shows up with a big round tray. He tries to balance it on one hand, but it wobbles precariously. They all watch as the kid dishes their food to them off the tray. "Anything else?" the waiter asks. He looks square at Lila.

"No, thanks," she says.

The waiter is barely two steps away before the others start to giggle. "No, thanks," Tim says in an exaggerated mocking tone.

"C'mon," Clay says. "Leave her alone, Tim."

They fall silent, all four intent on their food. Alicia breaks the mood. "I don't know how you can eat that," she says.

It takes Lila a beat before she realizes Alicia's talking to her. She points at her coleslaw. "This?"

"When I was pregnant with Amber I couldn't touch anything with mayonnaise in it. I'd be heaving in the bathroom about now."

Lila stops, the spoon halfway to her mouth. Alicia keeps talking. "Especially in this heat. Hot mayonnaise. Makes me sick now to think of it."

"Did you throw up a lot?" Tim asks.

"Oh, yeah. Every day, for a while. When I got as far along as Lila, I felt a little better. Just couldn't eat that slick mayonnaise. It felt like eating raw eggs."

Tim laughs. Lila puts her fork down. Clay turns to Alicia. "You think you could haul off on the sick talk?" He nods his head at Lila.

Perhaps the only one more surprised than Lila at Clay's tone is Alicia. "What did I do?" she says.

Before any of them can think what to say or do next, Alicia scoots back from the table. She shoves it so hard with her hands that Clay's iced tea slops over into Lila's coleslaw. Clay grabs for the glass and knocks his plate off onto the floor. It clatters, luckily does not break, but the meat and bun and ketchup fly all over. Alicia stands, throws her napkin on the table, and rushes from the room.

Bewildered, Clay throws his hands up in the air just as the waiter bends over with a rag in his hand to wipe up the floor. Clay hits the kid in the face, the boy's nose flowering into blood.

"Oh, hell," Clay says. Lila can't stop laughing.

"You better go after her," Tim says, yanking his head toward the doorway.

"Go on," Lila says. She's already up out of her chair. She's got the waiter sitting down, his head tilted back, holding a napkin to his nose.

"Sorry, kid," Clay says.

The boy mumbles something unintelligible, his eyes locked onto Lila. She's decided he's even younger than she first guessed, maybe thirteen, don't they have laws about child labor in this state? While she's holding the napkin pressed to his face, she realizes there's a red blob on the front of her shirt. She reaches down with her free hand, wipes it off with her fingers.

Tim grabs her arm, but too late. She's already stuck her red-blobbed fingers into her mouth. "What're you doing? He could have AIDS."

She looks at Tim's face, his dilated pupils, his shaking hands. She's got the kid's blood all over her hands from the napkin she's pressing to his face. "Don't be an idiot," she says. "It's ketchup."

George

He does not approve. Lila, in her condition, has no business running around with Clay and Tim Pickford. There's no doctor on the staff at Fort Robinson.

"Crawford is only ten miles from the fort," Toby says.

She hands him a cup of coffee, steam rising, and he sets it on her kitchen table. He's seated there, which is unusual. He doesn't often sit at Toby's table, in Luther's house. He prefers his own home, his kitchen. He's left John sunning on the porch, facing east. He's come, in the early morning, because he needs to talk to Toby. He did not plan to start the day with an argument, but he saw Lila climb into Clay's pickup, Tim Pickford hauling himself up after her.

"Ten miles is ten miles," he says.

She turns from him, stands at the sink and washes dishes. He realizes, too late, that she is worried. She always falls to cleaning when she's upset.

"Well," he says. Clears his throat. "She's young. She'll be all right."

The coffeepot under the tap, rinsed, upside down to drain. He waits. She does not speak.

"Why don't you come sit down?" he says, keeping his voice gentle. She needs to talk more than she needs to be told anything today.

She turns and leans back against the counter, dries her hands on the dish towel. The corner of the towel is embroidered with a girl child holding an umbrella, *Wednesday's child is full of woe.* It's Tuesday, but she's not the kind to match her days to an embroidered epithet. She pulls out a chair and sits, rests her forehead on her propped arm. "Don't start with me," she says.

He takes a sip of his coffee. He lets time go by, salve over the wound from that remark.

"Where's Gertie?" he says.

She tosses her head, the old impatience. "Howard didn't know Gertie Saturday."

He sips from his cup. Watches her over the rim. She's having trouble looking at him, her eyes shifting around the room.

"That the first time?" he asks.

"He remembered a picnic that we went on. Howard and me. Up to Crescent Lake."

George says nothing.

"It was in the spring. Two years after David and Momma died. And Howard . . . he wanted to go on a picnic. Just him and me."

Toby stands then, rubs her hands down the front of her jeans. She looks around for something to do. He thinks it's too bad that she's not Catholic. Running her fingers over the beads of a rosary would help. He decides that he will play the role of her confessor. Even without the rosary.

"So?" he asks.

She sits once more. Her fingers flutter along the edge of the table, then play over her lips. Shoulders move up and down with her breath. "That's it. Nothing happened."

He sighs deeply. All right, then.

"That's over," he says.

She shifts back in her seat. Stands again. Walks to the window and looks out. With her back to him she goes on.

"We didn't tell Gertie. We didn't invite her. We sneaked off. And even though he didn't say anything or do anything, I knew . . ."

"That he was in love with you." George says this matter-of-factly.

Toby bends slightly, as if she's been punched. She nods. Then she breathes the worst of it. "I enjoyed it."

"Is that all?" George asks.

She turns. Her face stricken. "All?"

She looks down at her hands. Picks at her fingernails. Finally lifts her face to him. "I hoped Gertie would never find out."

The trouble with this family, he has known for a long time, is that they all choose to be alone. Gertie has been poisoned by the secret knowledge that her husband did not love her. But they all knew. They only pretended not to know. And now how will Gertie live without this pretense? He wants to tell Toby that this is an opening. She and Gertie might stumble toward each other, find forgiveness and share their sorrows. But he knows it's just as likely that shame will drive a deeper wedge.

"She doesn't hardly speak," Toby says. "Sits in front of that TV in the living room. Disappears upstairs."

"Does she eat?" George asks.

"Yes."

"Mmm," George murmurs. Gertie's a survivor. He wonders if Toby knows that. It may be the one thing these sisters have in common.

"She blames me," Toby says.

George raises his eyebrows. He purses his lips but says nothing. Silence, he has learned, is a great encourager.

"She thinks I did it on purpose."

"Did you?"

Toby shifts in her chair. "I don't know. Maybe I did. After that year, after David . . . maybe I wanted to hurt her."

"But you said you hoped she wouldn't find out."

"The picnic. Yes. But the rest of it." Toby waves her hand in the air.

He decides to help her after all. He decides that he would not make a good confessor, not when he loves the penitent. "You were barely more than a child. Howard was a grown man."

He watches Toby struggle for a place of rest. Forgive, forgive, he wants to say, but he knows it is not that easy to let up on yourself.

He drinks from his cup until it is empty. Toby sits quieter now. His arms rest on the tabletop, brown sun-spotted hands folded. He's noticed lately that some days his fingers tremble, but not today. Toby places her open palm on his knotted hands.

"Lila asked Julia to take her baby," she says.

Surprised, he hauls in a sharp breath of air.

"She said no, of course," Toby says. She removes her hand.

"When did this happen?" he asks.

"Sunday night."

"It's Tuesday." He's hurt and knows it, but it's recrimination he lets ring in his voice.

"I told Lila about Paul. I thought I should."

"What did she say?"

"Nothing. Hasn't said two words. This house is a tomb."

"You could've told me."

"I am telling you." Her voice rises.

He stands. He can't help it. A whole speech rips through his mind. He senses danger, the smell of a wounded animal, but he doesn't care. God, when will she learn!

He walks with his coffee cup to the sink, dashes the sooty

dregs against the white porcelain. Carefully, with absolute precision, he sets the cup on the countertop. As silently as day falls to night, he walks out the front door.

Lila

It doesn't take her long to ditch Tim Pickford. Clay and Alicia have disappeared somewhere in Alicia's car. Tim tries once or twice to lay his hand on her arm, grabs at the back pocket of her blue jeans. She swats at him, the way she would a fly. He follows her numbly from building to building, sits on the steps outside while she goes through the exhibits. She likes best the officers' quarters, can't believe the life these people lived on this remote patch of prairie, teas and dances and calling cards. She tries to engage Tim in a conversation about the POW camp not far away, where Germans were held during World War II. Tim only grunts and mutters something about Krauts. She tells him about the canine troops trained here, but he's not interested.

She turns on him at the entrance to the natural history museum. "Why don't you get lost?"

He chews on the blade of grass he's put in his mouth. "Can't."

"Why not? You don't care about any of this stuff."

"Promised Clay."

"Christ, I don't need a babysitter."

Tim looks away. She can see he's struggling. She wonders, briefly, if he's got it in him to be violent.

"Okay. Just make sure you're at the pickup by 6:00. We're heading back then."

"I can tell time."

She watches him swagger away. She'd bet anything he'll be looking for a dark corner to nurse his habit. She doesn't know how she missed it before, his edginess, inability to focus. She waits until he's out of sight before she heads for Soldiers Creek. It meanders along the south edge of Fort Robinson, in and out among a few Russian olive trees. The campground is rigged for RVs, a few slabs of concrete, electrical hookups. On this hot August day there's only one camper, a clothesline strung and weighted with damp towels, two camp stools beside dead fire embers. Down a little hollow, the gravel road passes through the creek, the amount of water reduced to a trickle. She threads her way, stepping from mound of mud to tuft of grass, finds herself in an open field edged on the north by the curling creek and trees. Across the field targets are set up for archery. On up the road, around a bend or two according to the map, she'd come upon the original Red Cloud Trading Post site. Tired of walking, she sits under a tree to rest.

She's braced against a rough cottonwood, watching the erratic flight of a dragonfly, trying not to think about things, when Alicia's car edges through the muddy creek. Clay's driving, and she watches while he crosses the field, parks on the far side. They don't notice her, and she's wondering whether she ought to get up or whether she can just sit here while they have at each other. It's no secret to her, what they're doing. She lets her back fall against the tree trunk, leans her head, and closes her eyes.

She doesn't rest long before she hears shouting. She stands now, shields her eyes from the glare. She sees Alicia get of the car, stomp around to the driver's window, scream at Clay. Clay doesn't move, one arm propped on the window ledge. Alicia beats on him. Soon she bends over and bites him. Clay lets out a yelp. Lila is about to call out, do something, when Clay opens the door. He shoves it so abruptly he nearly knocks into Alicia, but she's quick. He steps out of the cab, and before he can rally, Alicia sidesteps him and slams herself behind the wheel. Clay leans his head in the open window, pleading now. With more spunk than Lila would have imagined, Alicia starts the car. She pulls away from Clay so fast that his head bangs against the door frame. He's left reeling, while she makes a wide circle in the field grass, spins out, flies through the muddy creek, her wheels tossing mud in long arcs, some of it spattering Lila's feet and jeans.

Lila watches all this, her mouth agape, thinking it will be better for Clay, and yet feeling sorry for him. He's standing in the field, his arms hanging limp at his sides, shoulders heaving. He's bawling like a wounded steer.

Lila makes her way to him, lays a hand on his shoulder. He pitches into her like a runaway who has found shelter, and she holds him in her arms. His head shelved on her big belly, his arms wrapped around her waist, it's all she can do to stand upright, but she lets him cry. She pats him on the back, thinking it's a good thing he showed her how to drive a stick shift. She'll collect Tim from whatever hole he's crawled into and she'll spoon Clay into his own pickup, and then she'll move from first gear to second to third and guide them home.

George

Tuesday night. Late, and he wakes to the knock on his door. Something's wrong, terribly wrong. It's her voice calling him. He slips into his bedside moccasins, pulls his jeans on over withered legs. Around his shoulders he throws a light blanket.

"What's the matter?" he says, his eyes riveted to her stricken face.

"Lila's not home yet."

She walks straight into his arms. He rests his chin on her head, closes his eyes, and breathes in her scent. They stand that way for less than five seconds before he sits her on the sofa. Without waking John, they leave in Toby's car. An accident. Runaway. Foul play. Arrested. They don't speak their fears. When he turns north onto Old Hill Road, past the stretch where David and Rosemary died, her hand flutters toward him in the dark, comes to light on the seat between them. He keeps both hands on the wheel, his eyes on the road, but his heart reaches her. There's no need to speak at all.

Lila

She tells herself not to be afraid. Someone will come soon. It's not like they'll freeze to death here in the ditch of this seldom-traveled road. None of them are badly hurt. The boys are out, Tim stoned, Clay drunk, both sleeping it off. She never should have let them talk her into going into Crawford, not that she'd had much choice. Clay insisted, and she felt sorry for him. Sat himself down in the Wildhorse Bar and drank until he was stinking. At least he had sense enough to let her drive.

She can't get comfortable here on the ground. She looks up, searches the sky for Rosemary. "Wish I may, wish I might . . . ," she begins. Then stops. There's a sob at the back of her throat. The sky is too big, and no one is looking for her. Not yet. It happened fast, the crest of a hill, headlights on the wrong side of the road, and she panicked. Wrenched the wheel and tumbled into the ditch, the pickup lying over on its side. The oncoming car lurched but didn't stop, the driver drunk or grief-stricken or underage or just plain callous. She'd bumped hard into Clay and then Tim, but she's glad she wasn't on the bottom. Somehow Clay pulled himself together enough to scramble out through the tipped-up door, then help her and Tim. Now they're half-sitting, half-lying on the ground, leaned up against the truck bed. Her back aches. She can't see the road behind them, but there's no traffic anyway. Won't be until morning. She has to pee but is putting it off. She hates to squat in the dark, who knows what could be lurking in the brush?

The baby has moved a few times. She'd put her hand on her belly from the minute they were out of the cab, waiting. She didn't realize she was holding her breath until she ran out of air. When the baby finally stirred she cried, but there was no one to hear her.

She's reciting all the nursery rhymes she knows when she hears a car coming. She tries to stand up, thinks maybe she can flag it down, but she's been sitting with her legs crossed, and her feet are numb. First the car stops and then voices. What if they are thieves? Or murderers? She pokes at Clay, tries to wake him. He snorts, but can't raise an eyelid. She feels around in the dark for the shovel that tumbled from the truck bed. She holds it like a baseball bat, the blade up over her shoulder, and waits for the voices to draw near.

She sees only the flashlight at first, the light blinding her to who's holding it. Then she hears her name, and someone throws arms around her. She's sobbing before the thought reaches her mind that this is her grandmother. She rests in the smell, lavender and vaguely antiseptic, old people's scent.

"You found me. You found me," she says.

Her grandmother slides a trembling hand over her cheek and says the perfect thing. "We would never have stopped looking."

Gertie

John Brown's body lies a-mouldering in his grave. This is the phrase that plays and plays in Gertie's head, *a-mouldering, a-mouldering, John Brown's body lies a-mouldering.* Everything she sees makes her think of death. She slides her feet across the pine boards of her upstairs bedroom, *step on a crack, you break your mother's back.*

During the day she reads her Bible, holds the magnifying glass against the red-lettered sayings of Jesus, turns her head sideways to scan the words. She knows who she is in all the stories. She's the older brother in the Prodigal Son, the one who does everything right and still the pig-swilling wastrel is given the fatted calf. She's Martha, making lunch in the kitchen while her lazy sister sits at the feet of Jesus. She's the bent-over woman, suffering for years with unnamed maladies, reaching to touch the hem of a garment of any man who has promised to love her. She is Christ on the cross, shunned, spit on, abused, and hated.

At night she hears Toby knock on her bedroom door. She does not rise from her chair in the dark to answer it. Go away, go away, *a-mouldering, a-mouldering.*

She plots. She plans. She wills her escape. She hears the horned owl call into the night and wishes she could swoop down on her prey. Crush them in her claws. Her hands grip the arms of her chair. The nails long and thick and yellow. Knuckles swollen.

A-mouldering, a-mouldering, if only, if only Howard would

die and leave them all at peace. Die and be buried. He's gone from her now. Three thousand dollars a month to keep him next to his piano-playing floozy. She will end up poor and destitute, Toby lording over her. She cannot, cannot endure this life.

She could bring him home to their little house in town. She knows the plants. Monkshood. Nightshade. Would he eat what she prepares for him? Would he know the loving hand who passes him the bowl of his deliverance? *God, my God, why have you forsaken me?*

Toby

In Malcolm Lord's office the air-conditioner blows hard. The thermometer outside the bank registers ninety-eight degrees. Papers on Malcolm's desk flutter in the blast, small piles weighted down with paraphernalia, an eraser, a wad of paper clips. The air smells clammy, like an old fruit cellar. The room hums from the fan motor, as if they are inside a beehive. Malcolm sits behind his desk, fingertips tented in front of his sagging abdomen.

It's Monday, the week after Lila's safe return. Toby has been basking in gratitude. That night George had dumped Tim and Clay on his living-room floor, let them sleep off the poisons in their systems. Next morning they called a tow truck to retrieve Clay's pickup. Turned out, once they righted it, the engine took off. Except for the dents and the busted bumper, it was hardly damaged at all. The same couldn't be said for Clay. George said he was so beat down he hadn't had the heart to be too hard on him.

Through the window behind Malcolm, Toby can see Lila heading toward the *Elmyra Newsblade* office. Lila announced that she wants to invite Owen to her birthday party on Friday. Toby was glad to hear that. She's glad for a lot of things, not the least that Lila wants a birthday party.

"You look like you're in a good mood," Malcolm says.

Toby turns her attention to the banker. He's not going to dim her light, not today. "Still got that buyer lined up?" she asks.

"To-by, To-by," Malcolm singsongs her name. "Don't play with me."

An exhausted sigh escapes her lips. She can't help it. Why did God have to make Malcolm so irritating?

Malcolm leans forward across his desk. He studies her like a specimen. "You don't know, do you?"

"Know what?" She pulls at the front of her shirt, in and out, gets a breeze moving.

"Well, I don't guess it's a secret. I thought you knew already. Western Cattle turned out to be a bogus outfit."

"How do you mean?"

"They didn't want the land for ranching. Some developer planned to turn it into a toxic waste dump."

An invisible hand wraps around Toby's chest and squeezes her like an accordion. Her voice comes out raspy. "The Bluestem?"

"Guess they figured the Sandhills were so remote, nobody'd have to know."

"But the aquifer. . ."

Malcolm runs his hand over his jaw. "Yeah. I know. There'd have been hell to pay."

"How'd you find out about it?"

"Remember that Jack Wesson, came to Royce's branding? He look like a rancher to you?"

She pictures him, expensive alligator boots, string tie, dripping silver and turquoise. "Nope. He sure didn't."

"That's what I thought. So I had him checked out."

Toby's struck dumb – her ranch, poisoning the underground ocean – God Almighty.

"I'm sorry, Toby. I didn't know."

She feels drifty, and the room tilts. She forces herself to concentrate. Malcolm's face looms at her as she fishes for his last words from the roaring surf in her ears. Eventually the room holds still, and Malcolm comes into focus. "I believe you, Malcolm," she manages to say. She's surprised to see the relief on his face.

"You all right, Toby?"

Though he's half out of his chair, she waves him down. She drags a tissue out of her purse, pats her cheeks and brow. She'd like to swipe it under her arms, mop up the perspiration she can feel trickling down her side.

"It's close in here, Malcolm. You ought to get your air-conditioner fixed."

"Yeah. Gol-darned thing. Blows cold air, but doesn't take the humidity out. I bought it on the cheap."

She shifts in her chair, gathers her mind to the remaining problem. "Well, what now?"

"Dodged a bullet, I guess." Malcolm actually grins at her. He looks younger when his mouth isn't sagging.

"But the taxes . . . you got another buyer on the string?"

Malcolm slams his hand down on his desk. He squirms in his chair, then stands and hitches his pants. The belt buckle doesn't make it over the mound of his stomach. "Let's don't worry about that, shall we?"

"You loaning me the money?"

"Jesus," Malcolm mutters under his breath. He shakes his head side to side, lifts his palms, like Pontius Pilate in old Sunday school pictures, the perfect image of dodging responsibility.

"Malcolm Lord, you best tell me what's going on."

He looks at her, his beady eyes gone soft. "I can tell you this much. Your taxes have been paid."

"Are you out of your mind?"

"All 22,286 dollars. And your back loan, too."

"Who in the hell do I know has that kind of money?"

"Now, Toby, I can't tell you that."

"You damn sight better."

"Nope. I promised."

She's on her feet without thinking about it. She takes a step forward, and when Malcolm drops back, she allows herself a satisfying shiver of power. "I got a right to know who's poking their nose in my business."

Malcolm, fool that he is, draws his finger and thumb across his mouth, a mimicry of sealed lips. He looks as stupid as the Cheshire Cat. Toby doesn't know what to do or say. Fumbling, she picks her pocketbook up off the chair. She stops at the door, considers for a moment. She looks back at Malcolm, straight into his eyes. He shrugs his shoulders, but not before she sees the confirmation she is looking for.

Lila

On Tuesday after supper, she goes solemnly with Toby and George. They leave Gertie staring at the television, John tucked into his chair, and they walk together past the cemetery. Lila knows they are heading for the prayer wheel, but she does not let on that she has been there before. They do not speak but walk in single file, like scouts on patrol. The air tastes of dust, the hills badly needing rain. The dry grass swishes against Lila's jeans. Sandburs load her socks, prick her ankles. Socks and shoes and long pants, Toby had said. Wear long sleeves. The black flies bite in the evening.

Lila walks slower these days. She follows mutely behind her heavy belly, as if she is bound to a wheelbarrow. She thinks if the baby is a girl, she will name her Rosemary. Although Dr. Penny has said the adoptive parents will give her a legal name. Yesterday she and Toby sat on a couch in Dr. Penny's office and pored over pictures and statements from families who want children. They narrowed their search to two couples. One lives in Montana on a ranch. The other in Fort Collins, Colorado. Once Lila makes her choice, the prospective parents will drive to Elmyra to meet her. She still has the right to change her mind, she hangs onto that.

At night she puts her hand on the protruding knobs beneath her skin. Bless you, bless you, she says, her hand following the trail blazed by her baby across her belly, thinking of early childhood prayers when she used to kneel by her bed, God bless Mommy, God bless Daddy, God bless Lila. She stopped those prayers, knowing they were nothing but incantations to lure her into sleep and preferring her father's sung lullabies, but now she doesn't know what else to do. Bless you, bless you, her hand lingering to offer a beatitude and an umbrella of safety, as if by osmosis she could communicate her love. Sometimes she cries.

They reach the prayer wheel in the hour when day shuts its doors. The sun slants, yellow and diffuse. A few wispy white clouds dot the sky, and mourning doves haunt the air, *oowoo-woo-woo-woo*. Soon there will be a sunset. Lila knows they will head back before dark. Too many pitfalls to navigate, gopher holes, clumps of brush, forgotten jags of barbed wire. They move gingerly down the slopes of the grassy draw, setting their shoes sideways so they won't trip and roll to the bottom. A few rocks tumble before them, scrabbling like loose gravel.

In the middle of the wheel, Toby invites Lila to sit beside her on the stone bench, still warm from the afternoon sun. George folds himself at their feet, on the ground, his legs crossed Indian style. There's a formality to their arrangement, like chess pieces garnered for battle. Toby looks first at George, who nods.

"This is a special place," she begins.

"I know," Lila says. She wants to make it easier for Toby. She goes on in a rush. "Clay told me. He brought me here once."

"Clay?" Toby sounds surprised.

"He said Grandpa Walter showed him when he used to work around here."

"Walter showed him?" George asks. His hands rest on his thighs, perfectly still, palms down.

"What'd Clay say about it?" Toby asks.

"Said you and George built it. In remembrance. I thought it was for David and Rosemary. When they died. But it was for Paul, wasn't it?"

"George and I built it the spring after Paul died. Paul's not buried here, in the family cemetery. We hauled stones for days, from every corner of the ranch."

Lila's hand trails through the sand at her feet, curves and figure eights. "I knew you were pregnant with David's baby. Owen and me, we found the birth certificate."

"You did?" Toby doesn't sound mad. More puzzled. "But you didn't say anything . . . that night in your bedroom."

Lila brushes her hand against her jeans, flicks the gritty sand onto the ground. She keeps her fingers busy, busy. "I know. I thought you might not like us snooping around. But we didn't mean anything bad by it."

"Why would you be looking?" George asks.

"I was hunting up old clippings from the accident. Because .. . because I'd never heard about it before, and it seemed big. In this family. And Owen got curious. So he went to the court-house, and that's how he found out. He thought it might help me." She wags her head at her swollen abdomen. "You know . . . with this."

"I see. And did it?" Toby asks.

"Well . . ." Lila's voice fades to a whisper. She rubs her hands along the seams of her jeans. She feels young, about five, old enough to know the truth isn't what people want to hear, even if they punish you for lying. "You've been great. And everything . . ." Her voice trails off like a radio signal moving out of range.

Toby says nothing.

Lila tries again. "When you didn't tell me . . . I mean, I thought you were probably ashamed." She stops and bites her lip. She floats her hand on her belly. "And maybe ashamed of me, too," she says, her voice reedy and thin.

Toby makes a sound low in her throat. "That's why you wouldn't talk to me, when you got back from Julia and Royce's?"

Lila chews on her lip. She doesn't know what to say.

Toby stops and looks out across the hills. Lila watches her face. She waits, something she has learned from George.

After she has scanned the distance, Toby's eyes settle on Lila. "I had no thought of shame. I just wanted . . . I wanted you to feel free to decide for yourself. That's all."

Lila lays one hand on Toby's knee, and Toby throws an arm around her shoulder.

They sit, the three of them, heads bowed. A coyote howls in

the background. Crickets chirp. Lila, open and raw, tunes to the night, her skin awake and shimmering. The western sky is a box of crayons, painful in its beauty, while the hills on either side of the draw shadow them like hovering angels.

"Does my mother know?" Lila asks.

With her free hand Toby touches Lila's cheek, her hair, lingers on the lobe of her ear. "No. I don't think she does."

"Paul died before Toby ever met Walter," George says. "She was still a young woman. We tried to put all that behind us."

Lila looks at the old man sitting on the ground, his face twisted with emotion. She'd almost forgotten that Paul was his family, too.

"I knew I could never have more children," Toby says. "Too much scar tissue. So when I met Walter, I told him everything. He knew about David. And Paul. But I never told your mother. There never seemed to be the right time."

"Luther was still alive then," Lila says. She pictures her mother as a small child, the imposing figure in the wheelchair.

"Oh, yes," Toby says. "Luther was alive. He lived with us, Walter and me. Then later, after we adopted your mother. He never spoke of David. Or Paul. He pretended they had never existed, and we let him. Because it was easier."

Her grandmother looks away from her. "I don't know why we . . . I don't speak of these things." A slight shudder passes along Toby's shoulders and back.

"Did you choose a star for Paul?" Lila asks.

Toby glances at George. "That one," she says.

Lila leans to aim her vision along Toby's outstretched arm. She can barely make out the star's faint glow. It's low in the sky, not far from David's.

Lila has her face aimed toward Paul's star when she feels

Toby's hand on her arm. She turns, and her grandmother moves her face within inches of hers.

"I want you to know that I love Paul. Every day that I wasn't with him, I loved him, and then every day that I was. And now, when he's gone."

"I know," Lila whispers. She looks at her grandmother's wrinkled face, the dark circles under her eyes, the sag of her eyelids. She could fall into that face, live forever under its roof.

The three of them linger and wait for the night to gather. When it is time, they fall into walking single file around the spiral of the prayer wheel. They reach for each other in the waning light and move forward with arms stretched, hands clasped, heading for home.

George

She finds him in the cemetery, where he has gone to deliver fresh flowers to the graves of his loved ones. It's Thursday afternoon, and while he's been expecting this visit, he's nevertheless surprised. She carries a wide-brimmed straw hat, swinging it by the floral print ties that hang from it. Her arms are bare and brown, sun spots freckling the skin. He shields his eyes from the glare as he looks up at her from where he squats. The silver streaks in her hair remind him of lightning, terror and beauty. She stands back and waits while he lays cut zinnias on the sun-warmed earth.

He brushes his hands on his pant legs when he stands. He does not avoid her searching gaze. "Want some tea?" he says. His right hand wanders from his side, drifts through the air.

She nods, but says nothing. She falls into step beside him, past her mother's grave, past the four little girls who died of diphtheria. A magpie flutters off a fence post, its raucous voice a rude accompaniment to the stunning sweep of white-tipped wings. They walk toward his house as they have thousands of times before. This day is different, though.

John is sleeping in the rocker on the front porch. He opens the door for her, and she enters before him. He nods at the kitchen table and she sits, placing her unworn hat on the table to one side. "Iced or hot?" he asks.

"Whichever."

"I got both."

"Hot, then."

He puts the kettle on to boil. "English Breakfast okay?"

"Anything but Earl Grey. That stuff tastes like perfume."

He puts two cups on the table, old turquoise Fiestaware. He unwraps two bags of English Breakfast and dangles them in the chipped yellow teapot. He sets the sugar bowl on the table, rummages through a drawer for two spoons. He's buying time, and she allows it. Once the kettle announces that its work is done, he pours the hot water over the tea bags into the pot.

"You take milk?"

"You know I don't."

He gets a saucer down to hold the used bags. Then, when he can find no more excuses, he sits at the table. He pours their cups of tea. He watches while she takes a sip, her lips curling back from the heat. When she has returned her cup to the table, he starts.

"When did you figure it out?" he asks.

"In Malcolm's office."

He shakes his head. She's too damn smart, always has outrun him.

"Why didn't you tell me? Why didn't you just offer it?" she asks.

He's puzzled about her tone. She seems genuinely perplexed, not angry like he thought she might be. "Would you have let me?" he asks.

"Well. I don't like to be beholden."

He sits back in his chair. Not that he didn't expect it, but still, it makes him angry. "Is that what this is?"

"I am who I am, George. I suspect you knew that. You went to Malcolm behind my back."

He fiddles with his tea. He hasn't taken a sip yet. He's already dumped in one spoonful of sugar, but he adds another to have something to do while he decides whether to say what's on his mind. "Is it because I'm hired help?" he asks.

She's quiet for a moment. She surprises him by not answering his question. "Where'd you get that kind of money, George?"

"Does it matter?"

"I think it does."

"Nothing illegal, if that's what's bothering you."

"No, I know better than that."

"What, then?"

"If you've had that kind of money, what are you doing here?"

"Where else would I go?"

She ventures a small smile. It's tight, that smile, but he takes hope from it.

"Besides," he adds, "the money isn't really mine."

He realizes, too late, that he has made a mistake. He can see her turning this over. He's kept this secret from her for more than fifty years, and because he let his fool heart sail away on her smile, he's going to have to tell her. She doesn't speak. She puts her cup on the table, folds both hands in front of her, and waits.

"When Mary Jane and Cal took Paul, adopted him, Luther gave them ten thousand dollars."

She pushes air out through pursed lips. "That was a lot of money."

"In 1949 that was big money."

"I never knew Luther to be a generous man."

"Maybe he had a change of heart."

"But they didn't spend it?"

"Nope. They put it in the bank, never touched it. When Paul died they gave it back to me. I've never spent a penny of it either. Invested it."

"My god. Invested in what?"

"Savings at first. And then in 1965 I put it all into stock, the Standard and Poor Index." He pauses, then adds, "By now there's a lot more."

She shakes her head. "So you've been sitting on it all this time?"

"That's right."

"Why?"

"I told you. It wasn't mine."

"What did Luther want in exchange?"

She's caught him off guard. Again. He hangs his head, but only for a moment. So long ago, what can any of it matter now? "He made them sign a paper saying Paul could never lay claim to any part of the Bluestem. They were insulted, didn't want his money. But Luther insisted, so they signed the damn papers. I encouraged them to take the money, save it for Paul's education."

She turns her head, looks out the kitchen window. He goes on. "At first I didn't want you to be more hurt. After a while I didn't know how to bring it up. You and Walter were doing fine on the Bluestem, didn't need the money. Then after Walter died, I didn't know how . . . hell, I figured I'd die and you'd get the money long before things got too serious. I lived too long."

She turns then and looks at him, her gaze soft. "That question,

George. About whether it was because you've been the hired hand. I think the answer is, maybe so. I'm deeply sorry for that."

"Okay," he says.

"I never wanted to be like Luther. Funny, isn't it? What we don't see."

He swallows down his disappointment. My god, they're getting old, and she's still the rancher's daughter.

She stands then. She reaches and pulls an envelope out of her back pocket, unfolds it, and lays it on the kitchen table. "Now, George, you just sit here and think about what's in this envelope. I'll see myself out. I'm grateful for what you did, but that's not all the reason. This should have been done a long time ago."

The front screen door slams behind her, and he hears her say a word or two to John. He rubs his hand over his head and then picks up the envelope. Plain white, with an ordinary stamp. Mailed out two days ago from town, the office of J. R. Edwards, Attorney-at-Law. It's a copy of the deed to the ranch, the Alhambra, his house, all the outbuildings, and 7,240 acres. Her name is on it, Gwendolyn Bolden Jenkins, and on the same line his name, George Bates. She's offering him co-ownership. All he has to do is sign his name at the bottom.

He stands and moves unsteadily to the window, to see if he can catch a glimpse of her walking up the hill. That damn woman. Can't receive a gift without paying him back. Did she think he paid those taxes so she'd do this? My god, he'd like to shake some sense into her.

He slams out the door, past John, and moves around back to work in his garden. He yanks weeds, notes the lettuces the damn rabbits have gnawed to the ground. He's out there for more than an hour, cursing every ornery growing thing, and finally his head starts to clear. He's standing over a purple-throated gladiola when it occurs to him that his name on a piece of paper won't change a thing. He's left everything to her in his will. Who else would he leave it to? They'll just go on living here, the way they always have.

After supper, after John has been put to bed, George sits again at his kitchen table. He takes a ballpoint pen out of his shirt pocket. When he bends to write his name, his eyes leak water onto the page. He wipes it off with his fingertips. His handwriting is shaky, but legible. He blows on the ink to make sure it's dry. He folds the paper back into thirds, slips it into the envelope. It doesn't change a thing, he says to himself. But he sits there long into the night, his hands reluctant to part with this single page of paper.

Toby

She takes care wrapping the package. She has chosen paper with yellow sunflowers, ties it with a bright blue satin ribbon. It's late at night, and tomorrow is Lila's birthday.

Since Tuesday when they walked to the prayer wheel, she's been pondering Lila's question. Why hadn't she told Nola Jean? There never seemed to be a good time. She was an adoptive parent who had once given a child up, what could she say to explain that? Later she thought it would give Nola Jean more reason to hate her. Then she worried that Nola Jean might think she was asking for her pity. They'd never understood each other, her daughter and her. But maybe she hadn't tried hard enough. Hadn't given Nola Jean enough credit.

She's done a good job with Lila, Toby thinks. So far. The girl is

strong. And capable of compassion. She's gotten that somewhere.

Without looking at the clock, Toby stands and moves downstairs. She does not turn on the kitchen light. She lifts the phone
off its cradle on the wall, thankful for once that it has a lighted
dial. She pushes buttons and listens while the phone rings, waits
until she hears her daughter's sleepy voice.

"Hello."

"Nola Jean?"

"Of course it's me, Mother. Is Lila all right?"

"Yes. Oh, yes. She's fine."

"Is it the baby?"

"No. It's not time yet."

Silence on the other end of the line. She can hear the sound of
a lamp being switched on. Toby wishes she could hang up, but
she's come this far.

"Mother, it's the middle of the night."

"I know. I'm sorry."

More silence. She should have thought this through. She
should have written out what she intended to say.

"What is it?" Nola Jean sounds frightened.

"I wanted to say . . . I wanted to tell you that you've done a
good job with Lila. She's a good girl. She's strong. Has a fine
spirit."

"Okay." Nola Jean's voice sounds tentative, disbelieving.

"You've been a good mother. So far." Toby bites her tongue.
Why did she add that? She hears Nola Jean chuckle, can almost
see the roll of the eyes. "Better than I was to you." She adds this
last hastily, then bites on her lip. She hates it when women run
themselves down in order to force flattery. She's watched Gertie
do it for years.

"You like Lila better than me, so I must have done a better job. Is that it?"

Toby rests her head against the wall, closes her eyes. How like Nola Jean, to hear a reproach even where she doesn't intend one.

"I only meant . . . Lila's fine. She's doing fine."

A long pause. She can hear Nola Jean breathing.

"Thank you," Nola Jean says.

Two simple words, and Toby's heart leaps into her throat. She hears the dismay in Nola Jean's voice. How seldom she has given her daughter a compliment!

"Nola Jean, I know it's not my business. And even if it was, I've hardly earned the right."

"What is it? Something's happened to Lila."

"No, no. But Nola Jean, she needs you. When this baby comes, she needs you to be here."

"She doesn't want me."

"Of course she does."

Silence again. Toby hears Nola Jean sniffle into a Kleenex. She hears the chink of metal against glass. Bedside water? Or something stronger?

"What are you doing for her birthday?" Nola Jean asks.

"A picnic. Royce and Julia are coming. And Lila has a friend. A boy named Owen, from town. We're making homemade ice cream."

"That's nice."

"We'll be home all day."

"Okay."

"We're not going out."

"I heard you. I'll call."

"All right, then."

"What is she doing about the baby?"

"I think you should ask her."

"She won't tell me."

Toby pauses for a moment. Then she decides to risk it. "She's giving it up."

Silence again. For the first time Toby considers what this must be like for someone whose mother gave her away. When Nola Jean says nothing, she asks, "Will you come?"

"I'll think about it."

"Okay. That's good."

"Mom?"

"Yes?"

"I sent Lila to you."

"I know you did."

"I wouldn't have . . . if I thought you were a bad mother, I wouldn't have sent her to you."

Toby presses her fingers against her lips. Before she answers, Nola Jean rushes on.

"Talk to you tomorrow," she says. And then she's gone.

Toby stands with the receiver at her ear, listening to the silence and then the buzz of the dial tone. She's looking out the kitchen window, watching the moonlight and shadows play on the west pasture, afraid that if she moves she will start to wail and bring the house down.

Lila

The party begins. Even with the clouds darkening, they eat outside, under the cottonwoods, the picnic table dragged into a spot near a dried-out wash. Hollyhocks wave nearby. George has picked flame-red zinnias from his garden for the center of the

222

table, crammed them into a blue ceramic pitcher. The cloth is flowered, too, a riot of color on color. The paper plates are a left-over mixture, reds and yellows and greens. Royce and Julia have shown up, right before the food emerges from the kitchen. They help carry heaping bowls of salad and summer vegetables, a platter of oven-fried chicken.

"Don't know how long we can stay with this storm brewing," Royce says. He pours himself a third glass of sun tea.

"Bound to be lightning," Julia says. "We'll have to check the herds."

They need the rain, but still, Lila's disappointed that it threatens to ruin her party. First Clay couldn't make it. Now it looks like rain any minute. Still, Owen showed up early. And her mother remembered to call.

Owen sits beside Lila on one bench at the table. Julia on her other side. Toby sits straight across from Lila, flanked by Gertie and Royce. They're crowded, even with John and George in chairs on the ends, so that every time Owen lifts his arm to eat or stretches it to receive another bowl to pass, he brushes against Lila's bare shoulder. They all jostle each other good-naturedly.

The air hums with static. Royce teases Lila about her jewelry attracting lightning. "Might burn your ear. Or singe an eyebrow," he says.

Lila ignores the words and warms instead to the affection underneath them. This is a skill she has learned this summer. She feels old and wise, beautiful and hopeful. She stops, now and then, to lay her hand on her belly, as if to say Listen up. This is love. This is what I want you to know.

Royce lights the candles on the three-layer cake. Off-key, they sing "Happy Birthday," and Lila blows out all seventeen candles with one puff. They cheer, as if she's crossed the finish line of a marathon.

"Speech, speech," Royce calls.

Owen picks it up, banging his hands together.

Lila beams at them. "I don't know what to say," she says. "Except thank you." She's close to tears and worried that she'll embarrass herself when George comes to the rescue.

"Where's that ice cream?" George says. "We didn't spend a good part of the day cranking for nothing, did we? Owen, where'd you hide that stuff?"

They tease Owen then. Take him into the family. Owen stands, flexes his arm to show the muscle he's developed from all the cranking on the freezer.

Toby dishes up the smooth ice cream and Lila spoons the first mouthful onto her tongue. They all lean forward, awaiting her verdict.

"Mmm," she says. "That's heaven."

When they've finished the meal, it's time for presents. From Royce and Julia a set of placemats with scenes from the Black Hills. Perfect, Lila says. From Owen a book by Willa Cather, *My Ántonia*. I love it, Lila says. Gertie and John apologize for not thinking of a gift, but Lila assures them that their preparations for this party are gift enough for her. George has wrapped a silver-framed picture of two children. Lila looks closely at the black-and-white photo. There's Toby, she says, pointing to a girl about ten. And this? Yes, George says. That's David. I don't know what to say, Lila says. I can't believe you did this. And then it's time for Toby's gift. She lays the daisy-printed paper with the bright blue ribbon in front of Lila. A long narrow box. Lila raises the lid and gasps when she sees Rosemary's garnet necklace. Lila covers her face with her hands.

"Oh, now," Toby says. Owen slips his arm around Lila. Leaning momentarily into Owen, Lila pulls herself together. She wipes her nose on the back of her hand, then laughingly blows it into her napkin.

"Here," Julia says. She picks the necklace up from the box. "Turn around."

Lila turns her back to Julia while she fastens the necklace around her throat. It falls over the collar of the plaid shirt. Even though the sky is heavily clouded, there's enough sun to make the beads sparkle. Lila reaches up to lay her hand on the necklace.

"Toby, I . . ."

"That's all right," Toby says. She pats Lila's hand across the table. "I wanted you to have it."

"Is that Mother's necklace?" Gertie asks. She leans forward, head turned sideways, straining to see.

Toby's hand grips Lila's. "Yes, Gertie. That garnet necklace Momma used to wear."

"Well," Gertie says. Pauses. "Someone should have it who will care about it."

With Gertie's blessing, Lila relaxes. They dish up more ice cream, and while they are spooning it, the talk turns to taxes.

"What's going to happen with your ranch?" Royce asks.

"What do you mean?" Lila says.

"Taxes," Julia says to Lila. "Didn't you know? Your grandma could lose this place."

"What?" Lila says.

"Now, let's not talk about that today," Toby says. She heaps another spoonful of ice cream into Lila's bowl.

"How can they do that? You mean, they could just take it away?" Lila's voice rises. Her face feels hot.

"I lost my farm," Gertie says. "Lost it to my own relation."

"That's not going to happen," Toby says. She aims this at Lila. She waves her head toward Gertie, but Lila has no idea what she means.

"Price of land has gone sky high," Julia says. "Lots of ranchers are forced out because of taxes."

"That's terrible. Why didn't you say anything?" Lila hears the reproach in her voice. She wants to be sympathetic, but she feels left out.

"You had enough troubles," Toby says.

"Nobody tells me anything," Gertie says.

"I'm not a little kid, you know," Lila says.

The whole table erupts, all talking at once, all trying to reassure Lila, only making it worse, and they hardly notice the patrol car until the sheriff slams the door. He stops and hitches his pants, then walks deliberately over to the table.

Toby stands. "Sheriff," she says. "What is it?"

"I'm sorry, Toby . . ." He reaches up and takes off his hat. "I've got some bad news."

Lila watches Toby look around the table, her face a blank, as if all are present and accounted for. But Lila's one step ahead. "Is it Clay?" Lila asks.

"I'm afraid so," the sheriff says.

Toby lowers herself slowly, feeling for the table for support.

"Is he dead?" Gertie asks.

"No, no. He ain't hurt. He's, well, there's no easy way to say this. He's in jail."

"In jail?"

"Good god."

They fling their confusion and disbelief into the air, but the sheriff quiets them. George's voice is the last one heard. "What's he done?" George asks.

The sheriff runs his hand through his thinning hair. He wears an actual badge. Under it his breast pocket holds two pens, the pocket bottom smeared with blobs of ink. Lila thinks his wife must hate washing his shirts, while her nails bite into the palms of her hands.

"Seems he's been carrying on some with Alicia Wright. He says so. She says they was through. Anyway, he went to her house. She was home alone with Amber. She says he forced her into his pickup. Made her abandon her child. She was so scared that she opened the door and jumped out of the pickup, traveling down the highway at fifty-five miles an hour. She's lucky she wasn't killed."

"Was she hurt?" Toby asks.

"No. Skinned up some, is all. Scared. She waited 'til she saw an approaching car so somebody'd stop and help her. Old man Skinner, lives over there on the Becker place."

"That Alicia Wright. Everybody knows what she is," Gertie says.

"Hush, now," Toby says. "You'll make it worse."

"He's in jail." The sheriff stops to roll his hat brim in his hands. He shifts his weight from one foot to the other, pushes his glasses up on his nose.

"What charges?" Royce asks.

"Assault. And kidnapping," the sheriff says.

"My god," Toby says. Her hand flies to her throat.

"Gertie's right about Alicia," Lila says. She's standing, throwing her voice at whoever's handy. She hardly knows what she's saying. "They were having an affair. She was part of it. Clay wouldn't hurt her or Amber. He's in love with her."

She feels Owen tug on her arm, but she can't sit down.

"We got to go to him," she says.

"Lila's right," Toby says.

"There's more," the sheriff says.

Lila sits again. She's only slightly aware that Owen's hand is on her arm.

"We arrested Tim Pickford. Seems he's been dealing drugs. Had a crystal meth lab set up out there on Clay's place. Making the stuff out of paint thinner and God knows what else."

"Oh, lord," Toby mutters.

"What's he saying?" Gertie asks. She leans into John, but John doesn't say a word. "What's that about my place?" She says it loudly enough for everybody to hear.

Toby turns to her. "Gertie, it's Tim Pickford. He's been making some kind of drugs in that old trailer."

"On my farm?"

Gertie turns pale as the bleached bones in Julia's flowerboxes. Lila's stomach knots. She knew Tim was using drugs, but she never guessed he was making the stuff. And selling it.

Toby pats Gertie's hand. Turns her attention to the sheriff.

"Sheriff, you don't suppose Clay had anything to do with this drug business?"

Lila's got to hand it to her. She says it like she's outraged that anyone could imagine such a thing.

"Well now, Toby, it was Clay's land. And they was such good friends and all. We think he might be implicated."

"Implicated? What the hell's that?" Royce asks. He's on his feet now, too.

"That's all I'm saying for now. I thought you ought to hear it in person."

The sheriff starts to back away toward his car. Toby watches him go, and then in a robotic voice says, "Thank you, Dwight." The sheriff gives a little wave, and then he's gone.

Toby's already on her feet, gathering plates, cups. The wind has picked up. The corners of the tablecloth flap wildly. Lightning flashes to the west, too far away for the thunder to carry.

"Here she comes," Royce says, looking in the direction of the approaching storm.

"I'll get the truck," George says.

"No. We'll take my car. Holds more people," Toby says.

"Lila can ride with me," Owen offers. "I'll be right behind you."

They scatter, Royce and Julia offering their apologies, Toby assuring them she'll tell Clay they are thinking of him. Lila and Owen carry food and picnic leftovers into the house, while George revs up Toby's car. It's a while before anybody notices that John and Gertie are still sitting at the table. Lila's gathering her gifts, piling everything into a brown grocery bag she's brought from inside.

"John, can you get yourself home?" George calls from Toby's car.

"You go on. Don't worry about me," John says.

"Gertie, c'mon," Toby says.

Lila sees Toby tug on Gertie's arm. Gertie sits like stone.

"No," Gertie says. Her mouth hard and firm.

"Gertie. I'm telling you. You come with us."

Lila has never seen her grandmother this forceful. She marvels that Gertie doesn't wilt or turn into powder. But Gertie sits firm.

"Suit yourself, you old fool," Toby says.

Toby moves away, joins George in the car. Owen's waiting for Lila in his Chevy. The rain has started now, big drops pelting down, a lot of space between. Gertie raises her face to Lila, eyes red and swollen. She mutters something, and Lila leans in to hear.

"What's that?" she asks. The wind howls now. The vanes on the old windmill creak and whine.

"I told them," Gertie says.

"Told them what?" Lila asks.

Gertie looks confused for a moment, then shakes her head. "Nothing good ever came from a Pickford," she says.

Lila puts her hand on Gertie's back. She looks at John, and John waves his hand. Go, go, he seems to say, and she does. She walks away, and gets into Owen's car, and they drive west, straight into the storm.

Gertie

She can't take it in. Bad news about Clay. She has seen it coming. She won't go to town, stand over Clay while his mother (that hussy!) and that man she calls her husband hover nearby. No doubt they'll hire a crackerjack lawyer. Let them. Clay's young. He'll recover. It might be good for him. Force him to think about his life. Get him away from Tim Pickford and that tart Alicia.

What she cannot take in is what John whispered to her. After the sheriff left. While the others were carrying things back to the house. The wind howling. The red zinnias fallen over, petals bleeding into the tablecloth.

"Don't worry about the ranch," John said.

Gertie's mind shifted back. She felt like a scratchy record, the needle skipping beats. Then she remembered. Taxes. Something about owing taxes.

"What's that?" she said to John.

"George paid the taxes," he said.

"George?"

She thought she could not have heard right. Where would George get that kind of money? But there was John, smiling at her, half crazed, that look he gets that makes you think the best part of his mind spilled out on the floor years ago.

"Toby put his name on the deed. She told me."

She stared at John. The whole horrible scenario clicked into place. John, grinning like an idiot. He had never understood about George. How he had hated their father. George could get anything he wanted out of Toby. And now he'd gotten her ranch. Their ranch. Her father's ranch in the hands of George Bates.

"C'mon," she heard Toby say.

She shook her head no. No. She would not budge until she figured out how to straighten this thing out. She would sit there for years, if necessary.

Now John moves off toward his house, uses a cane. The rain is still sparse, but each drop splatters like half a bucket sloshed. Gertie decides she can sit and think inside the house. Why should she allow herself to get drenched because Toby has done this fool thing? She'll figure out a way to stop it. She tried to stop Toby from running off with David. She came by the ranch that morning for cream of tartar. Can't bake a meringue pie without cream of tartar. Finding nobody in the house, she walked down to George's, and that's where she heard them talking. Plotting. She drove home half-blinded, not sure what to do, fit to be tied until Howard came in from the field. She wanted to tell him, but he had that accusing way about him. Jealousy, he'd say, whenever the subject of Toby came up. Instead she told him to watch

Grady while she went to the Alhambra for cream of tartar, and she drove out of the yard. She drove past the entrance to the Bluestem, straight west, left the car by the ditch, climbed under the barbed wire fence. She found her mother and father sitting on the backboard of the pickup, drinking coffee as if they hadn't a care in the world, and she blurted it out; Toby and David have run off. Go on home, her father shouted, and she did, back the way she came, under the fence to her car parked on the road. She finished the lemon meringue pie with the cream of tartar she'd already taken from the Alhambra's kitchen that morning, and she never told another living soul what she had done.

Now, to get out of the rain, she opens the front door. She's across the threshold when the sky splits with a blistering crack of lightning. *The veil in the temple is rent.* Thunder shakes the windows until they rattle. *The trumpets shall sound.* She thinks of that triumphant passage, the rumbling bass notes, the anger of the Lord. *And the dead shall be raised. Be raised incorruptible.*

She's not aware at first that the lightning-struck tree has fallen on the roof of the house. She smells burning, wanders into the kitchen to check the stove. Her mind is full of images, wrath of blazing furnaces, twisted metal, her mother's waxen face, when she sees the first flames licking against the window frame. She moves closer, not trusting her failing eyesight, and the heat sears her face.

She puts her hand on the phone to call 911. She has rehearsed it, as old people do, knows where to put her fingers even if she can't see. The smoke boils outside the kitchen window. She has trouble distinguishing the smoke from the dark storm sky, but there's no mistaking the acrid odor. *Vengeance is mine, saith the Lord.*

She couldn't have known how that day would end. It's not her fault, not her fault, the ruin of everything, the falling in of the cellar door, broken panes of glass.

They won't get here in time, she thinks. They won't get here. And then the revelation comes to her. Softly, she hangs the phone back on the hook. This is what God has sent. This retribution. She prays now that the rain will hold off. Send thunder and lightning. Burn the house down. She'll be damned before she'll see George living in her father's house. At last, at last, her father will look at her, and his eyes will not burn with reproach.

She feels almost giddy with relief. She starts for the front door. She'll walk down to John's. She'll tell him she couldn't find the phone. She'll tell him, and he'll call, but it will be too late. Let them come and find rubble and ashes.

She hesitates a moment. Her mother loved this house. I'm sorry, Momma. Sorry, Momma. She wonders if she has time to get to her room and back. Surely, if she moves quickly. The tree must have fallen on the back side of the house, and her room is near the front. At the top of the stairs.

She moves as quickly as she can, her hand gripping the familiar railing. She puts her arm in front of her face. Coughs from the caustic fumes. She reaches the top, flames now at the end of the hall. But not here. Not yet. She feels along the chair, picks up her bag of knitting. She takes hold of the yellow blanket, the surprise she's been working on all summer, the delicate shell pattern in baby-fine yarn. See, Momma. See, I can knit like you. That's all she has ever wanted. To be like Momma.

She turns to start down the stairs. The smoke rolling, rolling. She's halfway down – what's that – orange and yellow flickers in the dining room. The fire must have burned through the second story. She'll have to hurry. She holds the blanket to her mouth.

Coughs, her lungs scorched. Swings her head sideways, but cannot see.

Sorry, Momma. Sorry, Momma. Her mother's waxen face, twisted metal of the car. Her father in that bed, a secret, never tell anyone what you did, his clawlike hand wrapped around her wrist, his putrid breath hot against her face.

She's at the bottom of the stairs when she realizes that she's not going to make it. She's not going to get out. She's trapped in her father's burning house. She's the sacrifice, she's Isaac on the altar. She watches Abraham bend over the prostrate body of his son, one hand on the young man's chest, the other raised and trembling, hand clutched around the handle of a knife, and with a sudden and terrible clarity, she knows why her father kept her secret. He wasn't protecting her. He needed her to feel guilty. He blamed her so that he could go on living.

She clutches her hand to her chest, the pain searing her in half. She's afraid, her heart cold and in a panic. She's alone. Abandoned. Over and over again, abandoned. Momma, Momma, she cries.

Through the smoke she sees, dimly, a figure moving toward her. She turns her head, tries to focus her scalded and murky eyes. Someone calls to her. Gertie, Gertie. She strains toward the voice.

The lamb. The lamb in the thicket. The lamb has been found. She reaches, her heart bursting with gratitude and love. "Oh, Howard," she says. "You came for me."

Lila

Dear Heather Lynn,

They said I could write to you and leave this letter in your file.

You were born a month ago in Elmyra, Nebraska. I'm your mother, Lila Raymond, and I'm seventeen years old. I live in Minneapolis, but you were born in Nebraska because my grandmother lives there. Your middle name is from my grandmother's name, Gwendolyn.

I'm sorry that I could not keep you and raise you myself. I'm not ready to be a good mother. I have met the Fengolds who adopted you. They seem like good people, and they are happy to have a new baby daughter. I believe they will love you with a firm love.

As for your father, I cannot tell you very much. His name was Wade Booth, as you can see by the papers. He was smart, good-looking, and a good football player. We loved each other, but only for a little while. We were too young, is all.

I'm going to finish high school, and then I'm going to college. My parents (your grandparents) are divorced, and I hope that never happens to you. My mother is beautiful, and my father is a musician. You might take after one or both of them.

I've enclosed my school picture from last year. I don't know if I did right to put that in, I look kind of scary. I'm not.

Maybe someday I'll write down the events of the summer before you were born. Maybe I'll put them in this file. I don't know if you will turn out to be one of those people who likes to know your history.

I know now that I will love you every day of my life.

Your biological mother,

Lila Raymond

Toby

On a late afternoon in October, Toby stands leaning against the railing of George's front porch. This is her home now. From here she cannot see the site where the Alhambra burned to the ground. The cemetery where so many of her family lie buried is only a stone's throw over the hill. Every day she walks there, stands with her head bowed over the recent graves of Gertie, John, and Howard. She's grateful that Howard did not know of Gertie's death. His illness insulated him from that final horror and loss. She's uncertain about an afterlife. Still, she comes here to tell Gertie things. About Clay, for one.

"They dropped the kidnapping charge," she says. "He's made some kind of deal. Pled to a lesser charge, they call it. Anyway, he's sentenced to one year in a facility down by Lincoln where he'll have counseling. He wasn't selling drugs, but he was into it. Wanda and Frank have stood by him. We all think this is a good deal for Clay. He's got a chance to straighten out his life. Frank's going to keep the farm going for him. It's his when he gets out, if he wants it."

She stands a while in front of her older sister's grave. She never was comfortable talking to Gertie about personal things. It's not any easier now that she's dead. She hasn't told her yet that Howard died. She figures she either knows that or it doesn't matter. She's relieved, actually, that she never had to tell Gertie about George's name on the Bluestem. Still, Toby's surprised how often she comes here, to stand silently or to tell Gertie that the tomato crop was fine, argue with her about the amount of sugar to put in chokecherry jelly.

She stops and lays a late blooming aster on John's grave. Poor Johnny, his life truncated by a demanding father, then a war that ruined him. Still, his last moments were brave ones, filled with love. She hopes Gertie knows he tried to save her.

Standing now on George's porch, she holds a coffee cup in her hand. She sips from it, lets the liquid warm her. It's too early to be drinking whiskey, but what the hell? She's drinking alone, she might as well be drinking early in the evening. She promises herself that she won't make a habit of it. She doesn't know if she is lying.

The air in the fall always makes her melancholy. Something lingering and sad, the meadowlarks wailing away in the dusk. She slips her hand into her sweater pocket, fingers the photo of the great-granddaughter she will never know. She misses Lila, too, a dull ache she will have to learn to live with.

She hears George come out on the porch. Without turning she tracks his movements, to the rocking chair, sit, lean back. He's slowed considerably. He's not ready to tell her what she already knows. Perhaps they will get lucky, and they will never have to speak of it. Perhaps it will come for him on quiet feet.

"Getting cooler in the evenings," George says.

Toby turns then. "Mm-hmm." She smiles at him.

"We've traveled far, you and I," he says.

She turns back toward the hills. "I talked to Lila this afternoon," she says.

"How is she?"

"Good. She likes school."

"I'm glad."

"Nola Jean has agreed to come for Christmas. With Lila."

"Is that so?" Surprise in his voice.

Toby laughs. "Penance, I think."

"Well. That's all right. Has to start somewhere."

She nods. She wonders if she could ask him to promise to be here.

"Toby?" he says.

"Yes?"

"Those rides you were taking this summer . . ."

She can't look at him. Can't.

"That's not the way," he says.

Funny. He's asking her for a promise. This is not what she had in mind.

"I know," she says. "I always knew that. It was just . . . I was fooling around."

"Don't."

"All right."

When she tires of standing, she sits in the other rocking chair. The sun is dying behind them in the west. They look out on the gathering dark. A sliver of moon hovers on the horizon. Behind the moon, in the vast silence of space, the hidden stars start to appear.

Soon they will go inside. They'll have a bite to eat. They'll sit by lamplight and read. They'll say good night. Soon. But not yet. Now, in October, with the grass dried to amber and gold, they sit on the porch, side by side, looking out over the land that has made them. They are facing east, where the sun waits to rise, and there is no need to say a thing.

In the Flyover Fiction series

Ordinary Genius
Thomas Fox Averill

The Usual Mistakes
Erin Flanagan

The Floor of the Sky
Pamela Carter Joern

Tin God
Terese Svoboda

The Mover of Bones
Robert Vivian

Skin
Kellie Wells

and "haunting and profound" (A. M. Homes). In *Tin God,* her writing can only be called . . . divine. "This is God," the book begins, helpfully spelling it out, and we are spinning on our way into the heart of a Midwest that spans spirits and centuries and forever redefines the middle of nowhere.

ISBN: 0-8032-4331-6; 978-0-8032-4331-6 (cloth)

Order online at www.nebraskapress.unl.edu
or call 1-800-755-1105.

Mention the code "BOFOX" to receive a 20% discount.

Printed in the United States
69873LV00002BA/415